Azarel

a novel

Károly Pap

Translated from the Hungarian by

PAUL OLCHVÁRY

STEERFORTH PRESS

SOUTH ROYALTON, VERMONT

The translator acknowledges the support of the Hungarian
Translators' House Foundation, Budapest, Hungary.

Library of Congress Cataloging-in-Publication Data

Pap, Károly, 1897-1945?
  [Azarel. English]
  Azarel / Károly Pap ; translated from the Hungarian by Paul
Olchváry.
    p. cm.
  ISBN 1-58642-019-4
  I. Olchváry, Paul. II. Title.
  PH3291.P282 A9313 2001
  894'.511332—dc21

                              2001001902

FIRST EDITION   PRINTED IN CANADA

My paternal grandfather was a Jewish wool trader. He bought wool from peasant farmers and prosperous folk who leased land on big estates and took it up to the cities to Jewish merchants. In the heat and the cold he made his rounds of the villages, and knew nothing but the harried pursuit of one's daily bread and what it meant, as he put it, to "serve the Torah." He had but one desire: to give up his rambling through villages and devote all his time to the Torah. A great teacher lay dormant inside him, he felt, and he was convinced that if someday he could immerse himself entirely in the Holy Scripture and commentaries for a few years, he could bring redemption nearer. Never did fate give him these years. His children were born one after another, tearing his each and every day into seven pieces; for that was the number of his sons. Slowly he came unhinged, living only in the hope that what he could not achieve, perhaps he could acquire for Israel by way of his sons; surely one of them would arrive at the degree of knowledge, service, and inspiration at which, he said, "Yahweh's merciful heart would move," somewhat easing the burden of Israel's exile, shame, and humiliation.

The hopes he'd placed in his sons were dashed early on: three sons were consumed by the business spirit and joined the service of merchants who knew Yahweh on Saturday only; the other three attended "pagan" schools and studied toward careers in medicine, law, and teaching. And so his hopes were pinned solely on the youngest — my father. He was the only one who desired the company neither of "pagans" nor of the business world, but was more amenable to initiation into the commentaries on the Torah. By this time my grandfather was beyond his desire for "mere knowledge," the "empty years" of the past having tormented him into impatience, he wished to introduce my father straightaway to true "immersion" — to the all-transforming power of absorption in a truth outside of the self, the power of inspiration, of ecstasy. Yet the road to immersion was through fasting. Father was a lank, hungry child, so the fasts soon broke his desire for inspiration and ecstasy. With Grandmother's help, one day he too disappeared from home. He enrolled in the high school one town over, from where, however, he later went to rabbinical school. Grandfather never forgave him for this. In his eyes the high school was just another "pagan" institution: those who so much as stepped inside "defiled themselves before Yahweh." And the fact that my father went from there to rabbinical school only heightened Grandfather's anger. Those at the helm of the school were, as he saw it, hypocritical heretics; for day in and day out they consorted with and lived with the pagans, whose hirelings they were, helping them melt the Jewish people in the furnaces of exile. Further, they were either evil or blinded and foolish; for they took the pagans' bait: "emancipation" of the Jews from restrictive laws and other pagan shams of similar ilk.

Grandfather wanted to hear nothing more of my father. Of all his sons he was angriest with him, for he had disappointed him the most. He wanted to hand Grandmother — who sided with my father — a notice of divorce, but the congregation leaders deemed a ritual censure sufficient. Then he didn't speak to Grandmother for years, and lost all interest in chasing after wool. He sold his tiny cart, his sacks, and never again set foot in the little grocery store Grandmother managed. All day long he sat lugubriously above the *Mystical Commentaries* and returned the letters, unopened, that my father kept bombarding him with. Only when Father's first child, Ernuskó, was born did Grandfather write; he had Grandmother deliver the letter. In it he asked my father to hand over his firstborn son to him at once, so that he could raise him; this, to ensure that there would be someone after all in the accursed family who could "stand before Yahweh."

"If you agree to this," he wrote, "perhaps someday Yahweh's will can change; and although I cannot forgive you, for you did not offend *me,* but *Him,* He can forgive this too, in the interest of the children. Think it over carefully."

This letter tore at Father's heart terribly back then. In my grandfather he saw not only his father, but Judaism's past; and in his solitary moments not only did he often admit that the old man was right, but sometimes literally felt he'd betrayed him. At such times he lamented the fact that he lacked the radiant, imperishable hope he had seen in his father, but at other times the old man's thinking struck him as nonsensical — nay, pathologically extreme — and he neither could nor wanted to understand the old man's grim passion. Never did he resolve this inner strife. The slackened bonds to his father tormented him constantly; he thought long and hard about the possibility of handing Ernuskó over to my grandfather after all. My mother, however, who in all other respects deferred to her husband, would not hear of it. She feared her father-in-law and the *Mystical Commentaries;* while she never dared say it to Father, secretly she was worried that the old man had lost his mind. Not only couldn't she love such people, but she certainly couldn't understand them; and so the last thing she was about to do was entrust her firstborn child to his care. Her own parents were well-to-do lessees, the manor Jews on Count Bártfai's estate. They valued progress more than they did the Torah and the commentaries; their way of thinking was diametrically opposed to that of Papa Jeremiah and people like him.

More letters came and went, but Mother did not relent; they did not hand over Ernuskó. Instead they promised to give Grandpa their next son.

In reply my grandfather wrote only this much: "Yahweh has made note of what you two have promised; and you have promised it not to *me*, but to *Him*. What you deny, you deny to Him."

Soon enough, Mother regretted her promise. When she became pregnant again the following year, she and Father kept fervently inviting the old man over for a visit, wanting to ensnare him completely, tie him to them — rather like trying to coax a truant flame back into a woodstove. They promised to subject themselves wholly to his will, to honor his customs, and give him a separate, furnished room where he could immerse himself as he saw fit in the *Mystical Commentaries*.

Papa Jeremiah only kept reminding them of their promise. He budged not a bit from his woeful, wretched nest.

The second child was a girl. Mother was relieved. They wrote at once to the old man.

Once again he answered in but a few lines:

> You promised me your second son. I shall pray that he is born all the sooner. I know full well the two of you don't want this, for you fear and tremble at the thought of anything that might bring redemption closer — and with it, the day of judgment. I'm old — every day I am that much closer to Yahweh, and you won't have the strength to deny my will! What fans the flames of life within me still? The son you promised! You were my dearest son, yet you've given me the least. You know how indebted you are to me, and you know that you must pay this debt before I stand before Him who is the Beginning and the End. The world is built on the repayment of debt, this you know; and those who do not pay up must do so in the form of their sons. You know I wanted to repay my debt through my

seven sons, yet I only piled up ever more debt before the Lord! Every debt equals another seven, and that again, seven times seven! My father, your grandfather, may he rest in peace, trusted in me as I did in you; every seventh son trusts in his own seventh son, like in the seventh star, on which the repayment of debt shines brightly, trampling underfoot all the gold and glittering riches of the heathen. Well, all this trust was in vain! I no longer want to wait — come what must come! If the next child is a girl, I shall raise it as a boy, and if it is a boy, as a man!

Similar, and increasingly longer, letters kept arriving. Mother dreaded showing them to Father. She feared Papa Jeremiah was on the edge of madness, and that Father would be distressed. She was at a loss for what to do.

Life knocked anew a year later. A third child was born. But then it died.

Sometimes, when I stand beside his grave, my thoughts surge down to him as surely as the roots of a shrub whose seed the wind might plant there. Perhaps my life had been meant for him.

My parents mourned their dead son. Now Mother wrote first to her father-in-law, as follows:

I was happy when your son led me to the altar, but I sensed that something was amiss even then; for you, dear Father, did not come to the wedding. My husband had already spoken to me about everything that had, unfortunately, distanced the two of you so early on. I am no authority on the Holy Scripture and the commentaries, no, I have but one calling: to love those who are mine. You mustn't take offense when I say I fear for my children before you. Children are not made to be sacrificed to the Torah and the Holy Scripture. My maternal heart cannot endure this, and the law of the mother's heart is at least as important as the Holy Scripture. All the anxiety and brooding that you, our father, have stirred up in my heart has killed our third child; the grief has been unbearable. My husband has a terribly guilty conscience, so I am not about to show him this letter. I beg you, please free our souls from the burden that has been pressing at our hearts every time I think of you, Father, and of our promise to you. Dear Father, release us in peace from our vow. Surely you don't want our worries to deprive us once and for all of parental bliss, do you?

My grandfather took his time replying. Only much later did this letter arrive:

At first I didn't want to answer your foolish letter. You too know full well: you are a married woman, and you did well to keep your mouth shut until now. You know that you are to blame for much of what is happening around my son; and not just you, for you are only a woman, but your father, that lessee, that wretch of a hired hand, of whom it is written: "And they lease the pagans' land." Your father always valued land and livestock over the Torah. "They swindle with the swindlers, torture with the torturers," give their daughter a dowry, and so on. . . . He's the one you should damn! Oh, you women! Children are not made to be sacrificed to the Torah? Oh, you *woman!* [My grandfather always underlined this refrain or wrote it all in capitals, which signaled either anger and contempt, or forbearance peppered with scorn.] Oh, you *woman!* What on earth is marriage for? For your pleasure, perhaps? And childbirth? For your pain, perhaps? Ask your husband, he'll tell you: all this exists, and is good and holy, only because it happens in the name of the Torah — without that it's nothing but filthy, obscene blasphemy! I want the child, and God gave you the dead little one so that your mind will at long last be cleansed.

What did Mother think after this letter? No doubt her red velvety room played host to some weighty deliberations following these lines. I can find their traces in Mother's notes, which she tended to jot in the pages of her prayer book. She worked hard all day, I imagine, with feverish unrest, constantly looking for sundry tasks to ensure that she would ruminate less and less often on my grandfather's letter. This came easily, for as tiny, timid, and haughty as she was, she was every bit as diligent. She had an insatiable appetite for household chores, thriftiness, and decorating; there stood behind her an endless army of wives in the past, who in their blood, as if in a single grave, dreamed unceasingly of the pursuits that had filled their lives as well — exactly as written in the prayer about being a wife. These women were always but frames, the pictures within these frames being their fathers' will; and this will was but a frame as well, girding tradition, the laws and legends of the Torah, its poems and commentaries — all of which the ancestors had written in the margins of the Torah under the strict inspiration of the Law.

Like all those other women, Mother, too, could be reconstructed from out of these poems, in such a way that the part of her that fell outside these poems only troubled her. Now these proclivities hastened to her aid in the distress Papa Jeremiah's letters had caused her, and she threw herself into their arms, toiling away as if intent on having work swallow her whole. Her hands became her own personal martinet. Instead of thinking her troubles away, she cooked tomatoes, dried fruit, and put enough of it into jars to last for years. Her pantry nearly burst at the seams. Her shelves, her closets, were pregnant with clothes she'd sewn and embroidered, whereas she herself only wanted to stifle her desire after the pregnancy. At the same time she was consumed by an exaggerated desire for cleanliness, constantly painting the rooms and rearranging the furniture. A sense of foreboding meanwhile filled her voice with whispering, panting overtones.

For a long time Grandfather gave no news of himself. Only

from Grandmother's letters could my parents gather this or that about what her husband was thinking.

"Patience, my children," she wrote, "something is sure to happen sooner or later."

But this something was terrible. Mother was in turmoil. Sometimes she caught herself practically wishing her father-in-law dead, and for hours she brooded over such a thought; had this wish in fact occurred within her, and was it a wish at all, or only a nightmarish phantasm, a thought? . . . Memories of her dead baby alternated with such inner wrangling as time passed. Mother figured that two children would be her quota, and that instead of a third, which she would have wanted, she would love the one that died.

But this was impossible. Her memories had no face but anguish and pain. She had no memory of him, no, with no memories there was no one to love.

ONCE AGAIN Mother only scribbled her worries in the margins of her prayer book. "My husband wants to hand Ernuskó over to him for a year or two . . . but I'm worried about even this much. . . ." "Maybe a new one, one I don't know yet . . . whose face I haven't seen. . . ."

Grandmother's letters soon began to change in tone.

"Your father is treating me much better," she wrote. "By all means come visit us. I'm not well enough to go anymore."

Father paid them a visit, while Mother, her heart beating frantically, waited with her children.

Oluska, my sister, was quite lively, high strung; Ernuskó cried a lot. Mother often kept an eye on them — a fearful eye, ever wondering where Papa Jeremiah's temperament might spring forth out of them, with all of his chaotic, mistrustful, sullen zealotry. But how could this be perceived in a child?

Before long a letter arrived from Father, at which Mother had to go away as well: Grandmother was dying.

By her deathbed my parents fell prisoner. Papa Jeremiah talked them into a corner they could leave only after agreeing to hand over their next son.

And so they wove my destiny far in advance, before I even set foot in this world. After my birth, Grandpa did not wait long; no sooner could I totter about and stammer than he took me away.

The longing with which he had waited for me for so long and so zealously had taken a heavy toll on the old man.

When he came to get me, my parents hardly recognized him. He was thinner, which made him look much taller. His expression was that of a cast-out bull: anger and scorn, mistrust and battle-readiness stewed in his black eyes, which solitude had deadened deep within. Father was both shocked and moved, Mother was only frightened. They would have liked to bargain, but at the sight of him all their resistance evaporated; they handed me over to him.

On seeing me it wasn't grandfatherly love that was kindled in Papa Jeremiah's heart. Instead his mind was consumed by the thoughts that, he felt, had at long last found a body to reside in; these thoughts came from the *Mystical Commentaries* — raw stones from which he had built himself a fantastic and menacing world, a world to which only he held lock and key.

Two saints will help bring redemption to the world; Grandpa was certain. One is to die at the walls of Jerusalem in battle with the devil, while the other no longer need bear the impure burden of battle, only pure dominion with the power of prayer. Until these saints can emerge, however, other, lesser saints must pave the road before them. Papa Jeremiah was contemplating these other, lesser saints when examining the body of the child that I was. Wool and bread no longer posed him one dilemma after another, as when his own children had been small. No sooner did Grandmother die than he divested himself of the tiny store and tiny house, everything, in fact, leaving all to the congregation; whereupon he erected a tent for himself in the yard between the synagogue and the cemetery, in a manner "worthy of the ancestors." In that tent he lived quietly, opening the synagogue for prayer, the school for instruction, and the cemetery for the dead.

On his shoulder he took me into the yard. Students from the synagogue were sitting outside around long tables under the trees, studying the commentaries. It was summer. Sometimes, when the sun shines as it did then, or if I see a tree that seems to have absconded from that very synagogue yard, I once again hear the students' wailing tones as they almost rock the passages, the words, within themselves, with singular, mechanical joy and pain.

At other times one of their faces flashes before me in some ghettolike street.* Back then, as a child, somehow I sensed even more acutely what I could articulate clearly only later — that by some odd circumstance all those students seemed to resemble one another, as if only one student had lived there, in numerous copies, as if one voice had been multiplied in the lamentations. Every time I hear this, I am taken back to Papa Jeremiah, to that yard between the synagogue and the cemetery, under the dusty locust trees, amid the wailing students.

These lamentations were my lullabies and wake-up songs, complemented by my grandfather's throaty prayers as he sat hunched up in front of the tent, his lap filled with books. Around him under the summer sun I rambled and toddled over the scorched, sparse, dusty grass and amid the weeds that choked much of the vast yard, growing thicker and taller toward the cemetery; the graveyard they had overrun completely. Thistles, broom, chicory, poppies, and thyme sprawled in drunken lushness among the tombstones. This motley sea of wildflowers rising above the graves was just as extraordinary to me as the incessantly billowing, lamenting voices at the far end of the yard, as Grandpa's guttural

---

*Here the author appears to be referring to Budapest, where he spent most of his adult life. Hungary's largest city, it is some 120 miles east of Sopron, the unnamed setting of most of this semi-autobiographical novel. — *Trans.*

prayers. I was afraid of it all — the colors, the voices. Afraid to stay, afraid to flee. The walls around the yard, probably erected by some congregation past, were full of odd-shaped hulking rocks. These were even more frightening than the path to the cemetery in the back of the yard, where, in a riot of colors, a thicket loomed menacingly. I believed these plants to be some sort of creatures who stood there so dense and dappled, so still, precisely to be all the more frightening — to block my way should I have gotten it into my head to flee Papa Jeremiah's growling voice and the students' lamentations. What held me in virtual captivity, however, were the rocks; as if the skulls of giants from times past were looking down upon me from the walls; as if the resplendent summer honeysuckles growing in the cracks were in fact grinning and glaring at me from within the giants' mouths, and from the blind cavities of their eyes. Indeed, it seemed the students were lamenting that I had to stay here amid these horrors until the end of time, as Papa Jeremiah's captive. What's worse, the frantic loving kisses with which Mother had bid me farewell still gushed in my veins, my nerves. Their mournful passion had filled me with a foreboding of some appalling danger; and so in fact I'd begun to fear her kisses just as much as these graveyard flowers, the rocks in the wall, the students' wailing voices.

The other memories I'd brought with me from home were no kinder. Above all I recalled my brother's and sister's whispers. Ernuskó and Oluska had sensed my parents' strange behavior. My prospective fate had awakened their curiosity. Every time Mother hugged me so fervently, preparing for separation, they huddled and fell to whispering. These hushed tones only heightened my fear, and I took them in my veins as surely as I did the silence Father imposed at home while preparing his sermons. In response, the flat was filled with whispers, just as during those frequent deliberations that took place day after day in Mother's red velvety room about my grandfather and my fate. After such sessions Mother would often fall deep into thought. Along with my future she invariably brooded upon my dead brother's grave, no doubt; yes, her mind intertwined the two in some odd, mournful manner as her brow darkened and her eyes filled with tears; then my brother and sister would huddle and fall into incessant whispering.

All of this — the deluge of silence, whispering, solemnity, and sudden bouts of rumination; Father's pacing with its inner tension and outward, pendulum-like monotony; the white curtains so thickly draping the windows; the dimness and faint noises from the narrow street outside, the daytime shadows and the deep nocturnal oblivion of the roofs vanishing in the distance — all of this drenched me again and again with countless, elusive fears and suffocating unease. Papa Jeremiah's appearance, my dreaded departure, and my strange new environment were but the culmination of being enthralled by all these impressions. Grandfather instinctively harnessed these fears to his own carriage, as it were, intending to hitch them before the triumphal coach of redemption. His grim, solitary figure would have made a perfect, cave-dwelling hermit. The fanatic pathos of his speech, which his tongue absorbed unnoticed from the Holy Scripture, only increased the strangeness of his presence. This is how he referred to me in the synagogue yard: "I have brought him from Babylon." (By this he meant my hometown.) "From the house of betrayal and paganism." (This was my parents' home.) "I have brought the last of the innocents." (This was I.) His heart was like a graveyard; a graveyard in which he had buried, along with his children, the larger part of his own life, and which was now haunted by the characters of an ancient world, the prophets of the Holy Writ. With them he awoke, of them he dreamed. He spoke their language, blending his words with all the dismal passion that his troubles and his wife's importunities had extinguished in him; and which now gushed forth like a volcano from the sea, spewing lava. As passionate as he was, he was just as blundering, helpless, and confused.

Early each morning he could be found sitting in front of the tent. He lowered his head in his lap, or rather, stuck his head between his knees, like an ostrich with its head in the sand. There he growled away in prayer. Bewildered, I meanwhile squatted motionless in a corner of the tent, where Grandpa had laid our beds of straw on the ground. For quite a while each morning around sunrise the only sound that came from the yard and from the tombstones was the buzzing of the bees, wasps, and other insects; for they'd long begun their exciting daily forays among the wildflowers. The forever sweet, heavy buzzing set my nerves atingle. In suspense I listened, always convinced that something extraordinary would happen at any moment. The insects' buzzing and Papa Jeremiah's growling came by turns. The bees sang of honey; Grandpa, of the bitter life he'd lived.

"Even the dust says you are nothing, Jeremiah. I know and accept this. I am old. I went from bread to woman, from woman to troubles, to children; I arrived, turned gray, maimed by anger and resentment. By the time my fruit fell from me, I'd dried out. All I ask is that you listen to me through my grandson! Let me breathe hope into him, for my hope is not yet maimed! For the sake of our hope, let me live! My hope is that of us all: redemption!"

These words, and perhaps the hues of the rising sun, the sound of his own voice, and the feelings this must have stirred in him sent him into a doleful trance. His voice catching fire, he launched into an anthem. This near-ecstasy was also full of unconscious recollections of the books he'd read; perhaps not a word of the anthem was his own. The words and sentences were scattered about in the books of yore as surely as the nation was scattered about in the world; not one word was his, only the feeling he wanted to fuse them into, only *that* was his.

"I rose each day with the sun, You know this well. I pursued my daily bread, I sheared sheep, carted off the wool. And when the sun stopped in the southern sky, I could not stop; when the sun set in the west, I could not rest. This is what I believed: I would raise my sons, and they would study with me. They would seek what all of us have lost — Your kingdom, Yahweh! But what did they do? They went off to join the blind!"

The blind — to Papa Jeremiah — meant the world, or rather, every bit of the world that was not Jewish. And here there was no distinction between north and south, east and west — all was blind. The town he lived in, the estates of counts, along the border; lessees and peasants alike; children — blind, every last one. Even the tools in their hands were blind. Back at the beginning, according to Papa Jeremiah, the very universe was blind. It was through the Jews that Yahweh had sent the Light which is the soul — the Eye — into the world. And since the Jews had not fulfilled this mission as they should have, Yahweh had scattered them, He had scattered the Light. The Light turned into dimness, the blind had sunk ever deeper into their blindness; and so the Light now had to struggle against its own dimness, not only against the darkness of the blind.

Ideas of this sort often sprouted from the lines of the *Mystical Commentaries*. Ideas are nothing. But in Papa Jeremiah all this became flesh and blood. It is impossible for me to recall exactly the feelings that Papa Jeremiah's morning anthems stirred in me. I could not grasp their meaning; only the sound affected me, the naked feeling that — mingled with the sultry heat of the straw I lay upon, the smell of the dried-sheepskin tent — enveloped my life. Never could time bury this indefinable sensation, but neither did it allow me to reach its depth. The sound of these morning anthems comes not from the past, it seems, but from an uncertain distant depth, from times unfathomable:

> They have abandoned me, but this *one* has remained. . . .
> They have forsaken me, but this *one* yet lives,
> They set a trap, but this *one* will save me,
> Glory be to the One, thanks and Salvation!

What was this *one*? Papa Jeremiah's God? Plainly it was the hope of an old man unable to perpetuate himself in any of his seven sons, as he would have wished, and who now wanted to transplant his hopefulness into his grandson. And what was this "redemption" he sought? The hope of a mangled body, which could never again heal naturally, just as he and his sons could never unite around Jerusalem, nor could the world unite around them.

PAPA JEREMIAH did not want to stay in B——. The tent and his entire lifestyle spoke of someone constantly on the move: He was making ready for Jerusalem.

The letter in which he notified my parents of this plan read thus:

> I asked for your son not to cause the two of you sorrow, but so that all of us could rejoice. This is why we must go to the Land of Truth, the Land of Fulfillment. There I will raise him, as it is written. I allow you to contribute to this journey.

Papa Jeremiah wrote identical letters to his six other sons, my uncles, whom he had neither spoken nor written to in decades.

The letter upset Mother terribly. She and Father came down to see me, and there, in the yard, in front of the tent, further deliberations ensued. Chacham Tulczyn, the local rabbi, along with members of his flock, also took part.

Chacham was round, burly, blue eyed, and jovial. His family had come from the Ukraine way back when. In his view too the world was blind, and Israel was the light — the light that struggled against its own dimness. Like some male nanny, he adored my grandfather. Chacham lived in the yard behind the synagogue, he and his many little kids, who often came over to our tent. At night their mother rounded them up.

Following the example of the teachers of yore, Chacham

Tulczyn did what he could to immortalize his name in the congregation through good counsel and occasional wise sayings, such as, "Avoid those you cannot lead," or, "There is a place whence everything seems laughable, ridiculous, and another whence everything gives cause for tears. The wise avoid these two places in their hearts."

Chacham did not extend a hand to my father — who in his eyes was half pagan — but he did allow him to shake his hand. Then they stood before the tent and deliberated. The sun was shining strong. Crouching next to the men, I was watching their shadows. Those long black blotches protruding from their feet in the dust held my attention completely. But then I stood up too. It must have been then that I noticed my own shadow for the first time: while they continued to deliberate, I occupied myself with this new discovery.

Chacham Tulczyn and the members of his flock advised Father to submit to his father's will. My parents huddled helplessly. Mother wept. Then they had Papa Jeremiah promise to write from the Holy Land once a week.

I fled in fear from Mother's parting kisses, and as my parents left the yard I watched their shadows.

Before long the money for the trip arrived from Father and his six brothers; they'd split the expenses so their father could travel to the Holy Land.

For the time being, however, Papa Jeremiah didn't touch the money. First, to the accompaniment of a ritual prayer, he purified the coins of the "half-pagan" hands that had handled them: he rolled them in embers and ashes, then buried them in the tent, under my bed. Suspiciously I watched the sparkling forints as they vanished from between his long fingers into the ground by the light of the oil lamp. Their glitter was blinding. Ever since I'd discovered shadows I'd been watching them every chance I got, and sure enough, this only increased my taut, stifled fears.

That night Grandpa was beset by doubt. He felt that first he must be cleansed completely. Only then could we embark for Jerusalem.

A few days later my parents came by to bring me clothing and playthings for the journey. Grandpa insisted on taking everything from their hands. Mother cried, Father picked me up and carried me to Grandmother's grave. The blazing sun and Mother's mournful sobs upset me to no end. I watched my parents with bitter indignation. Papa Jeremiah was a sullen witness to the scene. No doubt he wished my parents to be off, to leave him alone with his plans. The grave was thick with poppies and wild roses. I kept a wary eye on Mother, anxious lest she should fall upon me once again with her parting kisses.

Once my parents had left, Papa Jeremiah cleansed the things they'd brought for me just as he had the forints. As for the playthings, he cast them into the fire. I can still see this fire lighting up the old cemetery with its toppled, tumbled tombstones overrun with flowers and weeds, and beyond, the large yard surrounded by the tall, concrete, yellow wall, and the synagogue's Arab-style back door. The scene fixed itself inside me as ice preserves the dead — the ice of fear and aversion. The air well above the flames began simultaneously to move and tremble, nervously, as my strange new toys turned to ash. Hardly could I see them, and I was unable to express that which contracted within me there beside the pyre; my body, my arms were frozen still, I only kept stretching out my fingers involuntarily toward my vanishing toys. The fire frightened me every bit as much as the quivering dance of the air in which the tombstones, the walls, the columns of the synagogue — everything I'd feared until then motionless — was now dancing, slithering, swelling, slinking menacingly, and then flattening out in the air, fairly depriving me of my senses. Further off stood the stifling tent, in which I never got enough air, and beside me Papa Jeremiah stoked the fire. Even now he was performing a religious ritual. He murmured and moved about the fire as laid down in the *Set Table*,* although he felt that these words and motions came not from his memory but from his heart, as Yahweh had demanded; Yahweh, that stern Eastern despot of a god. Pious courtiers of yore had come up with that profusion of singular rules for Him, the rules collected in the *Set Table*. It was Him that Papa Jeremiah saw in the fire in which my playthings burned up. He saw Him in the ash, and in the water with which he washed my clothes; the great King, of whom the *Set Table* says the following:

> You cannot go before the King as you wish, is this not so? Or perchance may you spit about before the King? Or may you say those words and use those gestures that you do before the sons of other men? The court steward first tells you how it is you are to act, does he not? And only then may you step before the King. This is all the more so if you step before the King of Kings, before our God.

Although this book, the *Set Table*, was printed in Italy, it could have been written only by a Jew of Spanish stock; for it was the conduct of the Spanish despot-king that was midwife to the birth of the rites of the Jewish despot-God. Papa Jeremiah would have been dumbstruck to learn just how instrumental were the Hapsburg kings, the various Philips and their stewards, their codices, in giving rise to the *Set Table*! And just how many

---

*A reference to what is commonly referred to in English by its Hebrew name, *Shulchan Aruch:* the code of Jewish laws attributed to Rabbi Joseph Caro (1488-1575). It is important to note that Pap used not a single non-Hungarian term in the novel: Torah was "a Tan" (the Teaching), and even such terms as *synagogue*, commonly called *zsinagóga* in Hungarian, was *templom* ("church" or "temple" in a broad sense, meaning a house of worship) and rabbi was *pap*, which usually refers to Catholic priests but also carries the more general meaning of "pastor." While Hungarian Jews of the time certainly did know and use Hebrew terms, many — to be identified as "Hungarian" and not be stigmatized as Jewish — were just as apt to use their Hungarian equivalents. — *Trans.*

stewards of the Spanish courts lived on, strangely and spectrally, in Papa Jeremiah's movements as he lit the fire underneath the pagan toys.

Murmuring away, he followed with his eyes the paths of flames and smoke. His soul rose up too like a sooty flame, up above the clouds to where he imagined this stern, ritual-hungry despot to be; Yahweh, whom one may only sense, and who, in Papa Jeremiah's mind, resembled in so many respects those kings from the history of the East who so often turn faces to us, shrouded with bloodshed and destruction. As in the lives of his ancestors, so too in Papa Jeremiah's heart was it suffering, the terror of helplessness, that gave rise to the image of this warrior King, the cause of great afflictions, this King who used his earthly, despotic counterparts, time and again to lay waste the "nests of his beloved sons." The less the ancestors' power, the more they had to promise this God, only so as to assure that in times to come they might at least bring a smile to His face. They took on the yoke of the most devastated victims, and to Him they sacrificed the finest morsels of their food, the fairest yields of their soil, and the most flawless of their newborn beasts; and then in His honor they transformed the whole of their thinking, all of their movements, into ritual, only so as to soothe His fury-swollen nostrils. The smoke of my toys now rose in the yard toward the sky to a similar end. The ancients did not rise to new life in the heart of Papa Jeremiah, however, but remained just as they'd been, then they died. They lived on in him embalmed.

Papa Jeremiah didn't have a clue as to all this, however, but only prepared for the journey.

For him, this journey was writ with capital letters. This was the Way in all its symbolic profundity. The way that leads to the destination, the only way among all possible ways that leads there. To the Destination.

From then on he bathed at least three times a day, in a hidden, lukewarm niche of the gurgling brook that passed behind the cemetery. It wasn't a desire for bodily cleanliness that drove him to water, however, but the need for ritual. He would get into the water to forget his body, uttering prayers as he did so — prayers composed for this very purpose by the scribes of yore. Yet, in fact, Papa Jeremiah had no reason to protect himself from his body; the poor man was by now nothing but bones and sinews and his entire body was covered with thick black hair, like the sheep he had so often sheared. With grim devotion he lowered his spindly legs, worn out by years of rambling from village to village, into that flowing water, resting on his shins. As he saw it, this water was not water. It was an instrument of religious prescription, composed not of froth and foam as he stirred about within it, but of Hebrew letters. Moreover, it was a symbol — the *Water*. Not the lifeblood of Earth, inhabited by fish, frogs, gravel, and plants; not the wet exuberance of life; no — this was the water of dry land, which Yahweh had created on the third day.

His body recoiled with disgust. He scowled. Yet his soul splashed about in the symbol. The pious old man splashed water on his sour face — which was, however, veiled by somber, unflinching devotion. After a while he began dipping his gnarled bony fingers into the flowing water, fingers that branched like exclamation marks out of his hands. With these fingers he then went about writing mysterious symbols, as he had read in the *Mystical Commentaries*.

On the third day Yahweh created the water and separated the dry land from the seas. The sea: uncertainty, vacillation. The earth: certainty. The sea: incredulity. Halfway to paganism. Dry land: faith. This is true Judaism. So if you go into water, you must be all the more careful to keep every law, for doubt is underneath you. This is why those who sail a sea must be more careful than those who travel through a forest. And those who bathe must be more vigilant than those who enter the bowels of the earth. Careful, now: on dry land *one* commandment awaits each of your fingers; on water, *two*.

Papa Jeremiah sat down in the water, a bit deeper. Only his head was now visible.

How often since then have I dreamed this image, and in how many ways! Papa Jeremiah's head on the water as the brisk current tried incessantly to sweep his beard away.

Yet the beard did not go. There it floated about his chin, swaying to and fro in a manner decidedly frightening to my child's eyes. That beard frightened me, not just because it was long and grayish black, so exceptionally somber and cheerless, not to mention that it belonged to Papa Jeremiah, but because it resembled the moss and honeysuckle that frightened me also from their lairs in the cracks of the wall surrounding the synagogue yard. How many ways I was to see this later, in my dreams! How large that little stream did grow, into a giant river, and how large Papa Jeremiah's head and beard became! And how often did these dreams, in all their chaos, evoke in me the time when, thrice a day, I would sit by the stream wearing only my loincloth, and a prayer shawl tied tightly around my neck lest some bush snatch it away or the wind blow it off while I roamed about. . . . There I sat, practically naked, with standoffish eyes, rather like some trembling frog resigned to constant fear, as Papa Jeremiah looked upon me from the water with a wretched, prying smile. Having had seven children who'd all "betrayed" him, he was unable to smile upon even his youngest grandchild without intense suspicion.

No doubt he was constantly braced between doubt and hope while watching me. And as he sat in the stream praying ritually away, he did so just as much for me as for himself. He felt that I, too, was being cleansed along with him, and perhaps he took my fright, which hardly allowed me to stir, to be docility. Already he wanted to bequeath to me the merits of his prayers; after ritually splashing his body a few times, he beckoned me to join him in the water. This frightened me every bit as much as his beard and the flowers in the cemetery. Clasping me in his arms, he muttered ceaselessly away; but he was already much too old and much too worried about Jerusalem to be able to say anything in a language that a little kid like me would have understood. Cringing in his arms, I stared with fear upon the water that trickled underneath like hushed music from the netherworld; the billowing bubbles looked dangerously spry, as if they might do me harm; perhaps one would spring up suddenly and take a bite out of my leg. Knitting my brows, I rolled my eyes incessantly. Then Papa Jeremiah, punctuating the ceremony with various godly words, dipped me in the stream despite my sobbing and squirming. He only kept muttering the secret and blessed words; kept rolling, opening, and shutting his forlorn black, bull eyes; kept clasping me tight with his long and hairy, bony arms.

Although the water did me no harm after all, and Papa Jeremiah had already commended me to his God, I trusted not even the water and even less so, Papa Jeremiah. Shuddering in my sun-drenched body, I held the prayer shawl tight in my fist; this was all I dared hold on to. Before long there came the sound of cowbells ringing in the distance; somewhere on the far side of the stream the village cows had been taken out to graze. After a little while the faithful arrived, a handful of folks who so often became a multitude in my dreams in years to come. Old Chacham Tulczyn hurried on up front as if drawn by the stream, followed by the rest — mostly grocers, horse dealers, salesmen, and artisans. I gaped in fear from my vantage point in Papa Jeremiah's arms and imagined that if every last one of them resembled him, while drawn-out bellows came from the herd on the far side of the stream.

GRANDFATHER PUT off traveling for now. Something told him he should wait; he was not yet cleansed enough and I was still too young. My parents were delighted. They came by every week, sometimes with my brother and sister too. There they stood before the tent, while I sat beside Papa Jeremiah; all the fear and aversion I suffered day in and day out only drove the wedge ever deeper into the gulf between me and my parents, between me and the whole of my surroundings. We only stared at each other. Mother wept, and bickered with Papa Jeremiah while my father tried to calm them down. Once again Papa Jeremiah took the clothes and playthings they'd brought along, and they met the same fate as their predecessors.

Every day after emerging from the water Papa Jeremiah returned with me to his tent and there partook in a constant spate of ritual excitement until evening. He touched nothing without a prayer. He extended his prayers with pre- and post-prayer blessings. Later on he stopped going down to the stream, instead digging himself a bathing hole beside the tent. Each day he filled this hole with what he called the "living" water of the stream. No longer did he wash along with the others. No one was clean enough for him anymore. He hardly stepped out of the yard, and ate less each day. Usually he had a bit of ewe's milk and some sort of bread, which he himself kneaded in the tent.

Then he began the long fasts. At first he fasted only once a week, from Thursday night to Friday night; then twice.

A thought he'd been mulling over for some time took hold of him now — namely, that using money to travel to Jerusalem would doom the venture from the start. All the prayers and fasting led him to a state of mind where the natural order of things could no longer satisfy his desires, and he now clung tight to the supernatural. He awaited a miracle, one that would get him to Jerusalem along with me. Though Chacham Tulczyn and his faithful deemed this desire as flying in the face of God, Papa Jeremiah couldn't care less for others' opinions. He fasted, prayed, and kept to his tent; no longer did he want to talk to anyone. Before his tent he erected a sign: JEREMIAH AZAREL, SON OF ÁMON, IS PREPARING FOR A JOURNEY, SO HE IS FASTING FOR THE PIETY OF ALL JEWS AND IS RECEIVING NO VISITORS! He sat me down underneath the sign, and to keep me from wandering off he lengthened the fringes of my prayer shawl and tied the ends to those of his own. Then he slipped into the tent.

In spite of the sign, every now and then Chacham Tulczyn stopped before the tent. And he chided Papa Jeremiah.

"Is there anything you *don't* want? Is there anything the Ineffable Name *shouldn't* do just for you? Because you pray and fast? Or because you've been fasting more nowadays? Surely you feel your sins! How many have burned at the stake, have had themselves flayed alive, for *Him?* But not a single one has desired that He perform miracles just for them!"

He called on one of his students, a child, who promptly read — or rather, chanted, in line with custom — a quote intended for Papa Jeremiah's ears.

"Rabbi Aryeh ben Tov taught," came the words, "that we will get closer to redemption through patience and obedience, by humbly paying respect to the law, than through fasting."

Now Chacham called on another child, then a third, and a fourth. Standing all around the tent, each one sputtered out his quote. Papa Jeremiah did not stir in the tent, however, for he no longer wanted to argue with Chacham Tulczyn. He only waited for the miracle, the angels, that would take us to Jerusalem.

At which Chacham Tulczyn called into the tent: "Keep this up and you won't get to Jerusalem even after you're dead!" Not even then did Papa Jeremiah offer a reply. Dizzied and mulish from fasting and half asleep from age, he lay sprawled in that tent thinking who knows what. I can't even begin to say, not anymore, how he imagined this miracle he awaited from Jerusalem, how he imagined cleanliness and perpetuity. . . . I believe that all these thoughts flitted about inside him in some indefinable fog, like a lost traveler; and that in secret he desired above all a bit of rest somewhere or other, rest in a world without pagans, half-Jews, and betrayers like his sons, but populated only by those like him; in a world where children resemble their fathers, and even if they can't be perfect images of their fathers, at least they do and think the same as them. . . . Perhaps he'd even had his fill of praying, bathing, and fasting; yes, perhaps what he really desired was to fly, in the way that Chacham Tulczyn fluttered about in his ridiculously old, black, tattered caftan before the tent. . . . Just what he thought, I do not know. That which remained of him remained only in my dreams, in which he often surfaces, even now.

In such dreams he often seems out to explain something, probably the journey to Jerusalem; he displays all sorts of writings, before which, in turn, I invariably feel — in these dreams — like a child once again. Perhaps these writings were there too, in his tent. At other times it's as if he wants to teach me to write, and to read. Perhaps back then he did give it a try? I don't recall whether I ever did learn anything from him. In my dreams I always try my utmost to hide from him. Yet it rarely works. The flowers, the trees, the walls of the synagogue yard, are in league with him to this day. Like dreadful, multicolored little creatures, those flowers and trees overrun the path to the cemetery, and as for the stones that make up the wall, even today in my dreams they resemble giants' skulls. I brooded over these dreams often enough, and it was quite a while before I realized that my childhood memories had swathed themselves in their vaporous fabric. Sometimes I see him poking at the pages of the ancient books with his long, exclamation-mark fingers. Only an inventor, a chemist, or a biologist leans with such utter solemnity above his experiments as did Papa Jeremiah in watching the letters in those texts of yore.

He did not see actual events in the stories of the Books of Moses. As he perceived things, the entire Bible had a magical, secret meaning. The human characters, the stories were symbolic; and as for the letters and words, sometimes they signified numbers, sometimes images, and they harbored not only the past, but hidden in them was the key to every possible future and knowledge, the key to the mathematics of the galaxies.

Yet in my dreams I see Grandpa not only stooping over his books; sometimes he assumes the shape of one of those trees along the stream. No doubt long ago I occasionally saw in trees horrific shapes resembling him. These trees were lost in themselves as surely as was he, and they too had beards. Perhaps I expected that they would likewise begin to mutter unintelligibly, like Papa Jeremiah, or feared that they would snatch me up at an unsuspecting moment and dip me in the stream below, like Papa Jeremiah sometimes did, in the consecrated bathing water.

In yet other dreams I see him sitting with his books among the tombstones. Timidly, anxiously, I tumble about the honeysuckles and all the weeds around the graves. When he has clearly lost himself among the characters, I crouch behind a tombstone to hide. On the one hand, I don't want him ever to find me again; on the other, I am frightened when he doesn't come looking for me for a long time. . . . Sometimes I hear him calling me in Hungarian: *"Hol vagy?"* "Where are you?" And I hear my docile, cowardly reply: *"Sehol."** "Nowhere." And his retort: "Well now, if you're *sehol,* fine. . . ." He reburies himself in the book before his head springs up suddenly "Don't you dare say *'sehol'* to me again, because *sehol* is Sheol, and that is the abode of the dead! King David said, 'I could give no word from Sheol.' Yet David was not a clean king! Of course he could not give word from the abode of the dead!"

Then he calls me to his side and points to a tombstone: "What is this?"

"A rock."

"What is underneath?"

"The ground."

"And under that?"

"I don't know."

"Read it. Along with me."

---

*Pronounced *shehol. — Trans.*

Perhaps this is how I first pieced together Hebrew words. Papa Jeremiah helped.

"Mordecai ben Shir is underneath."

I am horrified at the thought, lying in the ground, a rock like this above! Yet Papa Jeremiah explained.

"It's not *him* underneath! Just his ashes — dust!"

"What dust?"

"That which man becomes!"

I look upon him.

"Why does man turn into dust?"

"Because it is His will!" Papa Jeremiah bows.

"He?" And I too bow — this, Papa Jeremiah has already taught me. "And why is it His will?"

"Only He knows."

"He, He . . ." I say, now with a tone of plucky defiance. "And why doesn't He say so?"

"Because He does not want to say! Because He . . ." and now Papa Jeremiah triumphantly opens his grim black eyes, "Because He . . . has already said all there is to say!" Again Papa Jeremiah pores through his book. He begins to read: "'I am the Everlasting who delivered you out of the land of Egypt. . . .' You must learn this book, and the rest is up to Him. Trust in Him!" Papa Jeremiah casts a gruff disdainful smile, then continues the lesson. Sinking a hand down among the honeysuckles, he takes a fistful of dust and recites the words of Scripture: "And the Lord God formed man from the dust of the ground, and breathed into his nostrils the breath of life; and the man became a living soul. . . ."

And he shows me how. Papa Jeremiah blows on the dust. All at once his expression turns serious. Perhaps he is pondering whether one may imitate Him this way, and so demonstrate Creation. Nor does Papa Jeremiah explain things any further. Or could it be that during this sudden pause he is reflecting how different everything would have been if he could have taught his children as he now did his grandson? . . . But back then he had to earn his daily bread, yes, he couldn't sit about among tombstones with his book.

Or perhaps he is thinking that when he finally could sit down to teach his children, they were hungry not for letters and words, but for bread? . . . Grandma was furious. Wool, meanwhile, was plentiful and cheap. Oh, the smell of wool! Sometimes the breeze carried that smell into the synagogue yard, and whenever this happened, Papa Jeremiah's chin dropped. Ah, it wasn't him who fleeced the sheep, but the sheep who fleeced his wings! . . . If he'd given bread but not taught, they'd have damned him. If he'd taught but not given bread, they'd have damned him just the same. Grandma only fretted and fumed: Learning's for the rich, they have time! Papa Jeremiah shot back: Foolish woman talk! By the time a man gets rich, his heart and mind have rotted away. And what good is learning then? Take his cousin, David, the count's Jew. He's rich. Yet what he studied, what he says, what's it all worth anymore? If you get rich, you'll be damned. If you stay poor and so can neither learn nor give bread — you'll be damned just the same.

Perhaps such thoughts made him so pensive and gruff, as I always see him in my dreams. Yet his words excite me all the same. With my wee hand I too take a fistful of dust, and repeat the words of Scripture: ". . . and breathed into his nostrils the breath of life. . . ." I too blow on the dust, as did Papa Jeremiah. He hardly has any breath left. The dust stays there in his palm, in that gaunt parched hand. When I blow upon the dust, however, it scatters every which way.

He stares at me reproachfully, then sinks his arm into the honeysuckles once again and draws a circle on the ground. "And the Lord God planted a garden in Eden, where the sun does rise, and there he put the man whom he had formed."

Pointing a finger at the ground, Papa Jeremiah shows me the two rivers of Eden. The tombstone in the middle of the circle, that is the Tree of Knowledge.

I repeat his words and motions. What he says goes completely past me, but I don't dare say so.

How often my dreams have conjured up this image: I stand there afraid of him, not understanding a thing he says. Then I notice that I am wearing a prayer shawl and that I cannot move, for someone is holding its end. I turn back and see Papa Jeremiah lying there, asleep, clutching it in his fist.

I often saw him sleeping that way, but now it seems he is holding my prayer shawl tighter than usual. Time passes. Terribly anxious, I begin calling to him timidly. He does not respond. Warily I touch him just so. He does not stir. Deftly I try tugging the tip of my prayer shawl out of his hand. He does not allow this.

Then I want to yank it right out of his hand. Impossible. How I'd like to go somewhere — somewhere, I do not know where.

I edge closer to him. To his head. I am surprised to see that his eyes are open. He is staring ahead. Praying, perhaps?

I am frightened at the thought that I've disturbed him. Once again I wait.

Again time passes. Finally I recall that he isn't in the habit of holding my prayer shawl during prayer. Again I edge over to his head. Now I notice: his lips are still. I look again: everything is still. Even his eyes.

I cry out in fright.

Probably this is how it happened that morning, when Papa Jeremiah dozed off forever in his tent.

How I GOT BACK HOME from Grandpa's tent I do not know; all at once I am at my parents' again.

Nor do I recall having lived here before Papa Jeremiah took me away. Everything is new.

I am sitting on a bed. Why is there no warm, sultry smell of sheepskin and straw? The air may be lighter, but it is heavier for me. What now? Why am I here, what do these people — my "parents," my "brother" and "sister" — want of me? They are strangers every bit as much as when they came to visit me in B——. Nor do I understand what I have to do with this room and with this bed. I belong to one place only, and that is the tent, the yard in B——; and to one person only, Papa Jeremiah, that fearsome old man. And so I wait in dread far greater than ever before, for I believe that he will come for me the way I saw him last, with that stony twisted stare, which the pallid dawn in the tent distorted all the more; and with those spasmodic, gnarled fingers looming black, fingers that simply would not let go of my prayer shawl.

I wait for the dead man. To him and him alone do I belong, just as he belonged to but one: that only Lord, Elohim, who tortured him to death. He, the dead man, is my Elohim; I hold the fringes of my four-cornered garment, my prayer shawl, tight against myself, lest there be trouble when he comes, sees me and looks for it on me. And I clasp my loincloth firmly too, the only other thing he allowed me to wear. Sitting here on the bed, I wait in dread, with probing, mistrustful, wide-open eyes, for the old man to appear once again.

My mother steps over to me holding a tiny suit. She wants to dress me up like my brother and sister, who stand nearby watching, whispering.

Me, put on these clothes? I cannot. Give them to Grandpa, I insist, he won't allow it!

Try as they do to reassure me that he won't be coming anymore, that he *is no more,* that he died, fell asleep forever that morning in the tent, I gruffly shake my head. I don't believe it, I don't, that he is no more, that he fell asleep. How can I, when I know full well that he'll be here at any moment, and I'll be in for it if he sees me in another set of clothes.

Mother coaxes and cajoles, my siblings try talking me into it. Now Father also comes in; he's a stranger just like the rest of them. I don't believe them, I don't want to get dressed. When they put their hands on me to add force to their words, I scream and throw a fit.

This image, of the first time I was dressed back at home, arises often in my dreams, then the rest pour in forthwith: The first time I was fed, given a toy, rambled about, slept, and was bathed back in the flat — all carry Papa Jeremiah's forbidding, foreboding curse. I dare not reach for either water, bread, or toy. He, that fearsome old man, allowed only one kind of bread, which he himself kneaded and blessed in his melancholic way; one kind of water, in which he himself had dipped me while muttering away! A fire springs up in my mind at the sight of a toy, the fire he had lit underneath my playthings back then.

And those flowers! The first time I see my mother return from the market with a bouquet atop her bag, the image of that cemetery in B—— springs up! The sultry smell of the graveyard weeds surges toward me alarmingly from lovely asters; I hunch up convulsively at the memory of those grinning tombstones, of the rank, menacing swarm of honeysuckles. Even the smell of flowers is enough, and already I am beset by the memory of that yard and cemetery in B——. If I so much as see a forint glitter in my father's hand, if a lantern or a similar light, say the Friday candles, are lit at home, I run in fright for help. No sooner does darkness come each and every night, but I already hear Grandpa's snoring, wheezing, murmuring; he is silence and darkness, beside me at once. I give a start. Where is he? And if he isn't here, why doesn't he just come already? The longer he stays away, the more certain I am that he will appear exactly as I last saw him, or in an even more terrifying form.

Just how I finally got into my clothes, how they convinced me to eat, to bathe, to play, to sleep — I do not know.

I only see the finished product; already in my new clothes, I am cleaner. What's more, I am eating — timidly, but all the more voraciously for that. Sometimes I even play, fitfully, ever on the alert for Papa Jeremiah's hand to come swooping down upon me.

My father shows me a picture of a grave in which, he says, Papa Jeremiah lies because he grew "old and tired." I neither recognize the cemetery on the picture, nor do I believe that he grew "old and tired." Besides, Grandfather was most terrifying of all, wasn't he, when completely still? Father adds: "His soul is in the sky," far above us, where he is "with God," and he will never return from there, for it is "good for him there." These words only make things worse; I rack my brain over that distance, that sky, that "above," over the notion that it is "good for him there." For hours on end I stare out the window, watching the sky between the rooftops; so is that where Papa Jeremiah's soul will come from, when it does?

Autumn has already begun. The birds are migrating, the sparrows are retreating among the buildings, yes, I see them here and there in groups, as I had in the dusty acacia groves of B——. Does this not signal the coming of Papa Jeremiah? Maybe, just maybe, he'll rap on the window out of the blue. Nervously I scratch about under my shirt for the fringes of my prayer shawl, and I cry out in terror after my missing loincloth: He's coming! He's coming!

I am condemned to relive the era of ancient man, when a god dwelled in every new phenomenon, terrifying and dumbfounding man. But for me he is the only god, *he,* Jeremiah, only *he* lurks in all new phenomena, the personified, inexplicable, great Terror, great Misery, great Comes-and-Takes-You-Away: Death!

Everything that is frightening enough to begin with evokes the old man's presence, rendering greater the fear: an overcast sky, windows rattling during an autumn storm, the roar of thunder, flashes of lightning.

He'll never come again, they say? Impossible. I can no more believe it than I can forget him. Yet not only the new and terrifying evokes his presence and so becomes more profound, but also the unusual and unexpected.

Whenever a guest arrives or caftan-clad visitors come by to

see my father, or when he heads off by carriage to perform a wedding or funeral, I think straightaway: He is off to meet with him. When my father is late getting home or Mother is out shopping longer than usual, when my brother and sister cuddle up without me, when it's gloomy at home, are they not waiting for Papa Jeremiah? When a beggar curls up beside the door, or when someone comes by whom nobody knows, won't it turn out to be him in the end?

And all those noises! The clatter of the printing press on the ground floor, the thrashing sound of women beating the dust out of carpets on the rack down in the courtyard, the sound of scrubbing from out in the narrow, open corridors that overlook the rectangular courtyard from all sides; barrel-organ tunes, violin and piano playing, girls singing! By the time I realized their origin and design, they'd evoked the old man. And so the freshness of my new experiences was obliterated by an early frost: the breath of Papa Jeremiah and his Elohim.

I'm constantly shivering and cold. I am suspicious, precisely because I am afraid of all that exists and all that happens around me. Yes, try as I might to keep an eye or ear on everything, from the furniture to the visitors, from the droning of the wind to the sound of violin playing, I cannot keep track of any single one for very long; for invariably I find myself waiting for him, Papa Jeremiah, to come simultaneously from all directions. I watch the doors and windows, and for that matter, keep my eyes peeled wherever there's a crack, metal grating, a nook, lots of shade, any potential hiding place. I watch, I wander about, first our room, then the whole flat. . . . My mother, my father, my brother, my sister, they're always looking for me, but I'm ever on the move. I stand by the windows and stare, my eyes constantly darting about, making everyone anxious.

My father, busy writing his sermon, suddenly notices me spying on him from under his table; or else I'm in my mother's way while she's sewing or cooking. Squatting, I hold some toy tight against me as I cast her a strange, sidelong glance; I'm in the way of the maid as she carries a heavy tub, or wood or coal; I'm in the way of my brother and sister, who've long been studying hard. And if someone stops me, I turn toward them with gruff suspicion: What's it you want? Who am I to you? And if they ask why I'm roaming and fidgeting about, I have one answer only: I'm looking for Papa Jeremiah. What's it *you* want? I don't have anything to do with you! — and I ramble on.

JUST HOW MANY SEASONS I passed back at home imagining myself in the aura of Papa Jeremiah, and just what banished him from my little universe — whether the futility of waiting for him to reappear in person or the time that passed as I grew — I do not know. Finally Papa Jeremiah really did die for me. Yet from that point on, once his spirit ceased to stir my tiny world, what then took hold of me in place of fear, which had ravaged my nerves so early on, as I say, what then took hold of me without delay, in a sort of backlash, was that other devil — boredom. How mournfully inert my whole life turned all at once! How the nooks and crannies emptied out, how shadows and objects froze, how people all stood *still, still, still!* My boredom grew by leaps and bounds. The flat simply didn't want to hear of becoming a house of magic, whose hidden and unexpected playthings would have kept me amused.

In vain I waited for a playful spirit to spring out of the furniture; in vain for the chairs to stand on tiptoes and dance about the big round table out of respect for me, for my amusement; in vain for the tall, cast-iron stove in our room to issue any sort of music besides a murmur reminiscent of Papa Jeremiah. In vain I shouted into the autumn breeze with tones so odd, it offered only this reply: *Hoo, hoo, hoo.* . . . This eerie music did not permeate the chairs, so that they might have danced a tender melancholic waltz or else leapfrogged crazily about. In truth, it is these two dances I awaited at the bottom of my heart. In vain

I spurred the chairs: *Giddy-up!* They only crouched and stood unmoving about their mother, the table. In vain I stared tenaciously upon the animal heads and paws carved on the table legs — ever since I'd stopped seeking among them the frightening soul of Papa Jeremiah, they'd revealed not a thing.

The guardian angels hovering above the cast-iron stove — engraved into its facade, that is — never, never I say, fluttered their wings; invariably they looked only toward the ceiling, and not one among them turned their big empty eyes to me. If only one had all of a sudden winked or whispered something in a voice befitting an angel, just once! Oh, what perpetual immobility! How much of the same, all the time — everything, everywhere! The bathroom mirror never showed anything but what I showed it; for all my attempts to contort my face before it, never did it amaze me with some magic; with utmost faith and certitude it cast back the most freakish of expressions in exactly the same way! And never did the tiny sewing table by the window emit any sounds of fidgety stirring, so that I might have caught the spindles, buttons, and needles red-handed as they gathered for some secret ritual, à la Walpurgis Night!

In vain I wandered ever deeper into the flat, into Mother's room, Father's, or into the spacious parlor; not even there did objects have any secret proclivity to play, any latent mystery or music they would have revealed only to me, no metamorphoses or dances I might have caught them at. Everything was utterly manifest, motionless, closed. The further in among them I went, the less awaited me what I desired.

Nowhere a curtain that might have unfurled as a butterfly and fluttered to and fro; nowhere a divan that, stretching out and sneezing, might have begun to shake its cover about; nowhere a clock from which there might at least have sprung forth a cuckoo; nowhere a bed in which the spirit of the goose down might have stirred; nowhere a thing that somehow might have satisfied my boundless sense of self-importance and longing for play.

Nor did the red-plush furniture in Mother's room sigh so much as a wee cloud of dust in my direction to indicate how gladly it would come alive for the sake of this child that was I, for *his* sake only; nor for that matter did Árpád and his seven Magyar chieftans who'd conquered this land so long ago deign to spring from their frame on the wall; this, in spite of all my beseeching gazes, my attempts to encourage them by jumping about, by singing and somersaulting away. Nothing moved. At most, Mother would come in from the kitchen and take me out there with her, to keep me from ravaging the rooms.

The moment she stepped in, the furniture came alive nonetheless. A change came over them, and with Mother's help they revealed their secret. But alas! How dispiriting this secret was! Completely devoid of play! Far from fawning on my own boundless self-importance, their secret rather smashed me down as a little nobody — when, with the help of Mother's moving lips, the furniture, the curtains, the couches, all cried out:

"We cost money, which *you* don't have! A lot of money! Precious money! Hard-earned money!"

The painting of Árpád and the seven chieftans now called from above my parents' bed in the very same parlance, yes, now they sprang from the frame, and the red-plush furniture shouted at me too: Don't pound away on us, for we cost money, don't wish for us to come down to you, for we cost money. And the divans: Don't wish for us to shake about our covers, for we cost money! One a bit louder, another more softly, but all sang the very same tune: Don't disturb us, don't wish anything of us, or we'll fray and crumble away, and another must be bought in our place!

Was there any difference between them at all anymore? All were the masked specters of the same accusation: "money, which we don't have much of" . . . "that your father works so hard to earn" . . . and "that you for one don't have, and . . . *hmph!* When *will* you?" And while they all whined this accusation, I tottered out of the room following Mother into the kitchen.

But how humdrum was this kitchen too! Although I listened to Mother, and although I watched her, I felt that virtually no part of her was mine.

Her sense of pride, apparent mainly in the way she crinkled her little snub nose, was directed at Father. All the diligence booming on her round, industrious face was directed at the kettles. And the cheeriness that sparkled again and again in her brown eyes was directed at the foods, at the vapor and the steam, the tastes and smells, that hovered above the stove.

What was left here for me? At most that wee bit of those foods that would be allotted to me — yet what was that compared to all I expected from Mother?

How could Mother's monotonous hustle and bustle around the kitchen stove, her incessant rounds of tasting, stirring, grinding, plucking, and peeling, her bottling of fruits and vegetables, not to mention tying of tomato vines, have soothed the wounds of my sensitive heart? For all this revealed nothing, absolutely nothing, about my own disquieting exclusiveness.

How could these kettles have possibly fawned over me, my exceptionality, seeing as how I not only wasn't allowed to sample from them but couldn't even push them about on the burners? How would all that steam have told me a thing aside from its usual stupid fuming and nonsensical sputtering? In vain I yearned to hear something else, say, "Away already with all those wooden spoons! We don't want anyone but this kid to stir us! And if we burn in this kettle, we burn for him!" But this chorus of kettles never sounded, the cooked foods never broke out in song, nor did Mother fall into a frenzy of pride over me, no, not at all; never did she put everything else aside, embrace me passionately and say: "You are my favorite child, the most special! I'll put everything else aside, come on, let's dance, let's do the waltz! The maid can beat the drum with the tomato cauldron! Hip hip hooray, I say!" Now *this* is what I call a mother with her youngest! The only thing missing from the scene is for the door to fly open and for Father to appear, then my brother and sister, for them to hold hands around us and sing!

What unfulfilled, forever unexpressed wishes!

Hardly had the heart conceived them but that its sullen wounds had already swallowed them whole. And I only gave Mother a peevish, distant look; no, she felt nothing, absolutely nothing, of what I would have wished. She was not about to make amends through dance and song for what the kettles and vegetables out in the kitchen, and the furniture in the rooms, had failed to do for my amusement. Amid her hustle and bustle she didn't even say this much to me, in light of my uniqueness: "I see you, my son, I know who you are, and I love only you: all these kettles, these flames, all this sputtering and stirring don't mean a thing to me! Nothing counts but *you!* And she would have fawned over and under and through me: "Oh, what eyes you have! Only *your* eyes are beautiful, *your* hair" — and she would have sometimes pecked me with kisses all over, not to mention that, amid all the sputtering, the hustle and bustle, she would at least have cried out passionately now and again: "Oh, my one and only! Promise you won't tell your brother and sister!" Or if she hadn't cried out passionately, she would at least have said, softly, "Alas, I can neither dance nor sing, because my legs aren't nimble enough and I just don't have an ear for music, plus I've got to cook, for eating is good, you know that, you do. But afterward I'll kiss you till you're dizzy, until the kitchen spins with you!"

But she didn't say even this much, and by now I would have settled for less. For *this:* "Alas, my son, I can't kiss you so the kitchen spins too, but I'll tell you stories, stories about this hen, when it was still alive and scratching about, and about this carrot, when butterflies still dreamed upon it. . . ."

Ah yes, I would have said, now this is more like it, this is music to the ears. I would have forgiven her for her legs not being nimble and for her not having an ear for music, yes, I would have forgiven her for her kisses that couldn't make the kitchen spin, for being unable to cry out passionately now and again. In exchange for such stories I would have forgiven every last object for being dumb and distant, I would have overlooked the time she spent in their company, and finally, the fact that I wasn't her only child.

How I waited for all this, waited and watched — in vain!

Her talk was directed at the fire only, as when she remarked, "It burns up too much wood"; at the lard, "I think it was a bit expensive"; and at the stewed vegetables, "I just can't believe how much flour it takes to thicken this!" Not even when it came to raw tastes and smells did she speak with me, but only with the maid, telling her about the butcher, who it seemed had "gypped her with all these bones again"; about the baker, who deserved to have his "sickly looking pastries thrown right back at him"; not to mention the market hags, "who have no shame!" And finally, about them all: "They take all our money, that they do, our precious, hard-earned money!"

Oh, how trite these tales were!

The butcher and his many bones, the baker and his sickly looking pastries, the market hags, and everyone who took "all our hard-earned money" — for all intents and purposes they'd wormed their way between Mother and me. In vain I waited for her to break out from among them one day and dash over to me — in vain! Instead every one had taken this or that bit of Mother, who in turn became increasingly a stranger, so that only her voice remained, and even that seemed to come only from afar. . . .

Oh, if only this voice from afar had said at least this much: No kisses, no stories, no songs, no music, forgive me, I'm just a simple housewife, nothing more. Don't expect anything more of me either, but now don't go pining for some other mother, no, love me as I am! . . . But no, not even that! This distant voice of Mother's that still remained with me couldn't say even this much. Indeed, I had to step over to her to get a close look at just how little I had left! Then she leaned toward me to give a passing kiss, and said: "Be a good boy and go on back to your room, but don't make any noise. Your brother, sister, and father will be here soon, and we'll have lunch."

Then, since I just kept looking round and round, she stuck a slice of buttered bread in my hand.

"Go on now," she said.

And I headed off. What a bunch of nothing, that kiss! What a bunch of nothing, that bread! Nonetheless I nibbled, still roaming about the empty flat, wandering sullenly from room to room without knowing what in fact had happened to me. The longing for Mother's kisses, stories, and dancing lived on deep underneath the wounds of my heart, perhaps even deeper. . . . The only signal I received from down there was a sense of anguish every bit as hamstrung by shame and haughtiness as it was jumbled. Perhaps I didn't even have a clue as to what I truly wanted, whether it was all right or proper to want more kisses, another sort of love, not to mention stories, dancing, songs, and fawning; for I knew nothing of other mothers or similar sons. It was like hearing a whisper one doesn't understand, or waking up only to forget a vivid dream. Only in such ambiguous terms did the common blood tell me, under its breath, what in fact I so desired from Mother. . . . If only upon hearing the words of this blood I would have *understood* what it demanded of me, what I must demand of Mother — why then, I might have run up to her and shouted: You've got to be like this! This is what I desire of you, this is what I wish! Only *then* will you truly be my mother! Yet I heard the whisper only, the whisper of the common blood. I didn't comprehend its words, but desired only; I desired without knowing what the desire was that swirled shapelessly about in the underworld of my heart. And so I trudged about from room to room peering down into the dark bottomless depth of my heart, hearing nothing at all from down there, nothing but the whimper of an unfamiliar longing; an anguished, yearning, languid moan.

Oh, terrible desire, excruciating desire! Why won't you rise up out of the depths of the heart into the luminance of reason and will? There you might become what you must and can become! Instead you only torment from the deep. How inconsequential the agonies of unfulfilled or even suppressed desire, compared to your dismal pain! You are the devil, the real hell! You, who with your unintelligible groaning keep the world ablaze from down below; yet you are not only fire and hell, a ravaging devil, but you fan the flames of memory too, where that soot-faced god, Hephaestus, forges away. . . .

By your fire I now see a child rambling from room to room, muttering away for his mother, racked by incomprehensible desire, muttering rather loudly: "That lousy butcher gypped me again. . . . I should smack him on the head with all the bones. . . ." Meanwhile my words grow increasingly savage and bitter, and in a corner of the parlor I cry out, now enraged, "They take all our money, that they do!"

Perhaps I was waiting for Mother to come running in on hearing this cry, to discern what *I* didn't even know; to decipher, to mold into intelligibility the shapeless phantoms seething at the bottom of my heart. Yet this is not what happened. Instead I began to cry — just why, I don't even know; and so I continued meandering from room to room, my tears dousing the muddled groans from the deep.

Having cried away all my tears, I shouted once again, now with frantic abandon, "They take all our hard-earned money, that they do!"

Mother ran in frightened. At which I laughed at her brazenly.

"What's this?" she said, "You go scaring your mother, then you laugh? What a bad boy you are!"

I cast her a doggedly treacherous smile, unaware of the questions that hovered on my face: How *bad* am I? Come on, guess! And why?

But she didn't guess. She only sighed as I went on roving

about the flat. "She is afraid, and she is afraid for me," I thought. "She is my mother. . . ."

THEN I WAIT for my brother and sister.

When the uproar sounds from the courtyard, where the elementary school is located, I am already eagerly lying in wait in the hall. And on hearing the clatter of Oluska's bag from the stairwell, I open the door. I wait for her to call out and wrap her arms fawningly around my neck, to say how much she missed me while she was in school and how very happy she is finally to see her little brother again.

Little do I think or feel that she is waiting for the very same sentiment from *me!* And so I only open the door and call, "Oluska!" While she says only, "I'm back."

Then we probe each other's eyes, which speak the same words: You give your heart first, then I'll give you mine. Neither one of us moves toward the other. Meanwhile Oluska has already taken off her bag and turned to head into the kitchen to Mother.

With glittery, eager eyes I follow. Having failed to find in her the sisterly heart I'd expected her to give me, I am bent on rummaging about for it in her bag, which is rattling enticingly. And so I snatch it away. Jealously she snatches it right back, however, as if to say: You didn't ask for my heart, so you're certainly not getting my bag! At first she wants to put the bag in its usual place, under the washbasin, but noticing me watch her so slyly, she goes about finding a better place. Oluska flits into the next room, then the second, and the third, lugging her bag and with me on her tail. Nowhere does she find a place so secure that sooner or later I wouldn't get at the bag. The more red she turns from anger, the more I laugh.

That poor bag, which now must compensate for the brotherly and sisterly hearts we've denied each other. Yes, it meanders in Oluska's hands all the way through the flat until finally arriving before Mother, who puts it on top of the tall closet amid admonitions every bit as distant and unmotherly as she herself is to me. How can I do as I am told when what I want is a big sister; if not a loving sister, why then, at least one that I can squabble with? And doesn't Oluska want the same thing when now she yanks away the chair I want to climb to reach her bag? In no time we are scuffling; her big black sparkling eyes flash, and her little nose twists with rage; her thick little pigtails fly about, the red bows nearly fluttering right off their ends, like a pair of butterflies. Springing up, I snatch them out of the air and run with them wherever I can. Oluska then dashes to the opposite end of the flat and takes my paper soldiers hostage. Then we stand facing each other menacingly, holding our loot tight. Finally, trembling with rage, we exchange our pawns.

We haven't even noticed that Ernuskó has meanwhile arrived with his own bag.

He sides with neither one of us. Straight to Mother he goes, me following greedily close behind, watching the two of them. On seeing him, Mother bursts out with coddling giggles. She always gives him one or two kisses more than me; she gives him nothing more, nothing at all, only that kiss or two and that laughter. No, not even for him does Mother dance, make music, tell stories — but how very much that kiss or two is to me! The sting pierces my heart to the core, but I don't want to hear of my pain. In no time I suppress it to that realm where all other puerile desires swirl about like clouds in shapeless absurdity.

"He's a good boy," says my mother the moment she sees me. "He doesn't go scaring his mother."

I listen gruffly. Oluska stands behind me. Has she also noticed that extra kiss or two, that laughter? Her eyes sparkle with envy.

"And *me?* And *me?*" she cries out, snuggling up to my mother. "Aren't I good?"

Mother laughs. "Not always, but usually." And on seeing my darkening face, she calls out: "And aren't you coming over to me? Aren't you my good little boy?"

I just stand there. Doesn't she know what she's doing? Doesn't she know I saw that kiss or two and heard that laughter? Could it be she doesn't know? Or is she just pretending? What can I say to her?

Stepping over to her, I think: Go ahead then, kiss me if you want.

She pecks me on the cheek.

"You're not bad, after all, just a little naughty."

I think: Don't go soft-pedaling on me. Why not just admit that you love Ernuskó more? If you don't admit it, just stay the way you are. And don't ask me for another kiss ever again. Just stay the way you are, and that goes for all of you.

I pull away from her. Ernuskó's face seems to say: I deserve more kisses, because I'm older and a good student.

Well, I think to myself, I believe you're pretty good and smart, as far as my parents and Oluska and your teachers are concerned, but to me you're neither pretty good nor pretty smart, for otherwise you'd come over to me and say: Mother kissed me more than you, but don't let it get to you. Here, I'll give you back the extra ones I got! Then he'd say: I'm older, and a good student, come on over here, I'll teach you to read and write as well.

But he says nothing of the sort. Nor has he ever done so. And so I have not a bit of his good behavior and smarts, and don't know if I ever will.

The last to get home is Father. Our mother's face brightens again, even more than on seeing Ernuskó. Yes, I think, it's really just the two of them she loves. But she loves Father even more than Ernuskó.

Father hugs us even less than Mother. He only pats our faces, but from the way he does so it seems as if he's thinking: I'm big, and all of you are little. He doesn't say, "My dear children, it's been so long since I saw you," but only: "Well, children, what's new?"

First Ernuskó goes about relating his day in school, the usual message beaming quietly from his face: I was good at answering the teacher's questions, since I'm smart and a good boy, and I always will be, that's for sure. At which Father's face appears to reply: Yes, that you are, as was I. And it's in the order of things that you should be.

I watch them suspiciously. I don't yet know for sure, but I suspect that Father also loves Ernuskó more than either me or Oluska. I suppress this pain as well, to the bottom of my heart, and keep it there under lock and key.

After Ernuskó, Oluska says what she has to say — impetuously, with a sense of urgency and envy, lest she should lag behind Ernuskó. From the way Father listens and watches, however, I suspect that what happened to Oluska in school can't be as important to him as what happened to Ernuskó, for the simple reason that she is nothing but a girl. Beyond this, though, his face seems to say: Even if you are a girl, I expect you to be a good student too, because I was in my day, and so is Ernuskó. You cannot be anything but.

Then he looks at me.

"Well, what about you?"

Mother bursts out laughing.

"He's always just up to mischief."

Maybe she doesn't want to hurt me with her ridiculing tone of voice, peppered with laughter; maybe she doesn't realize its effect on me, but it hurts terribly all the same. What happened with me in the morning is nothing but mischief to her?

"Well now," says my father, "we'll see what happens next year, when *you've* got to study too!"

He says nothing else to me.

We sit down to lunch. Listening to them talk, I think: Can I help it that I'm not yet in school? Why does he love me less because of this, why does he bother less about me than with Ernuskó? And less than even Oluska? Why didn't he ask me anything? Only those who go to school get to be asked questions? And those who don't yet go to school, aren't they the same as the others? Does he imagine that nothing happened to me today? If he were to give me a big peck on the cheek and ask me, I too could talk about what happened to me all morning. And how! So much happened, after all. I would tell him about this and that piece of furniture around the flat, how motionless they are, how there's not a bit of play or dance or sound in them, how they hardly even notice me, and how it's impossible to do a thing with them. I'd ask him why it is that not even my mother can kiss, sing, or tell stories, and doesn't even want to, though this hurts me so much. . . . Why is it that she talks only of things that cost "precious, hard-earned money"? I'd ask him, does it really kill him earning that money? And: How exactly *does* he earn it? I'd ask why Oluska is so spiteful, why Ernuskó is so proud of being a good student. Finally: Why do they prefer Ernuskó over me, and why do he and Mother love each other more than they do me?

Once I'd asked all this, he would reply, and even if he wouldn't say too much, maybe I'd be satisfied with even this: Parents love those children who are older and already in school. It has always been this way and always will be. Or: I can't really say why things are this way, my little one, but they are, don't let it get to you now, and forgive me, won't you?

But no — he doesn't ask me a thing. He couldn't care less what happens to me.

I don't want it to hurt, so I take this pain, too, and lock it away at the bottom of my heart. And I think: I couldn't care less about you, either!

Nonetheless I listen closely to his words. Throughout lunch he speaks with Mother, and it is terribly distressing to hear him, too, talk only of things that cost or will cost money. Besides wanting us to be good students, it seems to me that this is the only thing Father really cares about; and so I begin to think with hate but also fear of money; that thing which, it seems, my parents always have little of, whereas everything costs money, even that which we are eating at the table just now. How good it would be, I think, if I didn't have to eat, if I wasn't as hungry as I always am. Then I think: If we had a lot more money, would my parents bother about me more, kiss me more, and ask me too what I've been up to? All I know is this: I eat what they put before me with ever greater shame. Although I'm hungry, and really do like to eat, I don't ask for a second helping. Mother has to do a lot of convincing before I accept any more. I'd rather eat bread, and I suspect that Ernuskó and Oluska think the same. It occurs less and less often, I notice, that Father offers us more. Bread is food too, he says. When I was little we often didn't even have enough of *that!* . . . Thus I am even more ashamed of myself; through a fog of pain I recall Papa Jeremiah as he kneaded dough in the tent with his old, wrinkled hands, and fed me.

AFTER LUNCH my parents take a nap in the inner room.

Why they need to sleep by day is beyond me. I'm not the least bit tired. My brother and sister sit on the little bench and do their homework. As for me, since I can't leave the room while the folks are asleep, I listen. Upstairs someone is playing a violin; older students play music up there. Sometimes I meet up with them in the stairwell when my mother sends me down to the nearby store, or when I'm allowed to go down to the courtyard. They carry their violins in big black cases, but not one of them greets me like I'd want; obviously they figure that since I'm little and not yet a good student, they don't really have to bother with me. They only call out: Hey there, little guy, whatcha up to? Yet it never occurs to a single one of them to really speak to me, though I'd sure like that. I'd like to ask them about their parents: Are things the same at their place as at ours? And I'd ask them to play the violin for me a bit. But it's not just they who are like this with me: Everyone who lives in the building — the teachers, the cantors, and other neighbors — at most tweaks my nose and strokes my hair, but that's it, nothing more, no real talk; and I can't *ask* them to give me what I want, no, I'm too proud. Best that they just be on their way, I don't want anything to do with them either!

How it hurts all the same! Yes, the whole building, from top to bottom, adults, fathers, mothers, students, maids, not to mention those just passing through — all their faces have just one thing written all over them: No sense bothering about such a little boy! No sense *really* talking to him!

Nowhere does there open a door, nowhere a window, whence someone might cry out: "Come on now, no matter how little you are, I really want to talk to you!"

Yet why would they be any different from those who are my parents, brother, and sister? Am I supposed to go out onto the street looking for someone I can really talk to? A kid like me? Why, I hardly dare to leave the building. And my mother has strictly forbidden me to do so. Why? "Because you can never know who you'll meet up with! Maybe he'll beat you, throw something at you, spit on you." Would this really happen? Why? Mother says folks are mostly bad, not good, and children all the more. Is this so? She should know, because she's a grown-up already. Should I believe her? *She* is not even really my mother. Though I don't exactly believe her, I am frightened; maybe it's just like she says, and I couldn't take it. I'd rather not even talk to anyone down there. This hurts, terribly. Should I go over in my distress and disturb my brother and sister in their homework? My parents in their dreams? My father would only scold me anyway. How alone I am! . . . And for how long now! I don't even remember since when! It seems things have always been this way. And when will they be different? Never! A long, long time will pass before I am bigger — maybe I will never be bigger, and even if I am, things won't be any different. . . . Nothing will ever be different around here, no, these people will never be my parents, my siblings, and not one of all the other familiar faces in the building will ever really talk to me. And never will I dare go out and be the first to talk to them. It hurts.

Glumly I look about our room. What to do, what to do with myself? I don't feel like doing a thing anymore.

What toys I have, those paper soldiers, I've long worn out and gotten tired of. My father won't buy any more. And there's no going outside while my parents are asleep.

I glance at the window. Once, twice, thrice.

Whenever I make a move to climb up there, Mother always says: "Careful! If you fall out, that's the end of you, you're finished."

"What's that mean," I ask, 'end of me'?"

"It means all your bones will break down there, every last one."

"And then?"

"Then you can't get up ever again."

"And then?"

"Oh, stop asking so many questions. What else do you want?"

"And then," I add, "will you all cry over me?"

"Now that'll do a whole lot of good! You. And us too."

Watching the window, I think: *Now that'll do a whole lot of good!* Sure, I think, they'd rather not cry over me. That's why Mother doesn't want me near the window.

I imagine climbing up to the window and falling out; there's lots of screaming while I lie there down below, my bones all broken, "every last one," but that's just talk, as is her saying, "you can't get up ever again." I neither can nor want to imagine either, no, the only thing I can imagine is that I'm already lying down there, my eyes open just so I can see what happens afterward.

I hear my mother's dreadful scream, "He's dead, dead, done for!" Through her sobs she cries: Oh dear, I should have loved him more after all. Loved him like Ernuskó. I should have danced for him. And sung. Bought him more toys.

And my father? Crying? Impossible to imagine. Sad, at most. And he says: I should have talked to him like an adult, after all. Really. But now it's too late; he's stopped moving, that he has.

Ernuskó is crying too. So is Oluska. But then again, Ernuskó is thinking: I'm a good student, but I wouldn't dare be dead. Like him. And Oluska thinks: Who will cry as much over me? Now everyone cares only about him.

What then? I've never seen a dead body and known it. When someone dies he's buried, and then, just like in synagogue, my father gives a sermon; this much I know. There are big funerals and little funerals, yes, I know that too; rich folks get the big ones, and for this they pay my father more than for a smaller funeral, but just how much, now that I don't know, he never tells us kids. My father prepares in advance for a "big" funeral and gives a long sermon; at smaller funerals, or for poorer folks, he gives a shorter sermon; and as for those folks who can't pay a thing or "just don't want to pay," he says nothing but a prayer. This is really odd, for Father always says that the rich and the poor are equal before God. All the same, I'm not allowed to go asking all sorts of questions about this, for every time I've tried, Father has said: "That's not your business." All right, I think: I know full well anyway that you do this because you always need money, you always have so little of it. But why don't you just tell me?

Sometimes, though, I've noticed that my father doesn't pay attention to what he's being paid. But he does this only with those he calls the "truest of his flock," that is to say, those who are always there in synagogue — especially when he is preaching. My mother says these folks "lap up" what Father says, even when the weather's bad or when they're sick; and afterward they keep pumping his hand or come to pay us a visit the same day or the next, thanking him "with feeling" — so says Mother — for the "lovely sermon." At such times Mother sometimes even notices tears in their eyes. These "truest" of the flock always "side with" Father at the congregation meetings; they'd raise his pay and give him everything he might desire, and on the Day of Rejoicing they always send us a little something — if nothing else, at least a nice bouquet of flowers.

Whenever one of these folks dies, even if he or she was poor, Father says he gives a "really nice eulogy."

Some dead folk get more praise and others less, and then there are yet others he doesn't praise at all, not even if they pay for a big funeral. No, instead he says "just what he thinks of them," but, explains Father to Mother, "Don't you worry, dear, only those will understand who've got plenty of reason to." Other times Father doesn't even bother with this: "I'm not going to say anything bad about the deceased, though they'd deserve it for being so weak — but by God I'll let the others have it." These "others" are those sons and other relatives of the deceased who've "turned Christian." For these, Father says, there's no mercy, "not even at the grave. But at least there they'll be ashamed of themselves."

I know all this only by listening to my parents talk about it, however, for Father's never taken any of us to a funeral. And how gladly I would have gone, if for no other reason than to take a little ride, for at such times a four-wheeled carriage comes to get him. As he sees it, though, a funeral is not an occasion for a ride, and the cemetery's too far for a child to go on foot. My mother doesn't go to funerals, either, it would "really upset" her. This is all I know about death. I won't concern myself with all of this now, however; I wonder only what my own funeral would be like if I were to fall out the window.

All I can imagine is that everyone would cry a whole lot. And I would think: There there, it won't do any good anymore!

Taking another look at the window, I think again: Since I'll never be any different, never any bigger, why then, the least that can happen is that everyone cries, just like I would cry too if I weren't so proud.

Up there in the window I'll be afraid no doubt — everyone's afraid of falling out a window. But I'll do it anyway. Yes, I'll show them that no matter how little I am, I'll do it all the same. Then they'll all realize how much it hurts me the way things are.

I drag the chair over to the sewing machine in front of the window and climb up. Meanwhile I take a peek at my brother and sister. Ernuskó is still writing his homework; in no time Oluska looks up with envy. At first she doesn't say a thing. Only when I finally manage to get onto the sewing table does she begin.

"What are you up to now?"

I don't reply. For now I am only resting on the sewing table, dangling my legs over the chair beneath me. Oluska starts again.

"Hey, you're not allowed to do that! You'll be in trouble if Dad finds out."

What can I possibly say to her? Bitterly, I reply: "I stay out of your hair, so you stay out of mine!"

Already fuming, she rises from her bench. "I'll tell Mother on you!"

I don't say another word. In a rage, Oluska heads for the door behind which Mother is sleeping. Now Ernuskó speaks up too.

"I can't do my homework this way. Stop fighting, you two."

Oluska waits in front of the door. Gruffly, bitterly I watch them. What could I possibly say? Ernuskó cares only about his homework; he's smart to be sure, a good student, but he doesn't know what I want, nothing hurts him that hurts me. As for Oluska, she doesn't even know as much as Ernuskó, maybe she'd even be envious if I jumped out.

In no time I'm kneeling on the sewing table and beginning to open the window. It has four casements. First I see to the outer ones. Then I pause. Wait for the effect. Fuming mad, Oluska watches me from in front of the door.

"That's nothing! Just try the other ones!"

As good as done. The autumn air streams in the window; I hear carriages rattling by down below. My knees are touching the windowsill, which I can step onto if I have the guts. By grabbing the casement, I can stand up, and then jump.

But I don't have the guts to even stand in the window. How will I then jump out? The fear that comes with the awareness that all I need do is stand, take a step, and jump, and nothing will come between me and that which no one dares to do — this fear suddenly sweeps away all the day's hurt! Yet I want to go the very edge of my boldness. I stand. Placing a foot, just one, on the inner sill, and clutching one of the casements, I stand. But then I don't even dare move. With one eye only, I squint out into the autumn air.

"Careful," says Ernuskó, as befits a smart boy and good student, "come on down from there, or else you'll be in for it."

What else can I expect of him? No matter how good a student he is, not even now does he understand what it is I want. And what's worse, and hurts, it does, is the sense that I will not jump out after all because I'm getting scared, ever more scared. And to think how good it would be! Yet I don't dare, no. . . . My heart is beating wildly, my legs make as if to move, but I can do no more than tremble; I won't be jumping out, and I get this odd feeling that never in a thousand years will I dare jump out, and by now my eyes are clouding over. Maybe I'd cry, if at this very moment Oluska doesn't open the door of Mother's room. At this I come to my senses and hear my big sister's voice.

"Mama! Take a look! Look what Gyuri's doing! He stood in the window!"

Mother gives a start. "What's that?" and in fright she calls to Father. "Papa, did you hear that?"

Frantically they hurry over, Oluska close behind. The moment that Mother sees me she lets out a shuddering cry.

"Look!" and she turns so we don't have to see her press a hand to her heart.

"What are you doing?" cries out my father, his face flustered and pale. Running over to me, he grabs the arm with which I'd been clutching the casement and yanks me off the sewing table. Once I'm safely on the bench, he snarls, then slaps me twice on the face, first from the right, then from the left. "You just can't sit still in your own hide, you fool!"

I stand there trembling, my face red from shame and slaps. Red-hot shame wrenches my heart: I want terribly to melt away to nothing. But then this pain soon turns numb — my limbs, my body, my heart, all numb to the core. Insensibly, rigidly, clumsily I stand there staring at my father with awestricken hate. He goes on scolding me. I now look at my mother. Still pressing a hand to her heart, she says: "Ever hear of such a thing?! My heart stopped beating, just like that!" Then an afterthought: "Haven't you frightened me enough for one day?"

She is every bit as red as my father is deathly white, and her eyes seem moist. Don't tell me she wants to cry? Because of me?

"I don't get it," she says to Father, who is walking in exasperation back and forth around me, still, I suspect, ready to strike at any moment. "Seriously now, this child's not all there. Don't even touch him."

"Oh, he's all there, all right," says Father, "just that he can't sit still in his own hide!" Again he shouts: "Can't you find yourself some other plaything, you lunatic?"

Mother cuts in: "Let him be. Don't get yourself all upset. Next time he'll think twice." She strokes and then pats Father's hand. At which Father asks her, "Were you awfully scared?"

Mother smiles, but her eyes are still moist.

"Why of course! My heart stopped completely. But now it'll go away, only my head hurts."

At this Father gives me another furious look. Mother restrains him, then sits down by the table while he paces back and forth.

Although I've practically frozen by now and my sense of things is cool, sharp, and precise, my face is still burning. I figure that Mother kept Father from another round of slaps only because he's really pale, and she doesn't want him getting "all upset." For his part, Father would like to hit me once again, no doubt because I got them "all upset," but especially, I think, because Mother was frightened, and as he puts it, "Her heart stopped beating completely, and her head hurts."

They can be frightened and upset all they want, it's all the same to me. Maybe Mother's heart didn't really stop as much as she said — my heart has sure never stopped, my head has never hurt. Father's pale-faced agitation is both frightening and loathsome, exactly like his whooping voice. I don't feel sorry for them at all, nor for myself. You had it coming, I think — why didn't you jump out the window when you had the chance?

Finally Father slows his steps and Mother's face reassumes its usual hue. He stops before her and asks, tenderly, "Is your heart back in order?"

Mother nods repeatedly, then takes a handkerchief from her blouse and starts dabbing her eyes, which are glistening with moisture. Whether her tears are tears of fear, I do not know, I only suspect that somehow they are not quite meant for me. And this is precisely why I feel just a tad sorry for her; yet even this empathy fuses with my sense of shame and with the searching look of fearful scorn I cast upon my father. Soon enough, Mother's tears become all-out crying. Fearing that this will prompt Father to slap me again, I think: You've got to bear it. For now, however, he only shoots an agitated, burning look my way, with no little disdain as well. No longer does he concern himself with me. Instead he caresses one of Mother's hands; her other hand holds the handkerchief into which she cries, now rather loudly.

Her face contorts and turns completely red. Never have I seen her cry so much; maybe she's crying over me, too, just a little. Seeing her face all twisted up, so ugly, I'm a bit more moved. Father keeps standing there beside her trying to calm her down, while she says through her tears, "It's best if I cry it all out." But then quite suddenly her tears dry up. "Oh, just look at me," she says, now turning more toward Father than me. "How could he do such a thing? He's always been naughty, getting in the way all the time and wrecking the furniture, but never mind that. Sure, he fights with Oluska too, but *this?* I really wouldn't have thought he'd do this sort of thing."

Father turns to Oluska. "Did he pick a fight with you?"

Soft and timid comes my sister's reply, as if she's afraid of Father: "He only wanted my bag."

"And with you, Ernuskó?"

"Not with me," replies Ernuskó in a measured voice, as befits a good student.

"If he so much as lays a hand on either one of you," bids Father, "tell me at once, and I'll break his bones!"

Now he turns to me: "You'll learn what discipline is all about, you will! You'll learn how to keep still in that hide of yours! If you dare touch the furniture from now on, you're in for it!"

Mother speaks. "Leave him be now. Instead why not ask him why he did it?"

Father replies, "Because he can't keep still in his own hide, he's got it too good!"

I do not and cannot know that he is thinking of his own childhood, when, amid far scantier circumstances, he fasted obediently while studying the commentaries with Papa Jeremiah. I do not know that those memories are behind the blazing fire deep in his steel blue eyes as he stares upon me now, and that all the deprivation and suffering of his childhood, which have hardened his heart, haunts every aspect of his behavior toward me.

I listen.

Rising from the table, Mother says to him. "Come on, maybe I can get a bit more sleep."

They head off. While passing by me Mother stops and, shaking her head disapprovingly, strokes my hair. "Oh God, Gyuri, why are you so bad?"

I avoid her eyes. She adds: "So tell me, how could you have done such a thing?"

Does she really want to know, I thought, how hard things are for me? Casting her a suspicious look, I can't say for sure. Again she strokes my hair.

"Go ahead and tell us, come on, we won't do anything to you anymore."

Her face, so tender from crying, and her hand stroking my hair, go straight to my heart. Yet I am suspicious of her all the same, and afraid of Father. No, I won't tell Mother straight out. Let her figure out the rest. And so I only reply: "I wanted to fall out."

Mother is taken aback. "*Wh-what?* You wanted to jump?" Turning to Father, she says, "Did you hear that? Do you get it?"

They stand there gaping at each other. Soon Father gives a contemptuous wave of the hand and says, "Oh sure. Nonsense!"

But Mother persists: "Talk to him, for God's sake!"

Agitated, Father turns to me. "Don't you know you'd break every bone in your body? You fool! You lunatic! You think jumping off this floor to the street is like from a chair to the floor?"

I stare at them. So not even now do they suspect what is in me, no, they don't realize that I might have climbed up there for some reason other than "foolishness," or, say, because I wanted to frighten them. They don't know a thing, and I don't want them to know, either.

Mother practically whispers, "Oh God, could it be he's lost his senses this much?" And she mutters: "Maybe you shouldn't have hit him? We should have just explained things to him!"

I only go on listening as Father offers her soothing words.

"Don't you believe he didn't know that he'd get hurt! And don't believe he really wanted to jump! He's got more sense than that! It's just that he's unruly, and wants to upset us any way he can!"

These words only make me all the more ashamed for not having jumped out the window. Father knows even less about me than my mother and siblings. Him being the most distant from me, I've always got to be afraid of him.

He says a few more words to reassure Mother as to the state of my mind, then they retire into the other room.

All is silent for a while after they leave. Like a statue I continue standing in the same spot where Father struck my face.

A new storm rages within me. My aching heart spurs a thirst for revenge: I want to rip apart my brother and sister's notebooks, then run head-on into my parents, scolding and hitting my father just as he'd done to me, then run right out of our flat so as never to see it again, so I'd never again have to accept another thing from him, and never again have to say to him, *Father*. My heart is beating wildly, my whole body is trembling with resolve — yet I can't so much as budge. I am afraid of my father, for I am little, and shame plagues me as well, aware as I am that everything that happened, happened to me.

Feeling helpless, I try choking back tears. This makes me more ashamed, and scared. The last thing I need is for my brother and sister to realize how miserable I am. But I don't dare leave the room, either. They — Oluska in particular — might figure out that I left to cry. Nor do I want my parents to learn of my tears; they'd only be convinced that they were in the right, that I am repentant and desire their forgiveness.

I fight back the tears, and stay.

Now Oluska whispers away with Ernuskó, then speaks to me.

"See? Why'd you do such a thing?"

Her voice is now conciliatory, almost tender. I figure this is because what happened to me alleviated her envy. I don't say a thing. She begins again.

"Does it hurt a lot?"

There is curiosity in her tenderness and, I sense, envy anew, since I didn't cry in spite of Father's heavy blows.

"Well, if you don't talk," she says, offended, "I won't bother about you either!"

She falls silent. At which Ernuskó speaks, like a good student indeed.

"This happened because you two are always fighting, and because you scared Mother so much."

I don't answer him either. Little do I realize what their little world is all about, and that I cannot step beyond this world. No, I feel only that what happened, terrible and unjust as it was, nonetheless changed their behavior not in the least. I want to show that I am not as wretched as in fact I feel, and that I could care less about the blows, the scolding I received; and so I begin tapping away at the stove, humming softly to myself.

Now, I figure, I can leave the room.

While passing through the kitchen into the hall, I think: You didn't dare say and do what you wanted, so now you're even more alone than before, and the way things are hurts all the more. And you can't do a thing about it.

Again beset by the urge to cry, I slip quickly into the narrow lavatory at the end of the hall, bolt the door, and finally begin to cry nonetheless.

The sobs come ever stronger, but I take care so they can't be heard outside. My whole body is trembling. My puny, ungainly shoulders twitch away, my frail chest heaves, my breath starts and stops in fits. The pain subdues my strength. As if I've swallowed too big a mouthful of food, I nearly choke on my stifled tears.

As my tears now dry up slowly, once again I want more than anything to leave home, and if not necessarily bravely, while berating Father, why then, at least in secret, quietly. Yet I am afraid of this, too. Father would just be angry again if he got wind of it; yes, he'd be ashamed that I am off to search for other parents, and would never let me go.

Where could I go, then, where he could not reach me, from where he could not bring me back? Should I seek refuge with the neighbors in our building? With the teachers? Or upstairs, where the violin playing comes from? These people all know my father, their rabbi, really well; and every time they meet up with him they smile and greet him without delay. Not one would take me in, no, surely they would betray me to him.

Where to, then? People live in other buildings, too. This much I'm sure of; every Friday night I see them in synagogue. Yet these, too, would send me right back to my parents as surely as would those in our own building.

Where indeed? To those who "don't attend our synagogue," as Father is given to saying? I don't even dare think of this.

So much for escape. I must stay here, with my parents. From now on, every morsel of food, every piece of clothing, and every reprimand will hurt all the more, and they'll bother with me even less than they did before. It cannot be any other way. Why didn't you jump out the window? Why don't you have the guts to go outside, downstairs, ask someone for help? It serves you right, you puny little coward!

Utterly exhausted from all the anguish, all the tears, I only stared ahead.

Perhaps a half hour passed this way before I began mechanically cleaning myself, licking all around my mouth and otherwise doing what I could to wipe away my tears. This was all I was able to do so they would not see my pain.

I unbolted the door and stepped into the hall.

How sad this place had become! The window called to me: "You see? It's just too late."

The long wall was occupied by two dressers and a large chest between them, which functioned as a hamper; here I sat staring at the window, then at the long wall opposite and the imposing coatrack before it. This held nothing but Father's hat, his autumn overcoat, and his gold-handled walking stick. I stared upon them with listless hatred, and to counter the tears, which still held me firmly in their grip, I raised my legs, clasped my arms around them, sunk my head onto my chest deep between my shoulders, and kept staring like this for quite a while, until a sudden noise made me look up with a start.

The door of Father's study had opened up, and there he stood, on the threshold.

"Come in here," he called.

What more am I in for? I wondered. With fear, loathing, and shame I staggered off the chest and entered the room.

There was much more light in there, and this window also called to me: "See? It's just too late." Mother now sat in front of the desk, in the armchair usually occupied by Father. I stopped in the middle of the long, narrow room.

Father spoke. "It hasn't yet crossed your mind to apologize to your mother?"

I said nothing, but thought: So they want this too, do they? Isn't it enough that I've already suffered so much on account of them?

Now Mother spoke, in a soft, mournful tone. "You don't even feel sorry for your mother, do you? How much more should I cry over you?"

And I thought: So she really believes that she's been crying over me? That I'm the one who should be feeling sorry for her, not the other way around?

Seeing me hesitate, Father now spoke much louder. "Well, are you going to apologize?"

Mother lulled him with sweet talk. "He'll do it. Right, Gyuri? We only want what's best for you, you know. So promise you won't get Papa any more upset."

What parents! I thought. What a mother and father! They can think of nothing but each other, can they? And they dare say that they want what's "best" for me!

All these "lies" rekindled my languid will. And so I decided to tell them all the same just what I thought of them. Not only had they behaved wrongly toward me — so I would tell them — but they also thought wrongly of me. In short, they had no right to corner me into an apology.

I turned to Mother. "I didn't want anything bad to happen," I explained, "all I wanted was to really jump out the window. But not to cause trouble, and not because I'm 'not all there,' but because . . ."

Suddenly frightened, I stopped. Then I ventured, looking at them both: "You won't hit me anymore, will you?"

Mother replied, "No, just go on!"

And so I gave it to them straight.

"I wanted to jump out because things aren't good for me at home."

Obviously annoyed, Father scowled. This frightened me again.

"So," he said sharply, "things aren't good for you at home?"

Mother turned red — from shame, I figured. Worried that she'd start crying again, I was sorry for what I'd said. But it was too late. Father went on.

"And why aren't things good for you? What's bad about your home? Do you even know what 'bad' is? Is there anything you lack? Don't get enough to eat, perhaps? Don't have decent clothes? Nowhere to sleep? What's so bad for you? How dare you talk like this?"

Mother tried calming him down. "Wait, Papa," she said, addressing him as she often did. "We'll get around to explaining it all to him, but for now, let the silly boy talk."

And she laughed.

Yet this laughter did not come from her heart, I felt. No, she wanted only to calm Father down, lest he should get himself "upset"; and she wanted to conceal her irritation at my words, and the shame she felt for being irritated.

"Go ahead, then," called Father gruffly, for Mother's sake only, "talk."

Frightened and ashamed of it, I began. As much as I wanted to lay it all on the table — how I'd felt that morning, what I thought of them, not to mention of my brother and sister — through my fear all I managed to spurt out was this: "Not a single piece of furniture paid me any notice, none made sounds, moved, winked, or, more generally, showed themselves as I would have liked."

Father waved a hand dismissively. "Enough of this nonsense!"

Once again Mother laughed, however. Not only did she want to amuse Father and otherwise calm him down, but, I felt sure, she was outright making fun of me, yes, she was laughing at me as much as she well could! And this hurt not only my heart but my pride.

I fell silent.

"Did you ever hear of such a thing?" Mother cried out. "Hey, Papa! The things this child says! How funny!"

By now her eyes were sparkling merrily indeed, and her tender face had puffed up, she was laughing so loudly and truly. Perhaps it wasn't so much that she wanted to hurt me, I felt, but more so that she simply didn't understand me, and, besides, that she just loved to laugh.

"Come over here!" she called, and took my hand. "Do you really believe that furniture can dance? Make sounds the way you like? And that the painting could move at your wish?"

I replied: "No, I don't believe it, I just want it."

Mother only laughed. "But how can you want such a thing? That's impossible!"

I said nothing. What could I have said? I only blushed.

Once Mother's laughter had ebbed, Father, suppressing a passing smile, looked Mother in the eye and spoke.

"This isn't so funny, you know. Your laughter is only egging him on. He'll think that what he's saying is proper and clever." Now he turned to me. "So instead of apologizing, you believe that you behaved properly and didn't deserve what you got? You take to explaining how bad things are for you! Because the furniture doesn't dance, the stove doesn't play the violin, and we don't do handstands around you? You think all of us, and this whole flat, exist for your amusement? And if we don't oblige, that you can scare your mother to death and turn the place upside down? Well, mark my word, I'll cure that little mouth of yours of such unruly, shameless talk!"

He proceeded to note that I had my choice of the paper soldiers and Oluska's dolls, and if all this wasn't to my liking, I could always begin learning to read and write, and if I didn't want this either, I should sit on my behind and not let out a peep. I'd better not go bothering anyone who's keeping busy, no, I had no right to do so, and every time this would happen, he'd smack me exactly like he had today.

Since I offered no reply, Mother spoke. "You see, it would have been better after all just to apologize, like a good boy, and not talk all that silly little nonsense. Well? It's still not too late."

At which Father said: "There's no point anymore." He looked at me: "You can go." With a wave of the hand, he added, "Now, once and for all remember what I told you."

Red-faced, I staggered out of the room. Mother called after me. When I paused on the threshold, however, Father sent me on my way.

"Go on, get about your business," he said.

And so I shut the door behind me. Yet as I stood there, I could hear Mother's words from the other room.

"Hey, Papa," she began, "aren't you too strict with him? He's so little, after all. . . ."

This line of defense didn't exactly flatter me. Nor did it soothe my sense of shame. Father replied, "I know what I'm doing! If we don't teach him right from wrong while he's still so little, to respect his parents and to love his brother and sister, to put the brakes on all his tomfoolery and selfishness; if we don't do this now, later on we'll never manage with him! If he already wants the furniture to play violin and to dance at his bidding, the stove to whistle for him, the paintings to jump from their frames — if he wants all this now, what will he demand of them later? His brother and sister are just barely older, but would either dare talk like that?"

He fell silent. Eagerly I listened for more. Judging from how he continued, it seemed that my behavior had roused his childhood memories like a stone does a bird from a bush.

"When I was his age, I was happy to have my fill of bread! Never would I even have dreamed that I might live like him! Never did I sleep in such a bed! Never did I have a nice new set of clothes! I didn't rack my brain wondering why the angels up there on the stove didn't wink at me; no, instead I wondered why the stove was made of iron, why I couldn't take a bite and eat of it. By his age I'd already learned whole chapters of the commentaries, just so I could be the best student, because old Chacham Tulcyzn gave the best a kreuzer on Saturday night! And then I could buy myself a little fruit to go with the bread."

"Oh," said Mother, "don't even talk of such things!" After a pause she added, "This is what you should have told the child. He might learn something from it. . . ."

No doubt Father shook his head.

"The little fool would think I'm sorry *he* doesn't live that way. . . ."

They fell silent.

I was shocked and ashamed. Sure, I thought, this must be really bad for him, but it's not like I can do anything about it.

With a sigh I left the door and sat back on the hamper.

I waited. Maybe Father would come out into the hall and suddenly talk to me in such a way that I'd forget all that had happened, and so I could cry away all my pain. Yet I waited in vain. It wasn't Father, but darkness, that came, descending upon me from above the two dressers, on either side of the hamper.

Ever so slowly the dark green stripes of wall faded away in the long and narrow hall; then the angels embroidered into two pieces of red silk vanished as well — the sort that could be picked up at flea markets, and which hung under glass on either side of the coatrack; and the long, disheveled trailers of the asparagus plants loomed as an increasingly dense mass before the window. Indeed, by now only Father's overcoat, hat, and walking stick were still distinguishable from the coatrack, and I went on waiting, until fatigue saw me, too, fade away. . . .

A strange brightness roused me awake. Father had entered the hall and turned on the light. He stepped over to the coatrack and was reaching for his overcoat when he noticed me.

"Don't sleep here on the chest," he said, "go into the room and lie down on the divan."

After the initial fright I muttered obediently, "Yes, sir." And so I climbed off the chest.

I watched as Father donned his overcoat, and then, before the mirror, removed his skullcap, slipped it inside his coat's long lappet, and carefully positioned his hat on his head. I opened the door to the study, went in, and sat down on the divan. Dusk grew ever stronger. Soon I stretched out.

Gradually the darkness softened all that had happened. The less I could see, the more the stern movements with which Father had yanked me from the window, the more his shouts and smacks, blurred within me. Behind all this there lurked a deep and, to me, incomprehensible love; and so I began to reconcile myself to him. Soon I took to imagining that the fast-disappearing sunlight had somehow found its way into Father, so as the darkness enveloped me, his heart, his form, slowly began to draw me in. His steely gray eyes now fixed themselves upon me in a sea blue hue, and I could feel his hand on my head in the very way in which he would bless me on Saturday nights. I still recalled all that "hard-earned money" that had distressed me so much all day long — but what a real, painful weight imminent nightfall now bestowed upon it! . . . There were plenty of these rays of twilight to go around for everyone. With love borne of fear and humility, I soon began to distribute among my family members what little remained of the sun, so that there would be people whom I could escape to from before the dark, which for its part was enveloping me increasingly in all its melancholy thickness. The thorns now dropped at once from Mother's laughter as, in the other room, she realized that she'd mistakenly switched the children's plates while setting the table.

Yes, all that remained of her laughter now was its lovely ring, straight from the heart; and this ring was now flooded with light. So warm was this light all around me that my eyes began to water.

And what had become of Oluska's envy? Hearing her voice from the other room as she and Ernuskó recited their lessons before dinner and bedtime, this voice was now *only* sweet. It had no biting edge, not anymore — no, her voice conjured an image of a big sister with big lovely eyes, a big lovely pigtail, not to mention a charming graceful gait. And what a fine example Ernuskó's aloofness — that of the good student which he was — was becoming for me to follow as I lay there in the dark!

Oh, how much brotherly and sisterly love the growing darkness lent to past admonitions! Sinking ever more deeply into the dusk, the pieces of furniture about the room reproachfully stuck out this or that familiar part of themselves, as if to say, "See how much you wanted? And now you're plain scared of us!" Indeed, no longer did I want anything of them, except that they should *not*, after all, begin to stir by themselves, *not* call my name! Trembling agreeably I thus clung to the voices streaming to my ear from the other room, and once every last one had been cleansed, illuminated, and heated to a comforting warmth, what was left for me?

In the darkness I yearned for them to be ever closer to me, and so I shuffled over from the divan in the study to the one in the bedroom. Afraid as I was of the dark, of sinking ever deeper into the menacing solitude of night, the hurt and hatred coiled up within me, my thirst for revenge and yearning to be far, far away, now began to die away, dissipating into the blackness. Self-accusation now held me firmly in its grip. In truth I was nothing but the evil-minded, evil-tongued child Father saw me as — this I now felt — and maybe even worse: as ridiculous as Mother deemed me, or perhaps even more so, more consumed by envy than Oluska, and more aloof than Ernuskó.

Certainly, I thought, I must not even touch the food at home before apologizing to them all. Meanwhile I could hear the rattle of the shutters in the adjacent room being rolled down for the night; and finally it came time for the windows by me. All at once the bedroom and I were enveloped by utter blackness. The desire for forgiveness arose in me as urgently as this darkness had come on, exactly like this: *Hurry, do it now, before it's too late!*

Suddenly there came the sound of Father's voice. He'd arrived home from synagogue.

Mother called out, "Suppertime!"

Now, now, I thought, shuffling in all my self-accusation and humiliation from the darkness to the light.

There they stood, already at the washbasin; I too muttered the usual grace while washing my hands. Every single word called out within me: *Hurry, or else you won't dare!*

But I only looked timidly about, and took my place at the table. The magic of nightfall had passed, I sensed, and with it, remorse; the light had driven away all these feelings. I looked into the light as if at a bird flying away; a bird that, the further it gets, appears ever smaller in the air. . . . And so my sense of self-accusation remained in darkness, as it were, locked away in my heart. With downcast eyes I accepted a plateful of food from Mother. Father broke the bread and said grace.

THE ONLY PERSON left to me in my haughty solitude was Lidi, the maid, so I set myself to making friends with her. One afternoon, when my parents were away and my brother and sister were busy playing, I tiptoed out to the kitchen door. To save myself the shame of her realizing how eager I was, at first I only peered at Lidi through the keyhole, then set my puckered lips against it and hummed away. She did not reply. Then, ever so carefully, I nudged the door open a crack. But I didn't look. Not yet. I listened. Warily I began opening the door farther, repeatedly sticking my head out and pulling it back quickly. Lidi was sitting near the window, sewing. Until recently I'd often been nasty to her, so now, hoping that bygones might be bygones, I chuckled amiably, invitingly.

She kept on sewing. Her big, bony, freckled face hung above the needle as if she'd neither seen nor heard me. Presently I opened the door the rest of the way, stood on the threshold, and advanced slowly toward her. I circled her a few times, watching. Her steely blue eyes were frozen still. I began to call her: "Hey, Lidi . . . Hey, Lidi . . ." and I kept circling around her like some wooing pigeon, producing all manner of sounds.

Finally she looked up at me.

"You can lay it on thick all you want," she said rawly, "but I know what you're up to. Now that everyone's had it up to here with all your mischief, Lidi'll do too!" And she sunk back into her work. I only watched.

It was awhile before she spoke again.

"What do you want of me? You can't be getting toys, or sweets — not from me! And if you want to make mischief, your father told me I should just go ahead and smack you! Well, I'll do it too!"

Silence fell again. She went on sewing. Little by little I managed to utter: "I don't want anything . . . from you. . . . I'm only watching you. . . . That's okay, isn't it?"

"That you can," she replied.

She fell back to sewing, and on I stared.

"Hey, Lidi," I asked, "do you like being here, with us?"

She was silent.

"Because *I* don't. . . ."

She cast me a stern look. "No kidding! Because they've gotten round to driving the devil from you, they have! So you don't like being here? Well, nowhere would suit a devil like you! When you were just *so* big" — at this Lidi held her hands apart about a football's width — "I rocked you in my arms! I even gave you my milk, seeing as how I was your wet nurse, and what did you do in return? You were always nasty to me!"

Suspiciously I listened. I couldn't remember those days.

"It's not true," I proclaimed, "that you rocked me, and the milk part isn't true either! You never said so before!"

"What would I have said? A devil like you doesn't care one way or other whose milk you sucked!" Again she resumed her work.

I cast her a searching look. No way could I imagine that I'd ever been smaller, as small as those kids who are pushed around in carriages. Through a confused, sidelong smile I spoke.

"You held me like Oluska holds her doll?" And I mimicked Oluska.

Lidi offered no reply.

"And I was as little as her doll?"

No reply even now. Incredulously, loudly I laughed.

"What's so funny?" asked Lidi. "What do *you* know who you were, and what? Why, back then you didn't have a brain in that head of yours! Not even now, but then all you did was suckle and sleep! Looking at you then, never would I have thought that just a year or two later you'd turn into such a devil!"

Her face changed not a bit. Again she sewed in silence. I began to waver, meanwhile.

"Hey, Lidi! Swear to God it's true, and I'll believe you."

"Believe what you want," she replied, "but you can ask your mother and father."

Could it be true? I thought. Suddenly something occurred to me, however, and I laughed.

"Ah! It's not at all true! You couldn't have given me milk, because you're poor! Mother said so herself. I can't ask you for anything, because you're poor, and you need to keep what's yours."

Lidi looked at me thoughtfully, it seemed.

"I didn't give you that milk the way you think! It's not as if it cost me money!"

"How'd you buy it then? How?"

"How did I buy it?" After a pause, she tapped at her bosom. "From here! Little'uns get their milk from here, not from the store!"

I contemplated this bosom she'd tapped so insistently. I saw nothing there. How it could give milk was beyond me.

"If you want me to believe it," I said, pointing to her bosom, "show me — show me the milk! Give me some now, too, if it's really there!"

For a while she said nothing. Then, suddenly and curtly: "There's no more! What do you expect? You're the one who sucked it dry!"

"Then show me where it was!"

"The devil I will! You saw it enough while you were nursing!"

"Then I don't believe a thing you said."

"As you wish," she said, and sewed on.

I edged closer. Touched her leg. She let me. Then I embraced her leg. All the way to her knee, as she sat there. Suddenly, though, she shook her knee.

"Off you go now! Give me all the sweet talk you want, but there's no more milk in this goatskin flask of mine. Like I told you, what there was, *you* drank up! Nozzle and all, dried up for good."

I began caressing her knee. Tiptoeing, I lay my face on her bony knee.

"Show me," I begged. "Come on, show me! How did you give me milk?" To further impress her, I addressed her with more respect.

"Please show me, please, pretty please, Lidi. . . . *Miss* Lidi."

She neither stirred nor spoke.

Now I tried wriggling my way between her knees, hoping to somehow reach a hand up to where she said the milk had been. But she only locked her knees together tight.

"Let me work already!" she said. "Those who don't believe, don't deserve to be shown a thing."

For all my trying to pry apart her knees, she did not yield. No, she only looked upon my efforts from on high, like a statue, with her bony face and raw, pitiless, steely blue eyes. She watched me tussle away around her knees, reaching my short arms toward her bosom. All red, I sweated and moaned. Now and then she gave way slightly, but just to take me in before locking her knees together with renewed vigor. Ever more rabidly I struggled, staring into her face. I couldn't read a thing on that face; neither whether she wanted to torment me, to get back at me for all my wickedness toward her, or perchance that not only was there no milk there, but that there never was, that she was lying, and didn't want me to know this.

All the exertion wore me out. I stopped, gasping for air. Squinting just a bit, she looked long upon me. Then she ran a finger across her lips as if cleaning, or rather, wiping away what it was she thought, but did not want to say.

"Had enough, have you?" she asked. "You'd do well to grow up a bit first! Slow down, little birdie! Oh, you'll pry at girl's knees plenty often, you will! You'll do enough mischief with them! That's the first thing a little gentleman like you does anyway on growing up! Little devils like you!"

Then she went back to sewing. Now imploring her, I promised never again to make fun of her for dallying with young men in uniform, never again to pinch at the soles of her feet when she washed the kitchen floor on her knees; nor would I leap on her back anymore. Nor, for that matter, would I smudge the walls of the kitchen stove all over with black varnish, or, say, smear ash on the pots and pans she'd scoured until they glittered. All I wanted was for her to let me in, at least between her knees, yes, for her to show me at least from there, where the milk she'd given me was from.

She neither said a word nor looked up at me anymore.

Suddenly I remembered the chair. There was one more in the kitchen. With great effort I carried it over to beside Lidi. She let me struggle my way onto it. From there I wanted to jump into her lap. No sooner did I jump, though, than she caught me, plopped me back onto the ground and shook me thoroughly, incessantly. I gave it another five goes more or less. She always let me but her hands and eyes never did soften up.

Thinking it might help, I staggered and fell, and remained on my belly while looking up at her. Lidi didn't stir. I cowered on my haunches and stared. She kept on sewing. Next, charging furiously, I tried falling upon her legs. Holding me at bay with a hand, she now chuckled rawly to herself. Then she picked me up and took me back into our room. Setting me down on the rug, without a word she locked the door behind her.

My brother and sister were still busy playing. For a while I pounded my fists. Then I cheered myself up by telling myself that, no, I didn't believe a word Lidi had said.

SATURDAY IS THE WORST day of the week. Whenever I touch anything on this day, straightway there comes a voice: Don't do that, today it's a sin.

"Sin?" I ask.

Says Mother: "Sin is that for which the Good Lord punishes man. That which is forbidden."

"If the Lord is good," I ask, "why does he punish people?"

"Because you mustn't sin," replies Mother.

"But if he's good," I press on, "why doesn't he let me do anything I want?"

"Well . . ." says Mother, but turns to Father. "Hey, you speak to him! He's always got a question."

At which Father says, "Be satisfied with what we tell you. You mustn't sin. And that's that. When you're bigger you'll learn the rest."

I think: "When you're bigger . . ." I don't get it. Instead of saying, "We can't explain this," they say, "When you're bigger . . ." It seems this is the best excuse to say no more.

Soon Mother adds: "A rabbi's child has got to pay more heed to Saturdays than others have to."

Such words only stir me to ask more questions. My father's a rabbi — that much, I know. But why him of all people? He ministers to the Jews, seeing as how we're Jewish — I know this too. But why are we Jewish, after all? When there are so many people who are not? A lot more than us. And they get to do anything they like, even on Saturdays.

Father replies that they have their own holiday, Sunday.

Very well, I think, Sunday; but that doesn't make Saturday a great holiday. Ernuskó and Oluska like it better than the other days, because they don't have to go to school, but it only bothers me.

Early in the morning I can hardly wait for Father to head out to synagogue, and I plop down on the floor in my nightshirt. And I watch the fire in the stove. Never was it as lovely all week long, through the six days up to today, never as golden, burning with such frightful rage, never as beguiling, exhilarating, as on this day, when one mustn't touch it one bit.

I crouch down before it, stand, then crouch down again, sighing angrily, bent on sighing Saturday clear away!

Never have I wanted to poke at the fire, to throw something in, as much as I do now. Yet I only watch the wood that Lidi has set beside the stove when we were still fast asleep. For Lidi it's okay; she's Christian.

This much is certain: This wood was never wood to the extent that it is now, so far as I see it. At other times it was just dumb, and even when it burned it stayed dumb. Although I'm not in the habit of looking at it for long, only for a bit, just now the whole spectacle promises to be far more interesting — if I have the guts to look. How gladly I'd watch it through to the end, until a whole piece of wood burns away.

But I don't have the guts.

Am I afraid of God? Maybe. Afraid of Father? That I am.

And of Mother? Were she to so much as see me by the fire, she'd yell at once: "Get away from there! That's caught your fancy on Saturday of all days?"

Yes, that's how it is. Yet more exasperating is this: even the *sound* of the crackling flames is more intriguing today. The fire is almost talking, which so many times before I would certainly have wanted it to do, but in vain.

"For the past six days," says the fire, "you haven't even noticed me, isn't that right? And if you did, I was nothing but a dumb fire. Someone you couldn't play with because I started burning right away. But now you'd gladly play with me, huh? Except that I won't play with you, not today. . . . My name is forbidden. . . . Then again . . . whoop! Just take a look at how I can dance, how I burn this way and that!"

Indeed, if I crouch down really well and watch, the flames shoot up so high and so helter-skelter every which way that you wouldn't believe it.

And how the fire hisses! Just like when Lidi combs Oluska's hair, and Oluska jerks her huge, unbound head of hair this way and that, prompting Lidi to grumble: "Oh, stay put! I can't comb you like this. I'll tell Madam about you."

To which Oluska replies: "Don't pull so hard, or *I'll* tell Mother!"

Lidi: "Go ahead. I'm not afraid."

Finally Oluska tears herself away and runs through the flat in search of Mother, her big head of hair streaming, tousled this way and that behind her, exactly like this fire, only that the fire's hair is not black, but red. And the breeze grumbles at the fire just like Lidi does at Oluska: "Oh, will you stay put already?"

I'd like to ask someone: Who combs the fire? I'd prefer to ask Oluska, but she's sleeping in the study, and to get there I've got to pass through Mother's bedroom; so Mother would no doubt wake up and immediately smell trouble.

Ernuskó is still asleep. Should I wake him up? Finally I do.

"Ernuskó," I say, "who combs the fire?"

He ponders the matter seriously, good student that he is, and only then does he speak.

"No one. You can't comb the fire. It's not a girl."

After a good laugh, I say, "And if it can be combed all the same?"

I press my point: "And who is the fire's *Lidi?*"

He offers no reply. "You see," I remark, "you're a good student, and still you don't know!"

Angry at my gibes, he is even less inclined to speak. I try to calm him down.

"Don't be angry, Ernuskó," I say. "The fire's Lidi is the breeze. So it's the breeze that angrily combs the fire's red hair. And the fire jerks this way and that just like Oluska does."

"Asinine," he remarks seriously. "Is this why you woke me up?"

"All right," I say, "now you've gotten back at me, so come on. Let's see how angry the Good Lord gets if we fiddle with the fire on Saturday."

He shakes his head. "Just so we get Mother and Father all upset?"

"No, not them! The Good Lord! Mom and Dad won't find out. Come on."

"Not me," he says. "Why should I?"

"Okay," I reply, "then I'll do it alone."

I'm still a bit scared. Then I quickly toss a piece of wood on the fire nonetheless. And I wait to see how the Good Lord will show his anger.

Meanwhile, though, I'm scared anyway. I keep my eyes peeled. And watch Ernuskó too.

"Hey," I say to him, "I've already done it."

"What do I care."

Then I throw on another piece of wood. And suddenly another. But by then I'm scared. Maybe the Good Lord has already gotten angry? I don't know, but to be on the safe side I don't touch the fire anymore. Having lost my courage, I leave the stove.

It's not just the fire that tempts me more on this day of the week than on others. Mother's drawers and little boxes are suddenly imbued with all sorts of temptations that I've otherwise gotten bored of long ago.

Just like the fire, all of them shed their everyday dumbness, their noiseless, motionless presence, which has caused me so much suffering all week, is now transformed; the objects I've come to disdain, hold in contempt, and grow tired of now become tempting playthings once again, as they must have been when I first saw them. The drawers in the sewing table invite me to open them, and as for what's inside them, well, only now are the scissors truly scissors; and the needles are really needles, sparkling, more primed than ever for pricking; and the thread on the sundry spools is practically begging to be torn; the chalk is ready and waiting to be written with, as surely as is Oluska's slate pencil or Ernusko's lead pencil and quill at the bottom of the large closet. And while Mother is still asleep, I hastily test God's fury on them all.

Before long I hear Mother's voice, then Oluska pops in half dressed, followed by Mother in her robe. Soon it will be time to wash up and get dressed; today we will all don our "best," for we are going to synagogue. Mother does not go to the market, since she can't even touch money, not today; nor will Father go teach after coming home from synagogue, but stay home instead. Seeing that we'll all be in the flat until it's time to leave for synagogue, time passes faster. I listen through the door as Father, in the big room, practices his sermon ; or else I spy on Mother as she struggles away before the mirror while trying to put on her corset. First she tries it herself, then Oluska helps, followed by Lidi; but neither manages the job. Mother, her face all red, whimpers away. As tight as it is around her, the corset still doesn't clasp, so finally she calls Father. How she can walk about in a corset so tight is beyond me. Not even Father likes it being so tight, but Mother points out that every "respectable" woman wears them like this. One of the clasps among the many suddenly pops off, at which Mother sighs.

"Oh dear God, do be careful, all of you, it's Saturday you know. This isn't a sin, is it, Papa?"

Father replies seriously.

"It's all right, it popped off by itself."

The problems go beyond the corset. Mother's shoes are awfully tight as well, so she tries on two or three other pairs, only to find that one is tight here, the other there. Every Friday she has her corn removed, mostly, but she never dares to have as much removed as she should. Lidi and then Father help with her shoes, too, and by the time she manages to pull on a pair, once again she is all red and "dizzy," with a headache coming on full force. Then she puts her hair "in order." Since today is Saturday, she cannot use the curling iron, and so she only kind of frizzes it with the "cold iron" before sticking rollers into her hair, mushrooming it up and inserting a whole bunch of hairpins. I watch her fixedly. So strange is the spectacle that I can't help but laugh.

"What's so funny?" asks Mother.

"Nothing."

What else can I say?

"Nothing?" she asks, adding, "Only little donkeys laugh at nothing."

In that case, I'll tell her. "I'm laughing because what you're doing to yourself, Mother, is all so strange." I point to the rollers, the hairpins, the curling iron, the corset, the shoes.

"Hey, Father," calls Mother, "this child is making fun of how I'm dressing."

Father smiles. "Shoo him away."

"Why shouldn't I laugh?" I say. "I mean, how would *I* look with all this stuff?"

And I too begin sticking the pins and the rollers in my hair, and frizzing with the curling iron. Now Mother really does shoo me away.

"That's enough. Scram."

Still laughing, I step over to Oluska, who happens to be standing before the other mirror having her hair combed by Lidi. At least now I can ask her the question too. "Who combs the fire's red hair?"

She can't answer either. Oluska also shoos me away.

A few minutes later, Mother having barely finished, the little bell in the maid's room rings. Ölschein, the beadle of the synagogue, has pressed the buzzer in the courtyard.

This means that the synagogue is already getting packed. We can be off. Father stays behind a bit; for he will go alone. The three of us, however, go with Mother.

Mother goes down the stairs circumspectly — so much so that I want nothing more than to laugh again.

Having passed through the little courtyard, then the big one, already we find ourselves at the synagogue. Here, behind the large door, the older students and men are on the ground floor; but we must go upstairs with Mother.

One step, two, then another. Though Mother goes slowly, I'm already upstairs and take a quick look down.

So many people, such a big room! Here, too, everyone sits on benches, like Ernuskó and Oluska in school.

We sit upstairs on both sides of Mother, behind metal grating. Further on I see more little boys and girls with their mothers, also behind the grating.

Ernuskó brought along his prayer book. Though he already recites the Hebrew text almost fluently, he doesn't quite understand it. To himself he softly pronounces it letter by letter. The two of us, Oluska and I, are more excited than he. My big sister's little pigtail jiggles to and fro as she keeps turning to whisper away with Mother. The others are whispering, too, as if a breeze were passing over the benches. Pressed right up against the grating, I only stare downward.

Though happy, I am afraid of the yawning depth beneath me. Nervous and red-faced, I shrink back repeatedly from the grating. After a deep breath I muster up my courage and make another go of it, gaping at the abyss.

In no time, I see Father step in through the big door downstairs! He proceeds between the benches slowly and silently, just like he does in our room when he thinks we're all asleep. He goes up a tiny set of stairs to the pulpit. What a big, dark, red velvety curtain I see there! Not to mention something golden up top, and those huge golden columns! All those burning candles left and right! They are much longer than the ones Mother lights at home on Friday nights. And right above the spot where Father comes to a stop, a lantern burns, some sort of red lantern.

"What's that, Mother, that red lantern? Why isn't it brighter?"

"That's the eternal flame. It's not supposed to burn any brighter; it's always got to burn just like that."

"And what's that big red curtain?"

"That's the altar curtain."

If it's really a curtain, why then, I think, there's got to be a window behind it too, like at home. But Mother says that behind it is the Holy Ark. I give a puzzled look. A closet, she adds, a holy closet.

I don't get it. Closet? Closet? Holy closet? No doubt there are clothes in the closet, maybe a robe, yes, maybe Father will change again beside that closet. At home he dresses in front of the closet too. I share my theory with Mother.

She smiles.

"Don't make fun of me," I protest. "Tell me instead: isn't there a robe in there?"

"No," says Mother, "that's where the holy books are kept. Now be quiet. *Shh!* The service is about to begin!"

Father has already passed the velvet curtain. Now he is standing at his bench to the right of the pulpit. He looks up, and singing voices suddenly ring out. Says Mother: Those are the older students. Then music, booming, and again the singing. Now only one voice sings, robust and deep, then it's as if the singing voices were carrying on a dialogue.

"What are they telling each other?"

Mother leans close to me and whispers in my ear: "They're singing to the glory of God, but quiet now. . . . *Shh* . . ."

"Glory?"

She waves a hand and nods, *yes, yes,* but . . . *shh* . . . *shh!*

God, I've got that much. But *glory?* That only swirls about in my head.

"What's his 'glory'?"

Mother waves her hand again and whispers, "I'll tell you at home — at home."

I turn to Ernuskó, for he looks as if he knows.

"Ernuskó, do you know what his 'glory' is?"

"I know too," Oluska rustles, "it's because he created everything!"

Ernuskó counts on his fingers: "In six days . . ."

All right, I think, but why isn't Father singing yet?

I don't like this one bit. Singing is something to be proud of, but he just stands there with his head drooping way down low, like we do before him when we're ashamed. Is he ashamed of himself too? Perhaps because he is not allowed to sing? A fleeting sense of suspicion passes through me: maybe he's not even the rabbi?

Mother only smiles when I say this. But Oluska is all-out mad: How can I even think such a thing? Ernuskó gives me a serious look. "Of course he's not ashamed," Mother now says, "he's just praying to himself. The rabbi doesn't sing, only the cantor and the choir do. The rabbi prays and then preaches; he teaches."

Relieved, I think: Oh, how dumb I am! And here I thought he wasn't the rabbi!

They're still singing. And I ask: "Is this the 'glory of God,' too?"

"Yes, this too is the glory of God. They sing it in different ways, from serious to cheerful, as necessary. But . . . *shh* . . . *shh* . . . I'd like to pray!"

Again I am at a loss. How can the glory of God be cheerful and all that? As I see it, the glory of God can only be along the lines of Father's expression — solemn. Surely not cheerful.

At this Mother laughs again. I say no more.

Father just keeps standing there like before. I've never heard so much singing. When it's cheerful I want to jump about, but that's not allowed; and when it's really sad and slow, hushed and deep, then I want to cry, but that's not allowed either. When it blares I am afraid: I clutch the grating and shut my eyes over and over again, but this is cowardly and so makes me ashamed.

By now the singing has given way to murmurs and whispers. All at once everyone falls silent. Then a deep, lone voice begins a song, which, says Mother yet again, is still about the glory of God.

Before long, Father and the cantor go over to the big dark curtain before that closet Mother calls the "Holy Ark." The cantor draws back the curtain, revealing a mysterious light. Something is there. Now Mother is singing too. Meanwhile two old men covered in prayer shawls, even their heads, go from the pews down below up to where Father and the cantor stand, and they stand on either side of the Holy Ark. According to Mother, they see to it that no trouble befalls the holy books, for that would be a big sin indeed, even bigger than when someone writes, tears anything apart, pokes at a fire, or argues, on a Saturday. . . .

Father is the first to reach inside that large chest. The cantor now falls silent and the two old men step even closer to the Holy Ark. All are watching to see how Father removes the holy books. My eyes open wide. I am awaiting a book that I've seen at home pretty often: big, black, old. That which Father now takes from the Holy Ark is completely different. Suddenly I cry out: "That's not even a book, Mother! What is it?"

Alarmed, Mother turns to me with a finger on her lips: "*Shh!* ..." A bunch of people look up at us. Even Father glances up. In my fright I try cowering behind Mother as best I can. Oluska is furious, Ernuskó stares at the floor. Slowly I come out from behind Mother, ever so warily pressing my face back up against the grating. Just now Father hands the cantor that which he removed from the Holy Ark. Again my eyes open wide, and I whisper: "It's a doll! Mother, it's a doll!"

That's just how I see it, too. It's wearing a skirt, like Oluska's doll, only the whole thing is much bigger, and its head is shining, even sparkling, strong; the cantor holds it the very same way that Oluska rocks her doll.

Mother lets me flounder about for a while. I keep repeating: "It *is* a doll! Are they trying to put it to sleep?"

Ernuskó offers no opinion. Only Oluska shakes her head: If Mother says it's a book, then it's a book, and not a doll.

Now the cantor starts off with the doll, Father just behind him. The two old men, still completely covered with prayer shawls, go behind Father. The cantor begins singing to the doll as they go down the steps and in front of the benches. By now, everyone in the benches has gotten on their prayer shawls, with which they now touch the doll as the cantor extends it their way. And so they proceed. I only stare. But I'm none too happy that it's not Father who leads the way, not him who carries the doll. Then they return the doll; not to the Holy Ark, however, but to the table before it. Everyone below sits back down, as does Mother. She whispers: "It's only from this far that it looks like a doll. Because it's written on a scroll." Mother draws a scroll in the air with her fingers. "True, you might say it's wearing clothes," she continues, "clothes of silk, embroidered with gold. Those aren't real clothes, though, but exist just to make the holy book more beautiful. As for what you see as a head, that's a big, lovely, silver crown, and that's there too so it will shine and be as beautiful as can be. When it comes down to it, though, it's really the holy book, with nothing but letters inside. In a moment you'll all see it. Just look! See?"

Again my eyes open wide as the two old men undress the doll as it lies there on the table. Just like we undress Oluska's doll.

Father helps them. The cantor meanwhile sings.

After they've removed the doll's velvet costume, one of the old men picks it up. Now I don't see a thing. No doubt they're removing her blouse, I figure.

Soon she'll be naked, and she'll scream!

But no. Now I can see it all again. They place the doll between the candles. Mother points, whispers.

"So, do you all see the scroll now? See it? Just pay attention! Now they'll open it up, and inside you'll see a bunch of letters! Just look!"

Ernuskó sees it already, and nods. Oluska nods too. The images of book and doll are still jumbled in my mind. I don't understand what a scroll is, and I certainly can't see any letters from my vantage point. Nor can I see the doll anymore, for it is completely obscured by Father, the cantor, and the two old men in prayer shawls. In vain Mother tells me that they'll now start reading from the holy book; for I only stare suspiciously downward, maybe Mother and them are secretly thinking the same, yes, Father and the cantor and the two old men are playing doll after all, and everything that Mother said, she said only so we'd all stay nice and quiet.

Ernuskó and Oluska sure aren't any help. They always want to be better than me. They only stare downward with expressions I can't figure out. They don't answer when I whisper to them. Mother now opens up another prayer book, and reads. With a wary smile I whisper to her: "Sure they're not playing doll?"

Mother chuckles to herself and says with a wave of the hand: "Can't you hear them? They're reading it already!"

Once more I look through the grating. The cantor is singing

again. I've got to face it after all: he *is* singing what he reads, and this doll *is* the holy book. So now I badger Mother thus: "And what are they reading?"

"Something different every day."

"And today?"

"Maybe about Abraham, our forefather."

"Forefather? That's Grandpa," I think — and say. Mother smiles at this too. "No, no. This Abraham lived a much longer time ago. Before even our grandfather's grandfather. You'll find out when, once you too study the holy book."

This new round of singing is not the same as before. It makes me neither sad, nor happy, nor does it frighten me. For a while I listen, paying attention; I want something else to happen, but nothing does — nothing, but that this monotonous singing puts me slowly to sleep.

There's a surprise in store when Mother nudges me awake.

"Listen!" she says excitedly. "Your father is talking. He's praying for the homeland and the king."

Again I press myself to the grating. I don't know much about the king. One time Mother showed me his picture. He had *two* beards — not like Father. He lives far away in a great big palace, and God created him, just like Father, to take care that everyone keeps the Ten Commandments throughout the whole land. The *home*land. I know even less about "home." Home: our flat and the courtyard. Mother says we'll find out the rest later on, but for now let's just pay attention.

Again Father is standing before the open Holy Ark, looking up with his hands clasped together on his chest. His voice is now completely different, like when he talks to us at home. But I just love it. Only a few of his words fix themselves in my head. The others fly right away, and I cannot hold them back.

All I hear is Father saying, in a more powerful voice: ". . . our sovereign, Francis Joseph, emperor of the monarchy and king of our country, our homeland, Hungary . . ."

Utter silence in the congregation. Everyone is watching my father. Being really proud of this, I smile. Everyone should know: I am his son.

All at once I see Father in the pulpit. Not even now do I understand what he's saying, but that's all right. It's enough for me that *he* is talking, that he is talking from so *high*, and that this high pulpit is so velvety, yes, its velvet hanging reaches all the way to the floor and is embroidered with gold just like the dress of the holy book. Even where Father rests a hand — all velvet. There, in the heart of the pulpit, as I stare and listen, Father grows ever larger! Especially when he stretches out his arms now and again, taking with them the arms of his gown, like giant wings, and he lets his surging voice resound, I am so proud to belong to him that I shudder with exhilaration, almost like I do when a military bugle sounds. I want to stomp about and shout — but this must not be done. I only sit there, my hands trembling with feverish pride, my feet pitter-pattering hard against the tile floor. Oh, Father, go ahead and shout, I think — shout, please do! Even louder! Louder! Spread out those wings more often, do, and while you're at it, don't forget to raise your hands up higher and higher, more and more! But when he suddenly drops his voice, I like that too. I find myself repeating some of his words at a whisper to myself, but then my blood freezes all at once: utter silence. Father bows his head. Thinking that he's forgotten his lines, like when Oluska sometimes trips up on one of the many lessons she must learn by rote, my breath stops in fear and shame; and only when Father finally resumes do I dare begin breathing, slowly, once again. Oh yes, he knows just what he's saying! All of you down there are sitting and listening to my father! None of you are rabbis, like my father! *You* don't even budge! *You* aren't even allowed to cough, not when *he's* talking, my father Why, you can't so much as whisper, for my father will look up immediately, fix his eyes on the direction the coughing came from — and silence anew! *Nothing* may disturb him! Haughtily I turn my head about, and when my father locks his eyes on the direction of some whispering, I do too, with uncompromising wrath.

Now his voice grows louder. I am surprised to see that the whole congregation stands up at once. My father's voice resounds throughout the synagogue one last time, he spreads his arms wide once again, then he clasps his hands and looks up: "So be it, amen," he says, then bows and slowly descends from on high. . . .

There is silence in his wake. These final words and gestures, and not least the utter silence that follows, make me want to stand up on the bench and cry out: "So be it, amen, I'm his son! I'll be like him too! No matter how little, how bad I am, I'll be like that all the same!" I'd gladly shout all this — but I do not dare. Instead I only look conspicuously about and show myself, but no sooner do I begin than shame compels more stealthy glances here and there, while I think: See me, everyone? See me? Hmm? You do, don't you, and you *know* that I'm his son!

The silence continues. "Now we've really got to be quiet," Mother whispers. "This is the main prayer, we mustn't even whisper this, no, we've got to say it completely to ourselves." But this is the last thing on my mind just now. I'm thinking of Father. My satiated sense of pride in this great silence sees me warm up to him. I forgive him for all of his prohibitions, his stern discipline, interrogations, unexpected appearances, the whole of his dominion at home; I forgive him for my getting everything I have, from him. I watch only him as he stands facing the wall, and amid the profound silence all my thoughts of forgiveness slowly become repentance and ardent devotion. I regret never having loved him as much as do Ernuskó and Oluska, and soon I begin softly crying to myself. But I am ashamed of this too, and so I crawl underneath the bench as if to adjust my stockings, and there I snivel away.

SATURDAY AFTERNOON we go out for a walk. Father's anxious dictums begin when we are still on the stairs. First he cautions us against getting too close to the wall, lest it should smudge our clothes; and once we're down on the street he exhorts us to stay out of the mud and the puddles along the sidewalk. And of course he takes care that the three of us children should be together, in a single row, with Ernuskó in the middle, me to his left, and Oluska to his right.

Father was displeased when anything upset this established order, and if a carriage rattling along at full speed nonetheless saw fit to upend this delicate agonizing family unit, Father would immediately offer sound and simple advice with which he reestablished family order. Everything that he kept repeating this way generally stood to reason, yes, even we knew as much, but no sooner did he actually pronounce it than it took on untold weight and began hampering my walk. Father was fond of calm, orderly walks: "Let's go on the other side, where there are fewer people. . . . We can go in a straighter line." Or else: "Best we wait until the sidewalk is completely free. . . . Sidewalks, not highways, are for walking. Walking exists so we can get a little exercise, and so there's no need to stop everywhere and gape. . . ."

Thus it was in vain that we might wish to have stopped now and again to mull over some building being built, to gaze in wonder upon a splendid-looking carriage, to take a peek into a park at all those kids and perk our ears at their hullabaloo; or, say, to glimpse into a tavern courtyard or even up at a flowery branch. Nor could we stop to look at soldiers or at those funny-looking synagogues with crosses on top, and not even at the Orthodox Jews who, wearing caftans and huddled in a group on a corner, excitedly deliberated matters. . . . And whenever Mother — who for her part was also partial to gazing at this and that — sometimes managed to get Father to stop momentarily, he invariably broke the spell straightway with an instructive, edifying comment: "One should stop only where one has some business stopping." ... "A building will rise without our help." ... "You won't see anything of the carriage, anyway." . . . "Both the children and the park are strangers, you can't go in anyway." . . . "Those loafers and drunks in the tavern sure aren't worth staring at." . . . "That flowery branch that sticks out from behind the fence is someone else's. You can't touch it, anyway." . . . "It's neither appropriate nor necessary for the families of Jewish rabbis to be peering inside Christian churches." . . . "Those men in caftans can't help being the way they are, they're backward, that's all, and there's no sense staring at them. . . ."

Mostly we walked the same route. Across two squares — Fő tér, this being the green, spacious main square; and Orgona tér — to Katona Park. There, in the park, we would sit down. Our parents would let us kids go around the park once or twice, then we too would have to sit beside them on a bench, all three of us, in the same order in which we walked. Now that he'd sat down, Father also began to notice the trees and the bushes; he pointed his walking stick this way and that, and if Mother called his attention to a bird rustling on some leafy bough, he gave a nod of acknowledgment and a smile of satisfaction. No doubt deep down Mother would gladly have scampered about as she had as a girl on the bank of the stream where she grew up, but by now she'd forgotten that time; she was a rabbi's wife, and of course it is most unbecoming of rabbis' wives to scamper about. Her long corset squeezed her full, low frame into a prim little bundle indeed. A high collar encircled her neck, and her head was topped off by a hat with a brim so wide that it all but concealed her small, girlish face. Her eyes sparkled diligently from underneath this hat into the flowery, sunny afternoon; only her eyes could scamper about while she herself kept sitting there on the bench, as befits a lady who truly knows she is a rabbi's wife. Only in her giggling and in the sparkle of the eyes with which she accompanied the singing of the birds — only in these could her little-girl's soul be perceived anymore.

But what did I know of all this, back then?

Caught as I was in the drizzle of Father's admonitions, not for a minute could I escape the consciousness of my captivity, my littleness. Grass, trees, flowers, sky, and people: all this served only to remind me even more of my wretched lot. A prisoner, I was. These flowers, these trees, this sky, the whole of my hometown, with which I became acquainted on these walks, were fast becoming the silent witnesses of my helplessness and shame, and thus even now, so early on, they had begun to wither in my heart.

FINALLY THE DAY arrives: Father will take me to enroll in school. Starting now, I think, I won't be as small as in fact I still feel. While Mother goes about dressing me, I think: I'll do my best while enrolling to come across as proud as can be. I don't want anyone at school noticing how little attention is paid me at home, how much I've wept in secret, how often I've wanted to run away, to leave my parents.

I don't like Mother dressing me. In the touch of her hand, in her voice, in her eyes, I sense belittlement. Try as she might to smile at me with charm, to hustle and bustle about while sprucing me up, I feel that this is directed less at me and more at my undershirt, which is "so nice and white and didn't cost too much"; at my shoes, which "look so spiffy"; and at my trousers, which are "really something, but don't go leaving them open now." And as she goes about tying the rosette on my neck, then contemplates it so mincingly, I feel that never was she so delighted with me as with this pleated ribbon.

If she were to see me dirty and in tattered clothes, never would she look upon me as she does now. She loves the clothes, not me; she loves the school I'll at long last be attending. This is only a vague sensation on my part, but this makes it all the worse, and is exactly why I want her to finish dressing me already. She wants to do a lovely little job, though, to make me as comely as can be; and so I sweat in anguish between her hands, yes, I want to stamp my feet in rage and cry out, "Stop it! Leave me alone! Love my clothes! Hug my undershirt! Kiss my rosette! Caress my shoes! Twinkle your eyes at *them!* But just leave me naked, or however, just leave me, leave me be already!"

Yet I can't cry out like this. She wouldn't get it. No, she'd just get mad. She wouldn't even believe it, but tell Father, and once again I'd be called a naughty, selfish, unruly, foolish little brat. Even now, as she dresses me, the day they scolded me so much is still fresh in my mind. Since then, Mother can smile at me all she likes, for I know full well that at the bottom of her every smile there lurks the same laughter that then accompanied her words, "How funny!" But I don't say a thing. For all I care she can go on dressing me, thinking it's me she loves.

Then I rack my brain nonetheless looking for a way to tell her what I feel, what I know about her; I'll do it so as neither to upset nor frighten her, but so she'll understand all the same. Yet I can't figure out how. Finally I say: "Let me get dressed alone." But she doesn't let me, for now I've "got to be a handsome little boy indeed." So I must endure it yet, there's nothing to be done. What's more, I can see she's tired; every time she bends down she complains that the blood rushes to her head, then her back aches — but she goes on diligently sprucing me up nonetheless.

Finally she says: "Now you just be as good a student as Ernuskó, as long as I go through so much trouble over you!"

Yes, I think: it's the beautiful clothes she loves, and the good marks.

Sullenly, I swallow hard as she combs my hair, arranging things just right on my forehead. Having done so, she pronounces: "There! What a handsome boy you are!"

I think: You said this to the hairdo you made. Neighbors and visitors often compliment my hair: "Oh, how lovely . . . how charming . . . how splendidly long!" While I am proud of this, as Mother combs my hair and expresses her delight, I think: If only I had the guts to cut it, yes, in no time she'd be talking differently about me and my hair.

Often I've thought of cutting my hair, cutting it after all. Why, *then* I'd see just how much she loves me — how much, if my lovely head of hair is gone. And I've also wondered what would happen if I had the guts to be lame; this now occurs to me again as she considers my stockings, smartening them up as well. As she takes "one last look" in my ears, I think: What would happen if I dared be deaf? Then, as she wipes my eyes: if I dared be blind? Only if I had the guts to do all this could I really see how much she doesn't love me; and then she'd no doubt tell it to me straight, not like now!

Yet I sense I'll never do all this. I think about it, nothing more.

Finally Mother is done sprucing me up. Looking me over, she's clearly pleased with the product. Then she sits me down so I don't move about, lest anything should happen to me; or rather, to my clothes, my knees, my ears, my eyes; to the György, or Gyuri — people usually call me Gyuri — she has now made me into. As she arranges the rosette one last time while I sit there, a bit of what I want to say comes to mind after all. And so I speak.

"Mother," I begin, "does this ribbon love you like you love it?"

She gives me a bewildered look.

"What's that you're saying?"

I repeat my words, then add: "Do my shoes love you too like you love them?"

Clearly she doesn't know what to think. Should she be frightened at how foolish I am, or laugh at how silly I am? She does neither. Instead she blushes.

And she says: "And *you're* going to enroll in school? When you're saying such things?" She asks seriously, "Do you really think a *ribbon* can love?"

I give her a sly look.

"But then . . . if it can't love you, why do you love *it* so much?"

"Oh God," says Mother, "How silly you are! I love it because it's pretty!"

I laugh. "But you're pretty too, Mother!"

Another blush. "Don't you get under my skin now with such silly talk!"

I fall silent. At which she says: "And don't you go putting questions like this to your teacher in school, or else she'll laugh at you, and I can go be ashamed because of you."

Sullenly I reply: "No, I won't."

Then Mother goes out to the kitchen to tend to her business while I sit quietly waiting for Father to appear with Ernuskó and Oluska, who are being registered downstairs right now for their first day back at school.

Not so long ago, I recall, Mother dressed them every morning too. Especially Ernuskó, since Oluska usually got dressed herself. A little girl, said Mother, has to learn early on how to dress by herself. So she knows on her own what's pretty, lovely, and clean.

She devoted all the more time and energy to dressing Ernuskó. I watched them then, just as I watch them every morning. I watched and watched so much day in and day out that now I am convinced she doesn't really love Ernuskó either; or rather, that she loves him only because he's a good student and a good boy. But if he got bad marks, she wouldn't love him. And if he was what I would sometimes like to be, lame or blind, she wouldn't love him either, but would be frightened and ashamed. When she kisses him, it's not him she's kissing, after all, but the good report cards he's always bringing home, yes, she's kissing the A's. It's for the A's that she chuckles away with such delight while pulling up the stockings on Ernuskó's long legs; and it's for them that she ties such a neat rosette on Ernuskó's neck each and every morning. Why, Mother even ties his shoes each morning not for him, but for those A's.

What does she love about Oluska? Perhaps only the fact that she's a girl, like what Mother used to be; and then there's Oluska's pigtail, yes, Mother loves that too, because it's lovely, as they say, because it's thick, long, and black. Then there are her eyes, because they're also pretty, as they say, big and dark. Mother even loves her way of walking, it's so "sweet." Yet if Oluska had none of this, Mother wouldn't love her either, not one bit.

Such are my thoughts as I wait for Father to return. And I think: What good will learning do me? For even if I learn everything to a tee, I'll be alone just the same.

So that someday I can be proud of the marks I get? Proud of what I know? Like Father is proud when he preaches? Yes, pride feels good, that much is clear in how Ernuskó comes home from school brimming with it; if possible he'd complete two grades at a time, so he could be even prouder. Oluska delights in her pride as well, especially when she looks at her pigtail; as does Mother when she points to her many tomatoes, her jams, her bottled fruit, and of course the tub of lard all arranged so neatly in the pantry. Well, pride will no doubt do me good as well; though come to think of it, I don't know what good it will really do, for even then I'll be sad all the time, just like now.

Yet I'm excited anyway.

No sooner does Father arrive, however, no sooner do I hear his voice — "Is Gyuri ready yet?" — than I get scared. Ashamed too. It's always been like this whenever I see or hear him; or rather, ever since he whacked me that time, which I'll never forget.

He steps into the room. I stand. With utter solemnity he looks me over.

"Come on then," he says.

In the adjoining room Mother is already helping Ernuskó and Oluska change from their school clothes into casual wear.

Father and I head down the stairwell.

The school is in the same building, in the second courtyard, where the synagogue and the little poultry-butchering block are also found. The first courtyard is dim and sad. As we proceed through the narrow covered passage leading to the second, Father speaks.

"Do you know when you were born?"

"No, I don't."

He tells me: "September twenty-fourth, nineteen hundred." Then: "Say it after me, so you know if you're asked."

I mumble the words. We now step out into the big yard, and I keep saying to myself, "September twenty-fourth, nineteen hundred."

SHE WHO INITIATED ME into the cold mysteries of reading and writing, the schoolteacher, seems to step before me from the pages of a first-grade exercise book, just as some little girl, some student of hers, might have sketched her there. She resembles an ancient hieroglyph, flat and planar with birdlike legs, a trapezoidal skirt; rectangular and bosomless above; then a corncob neck ornamented with a bow as big on each side as a mule's ear; and finally, a birdlike head, and a birdlike hand with which she writes her name on the blackboard: Sarolta Ulrich, schoolmistress.

She has yet another birdlike hand. In it she holds a pointer, which seems glued to her birdlike fingers.

Thus she steps from the pages of the exercise book. She expands and begins to move and talk, but in vain: she still seems the creation of a first-grade girl. Rather than sitting on a bench, however, she is standing on the platform up front as she brings her birdlike hands together and says:

In God's name I do begin and pray,
May His grace show us the way. . . .

Then she shows us how to sit, stand, and reply, as "good boys and girls should." She should know; for she's remained a good girl, a forty-year-old little girl, all these years. And she shows us how to fashion letters, numbers; how to connect two letters, three, then four. The letters become words, and the words, sentences. Only that there is no connection between the sentences, no, a great big dot separates them from each other. It's always been like this, for more than twenty years, ever since she's been teaching.

Sometimes the children ask her to explain the connection between this and that letter, this and that word; between their little hearts, their studies, and life. Over twenty years she's gotten used to these questions, and for twenty years she's given the same answer: "You'll learn that in second grade."

How could she say anything else? She too inhabits this grade, this life of disconnections, and has for twenty years at that. Her own days and years are just as disconnected as what she teaches; they are separated by mysterious and immovable dots as surely as are the letters and words on the blackboard. Each by itself has its own meaning, way of being taught, but then there comes a ruthless point: the end of the day, the week, the year. At such times the schoolmistress stops beyond the threshold of the school, stares ahead with her yellowed, spinsterish eyes, and asks herself: Why doesn't it all make any sense after all?

She had learned how to sit and stand properly, to answer questions, fashion letters and words, and of course to teach all that to children; but never will her movements become motion, never will her letters come to life. This has been going on for twenty years.

Yet it must be said: she treated us gently, that she did.

Way back when, this tenderness must have been imbued with the yearnings of the heart, of motherhood. By the time I saw her, she was nourished by habit only. And duty. She'd gotten used to seeing scared little boys and girls who needed to be emboldened; she knew that their faces had to be caressed, their heads patted; and she'd gotten used to smiling tenderly as she looked into their eyes; for they are the little ones whereas she is the schoolmistress, whose duty this is.

As for me and my voracious little heart, which suffered so much at home from its self-indulgence — she positively dazzled me! I thought her smile was genuine, that her caress was meant for me alone. I became giddy from her duty-bound smile, from the affectedly tender, yellowish twinkle of her blue eyes. She would be my second and *real* mother, I thought, the one I'd thirsted for so often!

When she first patted me on the head, I asked her to step behind the blackboard.

Even now I can hear the curious, excited murmur of my little peers, as I could that day from behind the blackboard while muttering away about how bad things were for me at home, and as I asked if she would be my mother.

"What?" she said softly. "But you have a good mother!"

With cocksure insatiability I replied: "She's not enough for me!"

She hadn't even had a chance to respond when I noticed to my dismay that my conduct had set strange forces into motion. All at once there came cries from beyond the blackboard: "Me too! Me too!"

Angrily I peered around the board: "Jealous dopes!" I muttered.

For her part, the schoolmistress called out from behind the board: "Quiet, children! I'll be out front in a second!"

But they didn't quiet down. More and more called out, with increasing fervor, "Me too! Me too!" This was presently interspersed with sobs. The teacher stepped out in front of the blackboard. It took quite awhile for her to calm the waves of all those hearts I'd rashly stirred. Then she returned to me.

"See? You're not the only one who needs a second mother, they do too! If I were to begin, there would be no end to it. Everyone has got to love the mother they have. Do you understand?"

What could I have said? No, I simply couldn't believe there were so many who desired the same thing as I: at least two mothers. What's more, crying their hearts out so openly. No. My greedy little heart told me this: it's only because of all those jealous dopes in class sobbing away that she doesn't want to be my new mother. If only we could settle this matter of our feelings in private, I thought, no doubt it would all turn out as I desired. And so I said: "Do you want to talk after school?"

"Very well," said the schoolmistress. "We'll talk. Now go on back to your place. And be quiet, like a good boy."

Burning red with excitement, I sat back down. Greed and pride had led my imagination astray, and so I took the teacher's words to signal full consent. Soon what I wanted would be mine, I felt; my first bounty, a heart that beats for me alone, a heart that doesn't have two other children and a husband to trouble over, as did my mother, but one for whom I would forever be all!

But hardly had I sat down when the refrain rang out again: "Me too! Me too!" I cast the teacher a haughty, conspiratorial smile as she stopped before the blackboard.

"Children," she said, "do be quiet. That little boy" — she pointed at me — "called me behind the blackboard because he didn't have a handkerchief. And I don't have enough handkerchiefs to wipe all of your noses! So do be quiet, and let's begin again."

And we began again.

Her lying to my envious peers, lying for me, because of me, only reinforced my certainty that what I so desired was as good as mine.

For a while I scratched diligently away at my writing slate, but I could not keep my bursting sense of triumph to myself for long. All at once I whispered to my neighbor, practically before I even noticed what I'd done: "It's not true, you know. Miss Ulrich promised to be my mother."

At which my neighbor whispered back: "But you have one!"

And I: "I don't need the one at home."

The news spread slowly, in whispers, like a stifled fire, from one bench to another. Finally a girl raised her hand and pointed at me.

"That boy said . . ."

And after she'd related the subject of my boasting, the class burst out in an irrepressible chorus: "Me too! Me too! Me too!"

To my astonishment the teacher now stared at me with a reddening face, then struck her pointer furiously upon her desk.

"Quiet right now!" she cried out with unusual severity.

Then she called angrily at me: "Stand up!"

I stood.

"Didn't I tell you to stay quiet?"

True enough, I thought, and bowed my head; but the thought that everything would be different after school brought a secret smile to my face.

Yet she continued. "This little boy lied. I didn't promise him a thing. All I said was that I'd talk with him after school." Pointing at me, she added, "Right?"

True, I thought, she'd said that all right — and I knew why. "Yes."

Yet I still held firm in my belief, in my desire. Only now was I taken aback, when she held her pointer toward me once again, and shouted: "So you lied!"

Hesitatingly I looked upon her. One of my eyes still believed, the other didn't; one still recognized and declared my desire; the other was already blinking nervously and with shame — admitting that perhaps in fact I'd lied.

But the schoolmistress now continued mercilessly.

"I didn't want to embarrass you in front of the class. That's why I told you to stay nice and quiet, that I'd talk with you after school. But you lied. So now I'll embarrass you."

By now both my eyes were blinking. Yet in no time I got the upper hand over my eyelids, and stared upon her with sullen hatred, and with disdain upon the entire envious class.

"Come here," said the schoolmistress.

Staring fixedly ahead, I went over.

"Turn to the class!"

Rigidly I turned.

Whereupon she said: "A child who doesn't love his mother, and lies, is a bad child and belongs in the corner."

She pointed at the corner. With sullen pride I trudged on over. The teacher now turned to the class.

"Now all of you repeat the moral after me: A child who doesn't love his mother, and lies, is a bad child and belongs in the corner!"

The chorus rang out shrilly and with glee as the schoolmistress beat the rhythm with her pointer.

MY THIRST for complete and unconditional love was every bit as dour and yet unrestrained among my little peers as at home among my siblings.

No sooner did I enter their company than I expected them to recognize me as more exceptional than them.

As Jacob's true progeny, this singular selfishness — as guileless as it was boundless — dominated me without further ado, rationally, even religiously, it might be said. Everyone but pious theologians scours the Bible in vain for *the* forefather's merits, for *the* reason Yahweh found that exceptional soul, Abraham, so decent a fellow as to select him and, well before they were conceived, all of his descendents as his chosen ones; and so in a manner worthy of my forefathers, I too simply believed that by the sheer fact of my existence, of my faith, I deserved to be *what I believed myself to be:* worthy of love and exceptional.

Call this faith what you will — childish oversensitivity or the naïveté of a little savage from afar — the reality is the same.

Since my little peers did not approach me to say, "Be my brother, and all that I have is yours," I felt offended right away; sullenly I locked my heart and tried to be as proud as I could be.

While my peers boasted of how much their fathers had in their stores — my peers were by and large shopkeepers' children — and of all the nice new clothes their fathers bought for them, of how their shops' display windows were chock full of all the toys and sweets they could hope for, and how the cash boxes their mothers tended were full of money, not to mention how they got to take to school whatever they well pleased for their midmorning snack; while they said all this and more, I countered even more proudly with my father — how he was, when it came down to it, the most important father of all, for he occupied the best seat in the synagogue; and even if their fathers had so very much through six days of the week, where did they sit on the seventh, after all? Not up high, like my father, but down below. What's more, my father prayed and talked while theirs just listened in silence, like we did in school. Not to mention what a nice outfit my father wore on that seventh day! Which of their fathers had such clothes? Although some fathers had worn military uniforms, swords, and shakos, which was beyond doubt enviable, what good was all that when even *their* place in synagogue was down below with everyone else! Lots of men wore military uniforms, but my father was the only one who wore a gown and high velvet hat — he alone, and no one else! So what if the cantor had one, too? Of course he did, but it wasn't nearly as grand, and he had to do what my father said!

Alongside Father's primacy in the synagogue, his gown, his high velvet hat, and all the dignity he enjoyed, what became of those oh-so-harsh memories of his love? What became of the fear that took me at once in its grip if I so much as thought of him here in school, and the endless shame that this fear also imbued me with? Odd, but all these feelings only heightened my zeal to raise him ever higher on my pedestal of pride. Yes, my vanity ran even deeper than the puerile wounds of my prematurely frozen heart.

What did my pride *do* with those sundry reservoirs of pain that I enumerated to my heart day in and day out as grievances against Father? With the pain I felt when Father did not buy a new writing slate and booklets for me, but gave me Ernuskó's old ones? When all my clothes were my big brother's hand-me-downs? The pain that came with having only a few cheap playthings, and sharing even these with my brother and sister, which meant I could not take them with me to show off? The pain inherent in the fact that my entire store of treasure consisted of a few small carob seeds and some colorful pebbles? The pain of having neither any pretty little coins nor a single piece of taffy, potato sugar, licorice, jujube, or rock candy, because Father, caught up in his own brand of parsimonious rabbinical puritanism, held all this to be superfluous indulgence? Well, my pride readily transformed all this into fanatic praise, which I heaped on Father so generously and, by way of him, onto myself, that my eyes gleamed with zealotry.

Child that I was, but without knowing it, I acted once again the very same way as my forefathers, who, although their very own god gave them little more than wandering and weakness, fears and shame, in addition to a few paltry flocks of sheep, nonetheless heaped untold praise upon him, squaring him off firmly, audaciously, undauntedly against the world's genuine powers that be.

All at once the sundry traditions and customs I'd learned from Father with so much fear and boredom into the bargain, neither knowing nor understanding their origins, resurfaced in me with effulgent pride. Yes, now I lined all of them up round Father's primacy in the synagogue, like angels fluttering about some sort of god. Up against all the sweets, pictures, pen cases, pretty coins, and midmorning snacks containing *meat* that the other kids had, what could I boast of but — blessing? The blessing I said each morning with the fringed shawl, at noon while washing my hands, to the bread, to the swig of wine that consecrated the holiday on Friday nights, and at bedtime every night. Finally I became so mired in pride amid all my pain, so thoroughly contemptuous of everything I didn't have, and which I secretly yearned for so dearly, that before long not one of my little peers would willingly speak to me. The solitude I thus created for myself was every bit as painful and impenetrable as that at home, in the family.

As befits a bona fide self-tormentor, I was out to heal my lesser pain, selfishness, with a greater pain, solitude. Even the bell that ended classes and signaled free time managed to break through the wall of my pride and isolation for only a few moments as I ran out into the courtyard and shouted away with the others in a great big cloud of dust. Yes, intoxicated though I was by the hullabaloo once outside, caught up in the frenzied longing to mingle, in no time my haughty sensitivity shackled me anew, and alone I drifted from one group of playmates to another. Eyes sparkling dully from the stifled boundless yearning to play, I sniffed at the edges of each and every group, until, terribly bored and wanting vengeance for my solitude, I tossed about fuming with rage, only to think of Father afterward with even greater fear. And I wasn't off the mark.

For only a short passage separated the schoolyard from that smaller courtyard that our flat — or rather, the windows of our entrance hall, kitchen, and pantry — looked out upon. Now, wherever I happened to be in the schoolyard, Mother's or Father's voice might ring out at any time, as if to say to my child's heart roaming about this Eden of play, "Adam, where are you?" And so I was reminded over and again of the constant and strict supervision that fed my fear and shame. At such times the voice of the Lord — Father, that is — and that of his angel — Mother — cautioned me *not* about the Tree of Knowledge, but only about the Tree of Life; in short, about getting too caught up in the passion of play. But did not both knowledge and life in all its passion share the same curse? Nakedness, that is? Nakedness, which I noticed with dismay, a scared and shameful dismay, at the sound of Mother or Father's voice shouting from the kitchen window? Just as Adam had realized this when Elohim's voice thundered from above his paradise? Even the words were practically the same; the ancient question had been desecrated only to accommodate my youth: "Child, where are you? Why are you so naked? Why are the buttons missing on your trousers? What became of your shoelaces? And why are your socks torn? Lo! You have eaten from the Tree of Life, haven't you?"

That wasn't all. The eager child was driven from the Garden of Eden, ordered to go up from the schoolyard to join Mother in the kitchen. Meanwhile the other part of the biblical curse, about sweat and toil, sounded from Father's room: "When you buy your own clothes, then you can rip and tear them as you like!"

This ancient scene played itself out at least twice a week, during playtime; and amid such pain, which recurred so often that it left me numb, learning progressed slowly and bitterly indeed.

The letters of the alphabet were inclined to lend my little person not a scrap of feeling and respect. In vain I waited for them to reveal their secrets only because I looked upon them! The letters neither spoke, nor did the numbers pant with desire to acquaint themselves with me. We were shown pictures: a garden, a courtyard, various animals, trees, fruit, a house, a family, workshops. How headstrong they seemed, shutting themselves off to me so gruffly! And when, racking my brain, I finally did recognize them, they only went on staring at me with cold indifference. They signified only their names, nothing more.

This didn't change. Days, weeks, and months passed, yet we didn't grow any closer. Only when year's end came round, winter, and a curtain of darkness fell upon the schoolyard with the falling snow, and the gaslight burned in the schoolroom from morning on, and a fire blazed in the stove, only then did I begin to feel as if we'd warmed up to each other a bit — the letters, the numbers, the pictures, and I. By the warm, hazy glow of the gaslight, the crackling of the fire, I looked upon my peers with more forbearance: without knowing how or why, I cast fond glances at my classmates and at our lessons, and it seemed that they too, albeit faintly, perhaps only for the space of a breath, but all of them, even the pictures, were now reciprocating the quickening beat of my heart amid the frozen air and darkness of winter. . . . But how imperceptible and fleeting this was, as time seemed to have ground to a halt. The schoolyard had frozen over, and my spates of wild roving in the Garden of Eden had been enervated by winter into shivers.

No longer was there a need for that ancient call, "Adam, where are you?" during free time. No, with chattering teeth I trudged up the stairs willingly to Mother, who was in the kitchen.

The winter metamorphosis continued just as imperceptibly up here. There began a deceptive game staged by the cold-weather anxieties of my barren heart: an inviting breath, a warmer light and sound, passed through all of Mother's lectures, through "all that hard-earned money" just as surely as it did through her laughter, through the dumb pots and pans, through the food and through the maid, through the listless furniture, through my hand-me-down clothes, through my few and shared playthings, and through my even fewer sweets. The more snow fell upon all of this, thickly, the more it all seemed "truer" to me; in my eyes I had become a better son, a better brother, a better child even to myself, better than the unfamiliar, unknown fear of death.

NEVER AGAIN did I attempt to find a new mother, not least because my first attempt had come to light. By now, my parents said, the whole building knew how "depraved" their child was. Blushing, Mother said she didn't dare go down the stairs, so ashamed was she of herself.

However long it took, this too slowly passed.

Now I am in second grade. Although my teacher is still the same old schoolmistress, I look with rash disdain upon those still in first grade, who are still troubling with writing slates and the sponges that go with them. We second-graders already have ink, a promotion in rank not to be discounted. But however illustrious this blue liquid with the accompanying pen and exercise book may be, it is every bit as dangerous to a restless heart such as mine. All it takes is one careless movement, a sigh, and the inkblot is complete. Amazingly, the more I try to soak it up so as to stem its flow, the more it spreads in all directions, relocating from the exercise book to my fingers, my clothes; and already I see Father's stern expression as he examines me thoroughly with all the rabbinical puritanism he can muster, and Mother's fright as she sighs repeatedly, trying to calm him down. . . .

No matter. Up and at 'em, I say! Before I know it, I'm up to my neck in inkblots.

Yet beyond the dangerous and illustrious matters of ink, pen, and exercise book, there's another bit of news afoot: The words and the sentences are starting to cohere! Even greater news is what they reveal! I stir, perk my ears, and squirm about on hearing and reading that there were children and adults who did not wait in vain, like me, for chairs to dance, for the hearth to whistle and warble; and that there were mothers who died pining after their long-lost sons, though these sons perhaps vanished right through a window into some dark forest. . . . And there were brothers and sisters who left behind everything they had, their whole kingdoms, to save their little brothers! . . . So, too, I read that there were people at whom animals secretly winked in just the way I always desired, and cats and dogs and horses called these fortunate few "dear master." Oh, and yes, a grape spoke, a peach chanted praises to the sky, and weeping willows sang!

All this warmed the cockles of my heart the more I read such things. Yes, my eyes filled secretly with tears — tears of desire renewed, but now for the reality of stories. Or were they only tears of pride?

How could I have failed to be proud, when, behold — here in my schoolbook, set in print, I saw that all the furniture, all those animals, brothers and sisters and parents, for whom I'd longed so often and so much in vain — and because of whom, when I'd wanted to jump out the window, Father had scolded me thinking I was wicked, and Mother had thought me a fool — did indeed exist.

Undoubtedly my tears spoke both to desire and pride, but by the time I got home from school I'd already buried the desire, allowing only pride to speak.

First I hurry to Ernuskó. I open up the storybook and show

him the talking horse, the singing peach, and the speaking grape, not to mention the dancing chairs.

"You see," I pronounce, "here it is, just what I wanted. See? This stuff really exists! I got smacked because of this, and you didn't say a thing. And you already knew it. You knew it was true."

Ernuskó listens patiently to all I have to say.

"That exists only in the book," he says, "so we learn it and can answer the teacher's questions."

"Sure," I reply, "I know that's why it's here, and that it's not true, but it does exist all the same, and I got smacked for it, I did!"

Ernuskó refreshes my memory.

"You got smacked because you wanted to fall out the window and you scared Mother."

"True," I say, "but also because I wanted chairs that dance, and furniture that speaks, and this sort of fruit! And mothers who die of sorrow over their youngest kids!" Out of pride I neglect to mention brothers and sisters who leave behind their kingdom to go in search of their lost little brother.

Ernuskó only shakes his head. "All this," he retorts, "is only in the book. It doesn't exist and isn't true, and you got smacked because . . ." And he repeats what he's already said, shaking his head and muttering, "Why don't you get it?"

There's no getting anywhere with him. But there's Oluska too, her pigtail a bit longer, as is her skirt, now that she's in third grade. Her eyes are all but sparkling, and I see that she'd side with Ernuskó were I to take her on. Today, however, I'm in no mood to bicker; I'm glad to be in the right, as I see it, and I resolve to raise the subject with caution but pride in front of Father at lunch. Even now I'm worried that I won't get anywhere with him, either, and that Mother will laugh at me; but then I do it anyway, because they're obviously in a good mood. At such times I'm not as scared of Father as at other times, though it's not like I know just why he *is* in a good mood, no, he never does let on why, no, I've always got to tell from his expression.

After telling them what I wanted, things happen exactly as I expected: Mother laughs at me while Father says with a smile: "All of us know full well that in storybooks there are people, adults and children alike, who wish for chairs to dance and grapes to talk."

Brazenly I interrupt. "And they don't get smacked!"

Fortunately, Father's good mood endures. "Of course not," he says, "because they don't expect their parents to grant them these wishes!"

As scared as I am, I cannot help but be even more audacious, and so I read a quote from my storybook: "Father, give me a talking grape, for that is the only thing I live for!"

Father still doesn't lose his temper, though he's no longer smiling as much.

"Do read on!" he says, taking the book from my hands. And he himself reads words of a sort I never heard escape his puritanical lips: "'Oh, my dear one and only son, I don't have such a thing in my entire realm, so how can I give you one?'"

I only listen, not daring to comment on his words, neither by making a face nor through words of my own. Father reads on. "'Then the son said, "Father, don't be sad — I'll go find that miraculous talking grape, so that it will heal my little sister's heart!" And the son bid adieu, sheathed a sword on his side, and embarked on his journey. . . .'"

Father read these final words with oratorical finesse, then added: "That's the whole point. This child wants a talking grape and a dancing chair not for himself, but for his sick sister. And he doesn't turn the house upside down if they don't turn up, but goes off on his own to search."

This wasn't all.

"When you're also big enough to go off and search for it on your own, by no means will I stand in your way if that's what you happen to want — a dancing chair and a talking grape! Assuming there's nothing else wrong with you."

He said this with a measure of sarcasm, with the bona fide sarcasm and smile of a puritanical rabbi par excellence, like someone who doesn't exactly believe in this sort of journey and grape, and to say the least, deems such an undertaking neither opportune nor fitting for his own son.

Mother's strident laughter provided the background music throughout. This laughter returned to her heart with just as much abandon as it had gushed forth from there, without being able to move my own heart.

Silently I ate.

FOOD INVARIABLY stirred up animal humility in me. That which separated me from Mother all day long — the butcher, the grocer, the market women, the baker, the costly wood in the stove, and the dumb, sizzling fat in the kettle — benevolently brought us that much closer to each other when we sat round the table. The steam rising from the soup instantly imparted a freshness to Mother's face and took the edge off her otherwise ridiculing voice and laughter; what's more, I noticed that this very same steam, not to mention the meat and vegetables that followed, softened up Father as well. As lunch proceeded, his steely blue eyes turned increasingly gentle, communicative, and so it was generally at meals that I asked for favors, just as I'd seen my mother and brother and sister do. Indeed, at such times Father often agreed to buy some inexpensive little storybook. A little ribbon for Oluska. A new notebook for Ernuskó, say, and for Mother, to fund the mending of clothes or, say, to buy an embroidery or ornamental pillow for a wanting corner of a room. Now his usual patronizing attitude, condescension, and ridicule were nowhere to be seen. I saw him as my real father, and so his small promises and encouraging words filled me not only with animal gratitude but, owing to the harsh image of him that I bore in my heart, with the greatest shame.

Nor did it escape my attention that Father even had it in him to be good humored at mealtimes, lighting a cigar afterward and then reading a paper, say. Yes, after meals he often bubbled with glee at Mother's childlike, whimsical remarks; and now not even in this did I notice so much as a shred of insult or belittlement on either of their parts. Likewise entranced by the food now pleasantly simmering within me, I humbly melted into their laughter with a grin or two of my own.

As for any promises we managed to extract at mealtimes, all of us tried to redeem them without delay. After so many disappointments I slowly realized that this had to be done then and there at lunch, or immediately afterward; for these were the only minutes of the day when Father could open his wallet without annoyance, reproach, or admonitory words and cross-examination. At most he knitted his brows in a melancholy sort of way or else let out a fleeting sigh somewhere above his beard, and this I could somehow endure without shame.

Sometimes, however, not even meals could tame him. Especially if he came home in an angry mood.

In vain did I plead to the soup and implore the meat at such times: "Oh, dear slice of beef, never again will I say you're dumb so long as you're delicious to him, to this master of fear and humiliation, who surely isn't my real father." Often the soup and meat and stewed vegetables struggled successfully against his bad moods, whereas at other times success was not forthcoming; then Father would invariably have Mother account for every kreuzer of the allowance he gave her every morning for shopping at the outdoor market.

Most times Mother would try avoiding the issue or postponing it until afternoon, either by smiling away in that childlike, whimsical way of hers, or using her matronly powers to calm him down. This is not to say that she did so out of concern for our sensitivity, especially mine — how I suffered when she had to account for her purchases this way at meals! It's not as if she even knew. No, the sole reason she strove to delay such confrontation until after lunch or, better yet, evening, was her fear that the numbers would ravage the blessed nature of the food she'd taken so much trouble all morning to procure and prepare.

She also knew that a ruined lunchtime mood would cast a pall over the whole afternoon and maybe the evening too. Further — and of this I naturally hadn't even an inkling at that age — by delaying the account of purchases, she wanted to win time to come up with little white lies, which, as loath as she was to do so, she had no choice but to tell if she wanted to guard against vexing Father's overthrifty nature; and, as she put it, she wanted to manage the household and furnish the flat "appropriately," as "becomes a rabbi's wife." Despite the considerable assets she'd brought to this marriage, she herself had no access to money; and so — in the interest of restocking her kitchen cabinet or linen closet — she was inclined to pinch and put aside wee sums from her daily allowances.

On seeing something tasteful, lovely, lush — whether an "exquisite" slice of beef or a plump, corn yellow "lovely" hen; a thick, "gorgeous" vegetable or some Italian fruit; Norwegian fish or even some "splendidly colorful" flowers; or for that matter, some "delicate and subdued" English fabric or a Czech chiffon, French kidskin, Turkish silk, Persian rug or pelt, Saxon china, Czech crystal; or, say, a "genteel" piece of walnut furniture or some antique clock or "sublime" upholstery — on seeing anything of this sort she'd cry out in glee and her face would begin to shine, as did mine on reading "Snow White" or "The Glass Mountain."

This struggle was hard. Never could Mother decide which part of her passion to strive for: a table full of lush and lovely foods, a home full of lovely things, or a linen closet and dresser filled to the brim. Achieving even a little bit of each was completely impossible. Father was opposed to all such things at once; then again, he did have a certain weakness for fine foods. Like many a puritan, he too carried about within himself an epicure buried prematurely under childhood privations; however, he hadn't the slightest feeling either for my immaterial fantasies or Mother's fantastical materials. Unable to grasp either their beauty or lush fecundity, he saw in them only numbers — in short, the money they cost; and so their potentially beguiling pleasures remained but a secondary consideration. Was it the rational man of simple taste, the puritan in him, who acted thus, or the child who'd never seen comfort and had wandered in patched-up clothes from the lunch table of one well-to-do family to the next like a beggar student living on alms?

His pleasure-loving self and his sense of comfort and fell to battle at Mother's every wish with his counting self and his sense of necessity. The only thing he was at a loss to express was love of beauty and lushness. Whenever Mother cast her net toward some lovely fabric, instinctively she called on the help of the buried epicure in him, the lover of creature comforts, against the numbers; however, the puritan slave of simple taste and numbers stirred in Father with doubled pain at every movement within him of this pleasure-loving gourmet, and so at first he protested against Mother's passions with tender forbearance, then with gentle mockery, and finally with indignation that brooked no contradiction.

Mother struggled doggedly. And only when nothing seemed to help anymore did she resort to putting aside kreuzers she pinched from her food-shopping allowance, missing kreuzers whose effect she then strove with diligence and taste to offset. She was always on the trail of lower-priced but "lovely" food, and if this or that dish won Father's taste buds, Mother was heartened not only for the recognition of her prowess as a housewife, but also for the good mood that the food evoked in Father. She hoped that such a good mood would lull his alacrity for accounting into repose.

But how often, how tragically she got it wrong! Indeed, the more Father liked some dish, the more quickly he got around to asking its price. The bewitching nature of some foods worked against her, and she had to do the accounting straightaway. Yet if the food *wasn't* to his liking, Mother's route to defeat was even more direct; for the resentment a bad lunch stirred within him spurred Father all the more to call her to account.

At such times I saw with fear and commiseration just how strict he was with my otherwise ridiculing Mother. Well, well, I thought, just as he begrudged every sweet, toy, story, and wild romping of mine, he begrudged every "exquisite" cut of meat, every "comely" fish, and the higher-priced sugar and fruit that Mother laid her hands upon.

All three of us children skulked in shame as Father pulled forth a pencil stub and a no less frugal slip of paper from the depths of his Francis Joseph–style vest, and began writing as Mother was compelled to dictate to the kreuzer the prices of everything from the meat to the soup noodles. All of that which we'd already had the good fortune to consume, with animal gratitude, was now broken down to its elements before our frightened and embarrassed eyes by the numbers Father jotted down. Naturally, this simultaneously dissipated my sense of gratitude; as Father, and so too my brother and sister, once again became "unreal," and it seemed to me that I lived on a charity of sorts, though in fact I had no right to what I'd already consumed. Yet by now the food was inside me. What could I have done? The animal gratitude quickly turned into an inextricable fog in which I cowered in shame; and because of this shame, I looked beyond Father, whom I now held in utter contempt, to Mother, poor thing, as she fidgeted away striving to get her bearings amid the prices she herself was busy creating, only so that she might salvage the kreuzers she'd put aside.

Unsuspecting though he was, Father recalled the price of the meat, the lard, and the sugar all the more exactly, and when doubting his memory, he promptly pulled a tiny notepad from some pocket of his vest in which he'd saved yesterday's slip of paper or the one from the day before that, and which, it must be said, he'd put aside not out of suspicion or some conscious plan to cross-examine Mother, but owing merely to his love of order. Every single such slip of paper featured the very same punctilious, peaked, impossibly Spartan characters.

With her self-conceived prices Mother fled madly before these slips of paper, before these numbers, from one shop to the other. Every bit as unsuspecting as up to now, Father meanwhile, owing merely to his love of order, was right on her tracks, albeit with startlingly calm, curious devotion. His memory allowed him to get his bearings among the shops every bit as well as among the prices, and he would agonize increasingly about the grocers who toyed so "undependably" or even "brazenly" with the prices, "taking advantage" of Mother's "goodness or absentmindedness," and "testing one's patience." Often he resolved to put a stop to this and enter the stores himself, at which Mother, panic-stricken, suddenly recalled that the prices were a tad lower after all, or else fled in fright from the familiar shops to completely unfamiliar ones, to where Father could pursue her neither with his slips of paper nor his memory.

Shaking his head and knitting his brows, he stopped dead in his tracks. Father just didn't understand the spell that everchanging shops held over Mother. This spell was born not only of her inclination to put kreuzers aside. Mother changed shops not just to dodge Father's slips of paper, but to quench the thirst for variety that issued straight from her bones. Yes, she sought and cherished variety in loveliness not simply in the things she bought, but in the shops themselves — how they looked inside and out, not least the buildings they were in, the squares they were on; and not least, in the owners and helpers too. If a shop was painted "beautifully," if it was full of "lovely" crates, if the display window was "something to behold," if the shopkeeper or his helper was "smartly" dressed, had "fetching" gestures, or an "inviting" face or, say, hair or eyes with "such a comely hue" —

all this drew her to newer and newer shops. And it wasn't only beauty, but stupefaction — anything, for that matter, that fed her hunger for bursts of laughter, anything splendidly freakish, in short — which beguiled her to wander again and again from shop to shop. So then, how could this sort of tableside accounting have truly worked, with Mother up against Father's puritanism?

Mother's efforts to have Father understand her passion were by turns marked by laughter, staid explanation, and, sometimes, despair. Father listened with either a smile or a concerned, baffled look, but one always steeped in a brooding indulgent tenderness he could feel for Mother only; and indeed, the spectacle of her womanly ado was enough at times to see him acquiesce to fluctuating prices and shops, lovelier sugar, and more exquisite meat. At other times, however, nothing could alleviate his concerns. At some point he stopped following Mother, halted his pencil, shook his head brusquely, and, proclaiming Mother's shop hopping an all too costly, whimsical extravagance, so firmly that Mother blushed, he demanded that she settle on a single shopkeeper one could trust in all respects.

But where was such a shopkeeper to be found?

Father wanted him to be Jewish, modest, and nearby. An almost impossible wish! Sighing and red-faced, or at other times tearfully proclaiming her innocence, Mother acceded; and so the choice fell upon this or that shopkeeper. The aggravation and persecution had completely exhausted her, so every afternoon she took a much-needed nap in her room. Father lay down on the divan in his study, beside the bedroom. Curled up as he was in the placidity of digestion, I can only imagine that in the silence that reigned before sleep Father quickly regretted having so brusquely shaken his head and having made his more cutting pronouncements; while on that other divan Mother's ruminations extinguished her tears in no time. For all her love of lovely things, she looked with housewifely respect and wonder upon

Father's thrift. As much as she wanted to luxuriate in her own nature, fulfill her passion for material things, she yearned just as much to pay homage to Father's puritan nature, and to money. While she'd spent all morning downtown at the market and in shops feeding fuel to the fire of her passion, pangs of conscience now held her in their grip as she lay on the divan.

And so it wasn't long before new talks ensued between the two divans.

Father took back his harsher words and consented to Mother's continued shop hopping, whereas Mother passionately voiced her longing for constancy and thrift. She still, however, couldn't fall asleep. The more indulgent Father became, the more Mother felt that she was a bad wife, unworthy of her rabbi husband, and so before long she cried out through her tears: "I know I'm not really a good wife!" At which Father protested, "No, no, I should have been more understanding!" This was then followed by Mother confessing to the money she'd put aside, and Father giving his permission for a new carpet, tablecloth, or curtain, say, so as to make Mother happy.

Yet the heartrending forces that brought about these reconciliations regularly avenged themselves, with Mother tormented afterward by headaches. At such times Father commanded that we spend the whole afternoon in utter silence, with our homework. The knowledge that I could neither move nor call out rendered both homework and play unspeakably boring, and having to stay in the room all afternoon unbearable. If I so much as opened the door, Mother woke with a start from her light, nervous sleep, and Father appeared at once with a stern expression on the threshold. These quiet but thoroughly menacing afternoons, which recurred with increasing frequency every week, made me feel all the more like a captive. The second half of such afternoons, after my parents had already awoken and Mother had either forgotten or explained away her headache and fast-beating heart to herself in that way of hers, generally passed more calmly.

While Mother troubled with supper, Father took us to synagogue.

Supper was a quieter affair. Father posed fewer questions about prices, for the suppertime dishes were far less lavish and thereby less costly; and thus I didn't have to be as ashamed as at lunch. Yes, at supper there was invariably less on our plates, and selfish as I was, it never escaped my attention when my parents had something a tad more extravagant—say, meat—while we ate only semolina or rice boiled in milk, with a bit of sugar mixed in. Light food is best for children, Father often said on such occasions, adding that it's foolish to eat a lot before going to bed. To my gluttonous, lonely heart all this seemed but an empty excuse behind which Father, so I thought, was masking his stinginess. Thus every single meal served to remind me, even more than did the sundry events at other times of the day, of my little and utterly dependent state; and after every meal I longed again to be bigger, so that I might flee this excruciating, shameful condition of mine.

The only way of becoming big and free, said Father, was to do as well as possible in school. Thus I figured that every completed grade would bring me that much closer to freedom; and so I longed to pass through to the next grade all the sooner. When this finally happened, and I went from second to third grade, I tried my utmost to be even prouder than during the year before. Why of course! For I'd become *bigger* once again, more grown-up, that much closer to the day when I could finally do as I well pleased.

But on coming home from school it invariably turned out that the very idea that I was bigger, and that I would be even bigger yet, and finally free, was to no avail — a sham. For compared to my father and brother and sister, I continued being just as little as I had been up to now, and neither the gluttony of my conceit — still fueled by my flights of fancy — nor the wounds borne by my ever-present sensitivity, changed. In vain I steadily advanced in school, my throes of shame did not fade away, and once again I felt that there was no help, that newer grades and newer subjects were all in vain, that in point of fact I could not grow, I did not grow, and never would grow; that nothing would change.

Whenever I thus thought of myself and my wounds, time seemed to have stopped once and for all; only the next morning, once I stepped into the classroom and again found myself thinking of the subjects at hand, of all the romping about and the stories and midmorning snacks that awaited me in school — only then did time begin to race along again! Indeed, it raced imperceptibly until the next affront. Then time stopped again, for an eternity at that, so it seemed. Helplessly I tossed about between these two sorts of time, between the all too constant, inner time, and the ever-racing time outside myself.

BIBLE STUDY was the new subject that, most of all, made me bigger and prouder to be in third grade. While we went about translating the Books of Moses from Hebrew to Hungarian, Mr. Würtz, our teacher, stood behind us to see that none of us should hoodwink so many centuries of Hebrew learning by peeking between our fingers at the Hungarian text underneath the palms of our right hands. The more nimble-fingered among us, and those whose hearts did not beat as nervously as mine, had no problem outfoxing Mr. Würtz, whose eyes were already bad indeed. The square-headed man moved between our benches, shambling along on his fallen arches as though on rails: the tracks of the curriculum, as it were, amid the landscape of the given assignment. Reading any sort of emotion on his stiff, torpid, freckled face was all but impossible. As if his insides had begun to soften with decay, he was particularly inclined toward neither teaching nor discipline. Yet he taught all the same, like a machine that had been started up long ago and now kept clipping helplessly along, heated pitiably with the little pay allotted to a poor teacher like him, who, incidentally, had fathered five children.

I can almost hear him even now, as he raises the book up high, like he did that first day: "This is our holy book. We must learn this just as it is. Now we'll translate from it. Pay attention, and you won't have to ask a lot of questions."

His tone of voice suggested that he was thinking: "This wretched pay of ours is what I've got to feed and clothe five kids with, and teach so many other kids. And we'll just have to keep getting by on so little unless we can eke out a little raise from the congregation leaders."

On such occasions he'd often fix his eyes on his enormous flat feet, which he'd have to drag about the room to complete this onerous task.

"In the beginning, God created the heaven and the earth."

And if any one of us stared out the window at the sky, Mr. Würtz would say: "Now now, it's not the sky you're supposed to be looking at, but the book!"

Throughout the creation of the world we could look only at the book, and at Mr. Würtz. No wonder that this creation seemed every bit as freckled, old and spongy, and shambling as Würtz himself; or that nothing remained in me of this whole Moses-made world but the flustered struggle to render Hebrew words into Hungarian, along with the longing for transparent fingers and a braver heart with which to do so. . . .

The legend of the Garden of Eden followed the creation story, reawakening in me the memory of Grandpa Jeremiah. Again I saw him, distant and hazy among the tombstones of B——, yet I neither could nor wanted to remember him more fully; no, I was glad that he was gone once and for all, along with that period of my life. The oblivion didn't last for long, however, because the fire in which Abraham was set to sacrifice Isaac saw Grandpa Jeremiah's fire blaze up before me anew, that fire which, so long ago, had swallowed the first of my toys.

Yet where had God been then, God, who would have sent a ram, as he had to Abraham, into my grandfather's blazing fire instead of my toys? I couldn't resist asking the teacher about this great deficiency of my past that kept returning to haunt me.

My audacious and preposterous inquiry was greeted with joviality all around. Mr. Würz cast me a listless stare and said: "When human beings are as good as Abraham, then maybe God will perform more miracles."

Voices came from all directions.

"I'm good!"

"Me too!"

Mr. Würtz only gave a resigned wave of the hand.

"That's not enough," he said, "simply not enough. Among other reasons, because those who are good do not shout."

Oh sure, I thought, you're saying this only because you, the teacher, are supposed to. This God and this Abraham, I figured, are stories no different from "The Glass Mountain" and "Tom Thumb," only that they happen to be in Hebrew, like the prayer book, so they've got to be translated.

But, not wanting to anger him, I didn't say a thing.

Only in the next Bible class did I have a go at it: "You're only saying all this, sir, because you've *got* to, huh? This is just a story, like 'The Glass Mountain.'"

He didn't get angry, but only cast me a listless smile.

"Azarel," he called, "no wisecracks!"

I could tell from his voice that his heart was probably weaker than that of the schoolmistress in the first two grades, and so I mustered up enough courage to speak again.

"Mr. Würtz, sir, you're telling us to be as good as Abraham was, right? Well, it says here that he wanted to throw his son in the fire. Then *he* wasn't good either!"

At first he only said the same thing as before: "Azarel, no wisecracks!" Then he opened up the Bible to the Books of Moses and looked up, glancing down only now and again as he told us the story.

> His heart was heavy for his only son, whom he loved more than all the world, but seeing that God wanted this, he went and saddled up his ass. . . . God, meanwhile, who only wanted to see if Abraham loved him as much as his son, Isaac, sent a ram instead. . . .

"So then," said Mr. Würtz, "Abraham was a good man indeed. He loved his son very much, but he loved God even more. This is exactly why God gave Isaac back to him. We must love God" — so said Mr. Würtz — "more than anything, for he created all and freed our ancestors from slavery in Egypt, as we will learn shortly."

My finger shot up once more.

"But where *is* he, God?"

"That, we cannot know. God is invisible."

"But if we don't know where he is and what he's like, and if he doesn't show himself to us, then how can we love him?"

"As to this," replied Mr. Würtz, "everything is written in this book, as we will learn — in the Ten Commandments."

I vaguely remembered having heard such words before, that He — that is to say, God — had already said all there is to say.

Mr. Würtz turned to the Ten Commandments, read them aloud, and pronounced: "Those who do all this, as written here, love God, and God will love them too."

Again I raised a finger.

"And then . . . what will God . . . give me?"

"Now, now," he replied, "it would be really easy that way. We must love him unselfishly, or, in other words, not so we get something from him."

"All right," I said, "but he could at least show himself for once!"

"Azarel," said Mr. Würtz, "no more wisecracks. Sit down."

I smiled, and sat. What he said isn't true, I thought; he said it only because he's the teacher. And who loves "unselfishly"? Father loves me because he can then go ahead and boss me around, but if I wouldn't obey him, if I wouldn't want to go to school, maybe he wouldn't even feed me. And he's the rabbi, always talking about this God in his sermons. And Mother, my brother and sister? Why, there's no one who would give without wanting at least something in return! Of course not. When everyone knows, just like I do, that this God doesn't exist, isn't real, is only in the book, and is talked about only so that us kids learn, whereas everyone knows he doesn't exist and will never appear! It's a story, like "The Glass Mountain." But while my parents said the glass mountain doesn't exist, if I were to say that this God doesn't exist, no doubt I'd be in for it.

I couldn't resist the temptation for long, however; and so before Father — at lunch — I raised the subject of this God. Cautiously, though, like this: Mr. Würtz said . . .

"To be sure," said Mother, "a good child will keep the Ten Commandments. The important thing," she added, "is to love your father and your mother."

Of course that's important to you two, I thought. But then she added, "Oh yes, and your brother and sister too." After another pause: "If you love everyone else too, all the better!" And she burst out laughing. "But you don't look to be at risk of that, do you now!"

Father was in a gentle mood — he was enjoying the meal — and so he said only this much: "It's quite enough if you're well behaved, a good student, and go to synagogue. We never asked you to do anything more."

Half giggling, Mother leaned toward Father. "He'll convert sooner or later! Würtz" — she laughed — "will make a believer out of him! He'll be a good boy!"

"Well then," said Father, "we shall see."

Mother thought the whole thing was one big joke, this much was apparent. God and the Bible just the same as the stories and me. As for Father, just as I'd figured, all he wanted was that I obey him. But when it came to their never having loved God, or rather, never having loved him "unselfishly," and to the issue of this God not existing at all, they didn't want to say a word.

I really should bring it up, I thought. Not having the courage to do so directly, however, I slyly said only this much: "I'd gladly do everything, all Ten Commandments, if I knew he was *for real!*"

I waited for Father's response: whether God exists or not. But Father didn't say a word. Mother replied, in just as mocking a tone as before.

"You've got to have God right away? Won't settle for less, will you? What we tell you isn't enough?"

Afraid of Father, I dodged the question.

"That's different. But I'd still like to know if God's for real."

Father apparently noticed that I'd been trying to lay a trap for him, for he responded sternly: "Enough of this nonsense! Eat up, and I don't want to hear another word out of you!"

I fell silent, but thought: *He, the rabbi,* talks like this when asked about God.

Afraid though I was, keeping quiet was impossible. I'll be gentle, I thought, ask them as nicely as can be, yes, that's how I'll keep up the questions. In a mellow, pleading tone I began: "But Father, please . . . please don't be angry with me just for asking something. . . ."

He shot me an irritated look.

"If you ask politely, I won't get angry. But you're being a smart aleck, understand?"

Mother tried defending me.

"Now for once," she said, casting Father a cajoling smile, "he wasn't even so nasty."

"Just forget it!" Father replied. "He's not curious about God like other, well-behaved children you can explain things to and that's that. Who listen and understand. No, this kid here is being a little brat, as if he wants to give me the third degree!"

Mother tried smoothing things over with another smile.

Ashamed and afraid, I just sat there with downcast eyes, taken aback that Father had seen right through me.

"I don't want to give you any degree, Father," I finally said. "Please don't be angry. All I wanted to know is what you think: Is there a God or not? Besides, I wanted to know because we're learning about it now in school, the whole book is about this, and anyway, we're always going to synagogue and praying to him. And you're the rabbi, Father. Who *should* I be asking?"

Mother took it upon herself to reply. "All right, all right, but if your father doesn't like it, you've got to be quiet, like a good boy."

Now Father spoke, turning to Mother. "You believe what he said? That he wants to know something? A barefaced lie! If I say to him, there is a God, he'll want me to show him right away, before I've even swallowed what's in my mouth! If I'd told him to wait, because he's too young to understand just yet, he'd reply, 'Then why should I go to synagogue? Why should I study the Bible?'"

Mother only shook her head. Father shot me another irritated look.

"I know his kind!"

I said nothing, but thought: Go ahead and be angry if you want.

My thoughts went something like this: Oh yes, I've figured it out — there is no God! And I've also figured out that you, Father, know he doesn't exist either, but that you keep acting as if he does. Only because you're the rabbi, and that's where all that hard-earned money comes from that you two talk so much about! You talk about everything except this. All you say is: If I say this to him, he'll . . . If I say that, he'll . . . You say I'm too young to understand. Well, I understand full well, no matter how little I am. You talk all sorts of things, but not the truth —

that there is no God, but we've got to act like there is, because if we don't, you'll whack us good!

Once more I shuddered, however, on noticing that he seemed to have figured out everything I was thinking about him; for suddenly he turned toward Mother and explained things sternly indeed.

"This is the same with him as when he wanted the chairs to dance and the stove to play the flute for him! And the same as he does with the stories. If he doesn't get enough stories, he runs about like a little madman out there in the schoolyard and his clothes get all torn up! Now it's God!"

All at once he turned fully, menacingly toward me.

"Did you ask anything about God down there in school?"

I cringed in terror. At first not even I could recall what I'd asked Mr. Würtz, and in any case, what should I say now? How could I defend myself? And so I said nothing.

"Are you going to answer?" he yelled, and struck the table. The kettle clanked and Mother turned all red. As always on such occasions, her mouth opened just so, her teeth glittered, her eyes grew wider.

"Wait!" she called, "he'll answer."

I looked for words but only stammered, wanting to be forthright but my head was dizzy with fear. Finally I faltered out: "We just happened . . . to be learning . . . about God. . . ."

Mother turned even redder. "You see?" she hastened to say, "there's no sense getting all upset."

"That's not certain yet," said Father, lowering his voice. "I'll find out from Würtz, I will!"

Again I shuddered. Of course he'd find out — but what? I still couldn't recall what exactly had happened that morning in school.

Tears now came to Mother's eyes. "You two are just getting me upset," she complained. "Then I won't be able to sleep again. And get over the headache."

"I'm sorry," said Father even more softly. "There's just no other way to deal with this child. . . . He's become a real Korah!"

Mother tried diverting his anger to Korah. "Who was that?"

"A rebel!"

Father had switched to the tone of voice he tended to assume for religious instruction, in which there now mingled a certain degree of male tenderness and remorse toward Mother.

"Korah was the one who was satisfied with nothing when Moses led the people in the desert. According to the Bible, Moses did miracles for him in vain, in vain they found quails, manna, and a spring — all this was not enough for Korah. He only rebelled, until, says the Bible, the earth opened up and swallowed him whole."

"You see," said Mother, now to me, "the same will happen to you."

"We won't wait till then," said Father. "I'll go ask Würtz, and if" — he now turned to me — "you've been acting up in school as well, you'll see what's in store for you!"

Mother, afraid in advance of the evening upheaval, turned to me. "Admit it like a good boy if you said something about God, and then you won't get in as much trouble as if your father has to find out the hard way."

I couldn't have cared less what Mother said. Her voice felt cold, as if she neither wanted to nor really could protect me, as if she feared only for her own peace of mind and for Father's, lest he get upset. It seemed I still had a few whacks coming either way, so I preferred putting it off until a bit later.

I said nothing.

Father waved a hand in resignation. "He's just lying anyway. Anyone who's rude and selfish lies too. That's natural. But" — and again he turned to me — "if you lied, you'll pay for that too!"

To keep him from saying more, Mother now turned his attention to the food on his plate. "Just look, Papa, your meat will get completely cold."

She herself began eating, so as to encourage him to do the same. "See?" she said, "it's still passable."

Father took a mouthful too, but threw his fork right back on the plate. "It's completely cold," he cried out, "inedible!"

Mother would have run to the kitchen with his plate, but he motioned her to stay. "Leave it be. I'll eat it like it is. To hell with it."

After a few more mouthfuls he stopped in annoyance. "Enough, take it away!"

Though Mother again offered to warm up the meal, Father was already ringing the bell for the maid. Lidi and Mother cleaned off the table. Prudently Father drank half a glass of wine, then lit a cigar.

By now he felt sorry for Mother. He spoke: "I toil away all morning. Go from one school to another, teach fifty children here, forty there, breathe foul air, and all the while I don't even buy myself a single salt roll. Why, I ask? So this kid has enough to eat! Then I don't even have enough peace at home to swallow one or two morsels of hot food. And then you wonder why a man's upset? Is it worth lifting a finger for a brat like this?"

Mother now took pity on him. And turned against me.

"You're completely right," she said, "a child like this doesn't deserve what you do for him. But what's to be done, if that's just the way it is?"

"What?" said Father, "since fair-spoken words don't do the trick, I'll never say a thing to him again, no, I'll thrash him right away! Maybe *then* he'll change."

Fearing even more upheaval, Mother didn't find this child-rearing tactic entirely sound. And while she continued to be vexed with me, she tried talking Father out of it.

"Why, if hitting him would help," she began, "he should have gotten better long ago! But it makes no difference to this child! God knows what kind of hide and head he's got! He is incapable of either crying or being ashamed. And why's that? Who's to say? . . . The other two are perfectly well behaved. Such things would never cross Ernuskó's mind!"

To calm Father down, she began naming all the things she loved so much about Ernuskó. "He's so quiet and gentle, such a good student. Ever since he was born. Never does he utter more, or for that matter, fewer words than he should." She finished after a pause by adding, "He's just like you must have been. . . ."

Ernuskó listened with quiet pride. Since Oluska was already squirming in her seat, however, Mother went on. "And what a good girl Oluska is! Even if she does talk back sometimes, that's *nothing* compared to this child." And she pointed at me. "First he lost his senses with the stories, then during playtime out in the schoolyard, and now over God! You never know when he'll do or say something he shouldn't. Never-ending chaos! When we have enough problems in life as it is! We've got to be on edge all the time because of *him!* What will happen later on?"

She turned to me. Her wide eyes reflected the pain of warm-hearted maternal self-indulgence, together with true womanly fear and practicality. "If only I knew what a child like this thinks! Why, then I could get across to him what misery he'll assure for himself later on too, if he starts out this way! He figures he's always the one who's got to be talking, asking questions, and answering them, about everything under the sun! Not getting his father angry and his mother upset — that just doesn't matter to him!"

Ever so gently she clapped her lovely, soft little hands.

"If he really knew what misery awaits him, I do believe he wouldn't behave this way. If he knew how bad things will get for him, it's impossible to believe he doesn't have the brains to change! Impossible!" She looked at me. "It's not yet too late. . . . Listen to what we're telling you. There's no one else in the world who'll give you advice as good as we do, who wants what's best for you as much as we do! That's why we're your parents! Don't you understand that? Doesn't it trouble you?

That you've caused your father so much grief, when he works so hard for your good!"

Not bad, I thought — almost as if you were my real mother. But you're not. I've known that for a long time. What's it to me? Because I'm right when it comes to how all this began: There's no God, and you and Father know it, too, yes, that's why you two are telling me off; and as for everything else — what's it to me? Go ahead and talk all you want!

Father read my thoughts yet again. After a puff on his cigar, he said: "Talking won't do the kid any good."

Right you are, I thought.

After lunch, when as usual my parents retired for their afternoon repose, I heard Mother making huge sighs in the adjacent room. This scared me. Since her head no doubt hurt from all the fuss, she would be unable to get to sleep, whereupon Father, lying in the room next to hers, would hear her sighs and get even angrier with me. I shuddered at the thought of what would happen that evening after Father would ask Würtz about me in synagogue. In my intractable distress I didn't even dare whistle to myself. After every single sigh of Mother's I waited for the door to swing open and Father to run at me with a storm of verbal abuses and hand at the ready. But I didn't have the courage to leave. Every step, every squeaking of a door, would be my ruin. Sullen and scared, I sat down before my homework, but not even studying helped. I only kept staring at the Bible translation, reading how God had created the earth, reading first in Hebrew then in Hungarian, but I grasped even less than I had that morning in school. Before me was the secret to my woes and to the blows I'd suffered, that which begot me and oppressed me; here was the fountainhead from which my family had sprung, and along with it, that of all Semitic nomad families; yes, here was the key to my life, but to no avail. . . . Only letters and words remained, at which I stared mechanically. And I thought: Why this whole business of learning? Just so I could be whacked! So this is what God and biblical translation are all about! And why should I put up with this? So long as I can't and don't dare escape, wouldn't it be better if Father simply said: You obnoxious little brat, beat it! Go beg on the streets, go wherever you want, but scram! And he'd kick me out. I'd trudge away somewhere or other, anywhere, it wouldn't matter, but I'd trudge away, I would; for I'd have no other choice.

Before long the fear and solitude were unbearable and drove me to my brother and sister. Ernuskó and Oluska were doing their homework together.

"Hey, Ernuskó," I said softly, "I'm in for it again tonight. Because of God. But you know just as well that there is no God, huh? That he's for real only in the book."

He looked at me like a model student. "Of course I know," he said, "and everyone with some brains knows that he's only in the book. But why bring this up with Father during lunch, when he'll just get mad? I learned all this too, and I still am, but that doesn't mean I bring it up. Why don't you use your brain a bit too?"

At this Oluska spoke up too — much more fervently, of course. "Yeah, use your brain! Now you've got Father all mad, then he'll get angry at me too and won't let me go down in the yard."

They looked at me disapprovingly as I sank back into sullen anguish.

Suddenly Mother's sighing stopped. Maybe she's gone to sleep after all, I thought. Mr. Würtz now came to mind, and then I found myself thinking that I might go upstairs to his flat and ask him not to say anything at night about me.

As quietly as possible, I slipped through the kitchen into the hallway to the front door. But here was the rub: if I were to shut the door, I'd have to ring the doorbell to get back in, and Father might wake up. He'd discover that I was out. He'd grill me. If, however, I'd simply "forget" to shut it, well, it would stay open. And if by chance Father would wake up in the meantime and come out into the hall, he'd notice the open door, look into things just the same, and discover that I was out. There was no way out of this fix.

I chose the latter, asking the maid not to say a word to anyone and to leave open the door. Then I bounded up the stairs.

Mr. Würtz lived just one floor above us. But I stopped dead in my tracks in front of his door. How very different was this door from ours, how strange! And how different it was talking to the teacher down there in school from being up here about to ring his bell! Meanwhile my heart beat something to the effect of, "Careful! Maybe your father's already woken up downstairs! Hurry back, and put up with the whacks tonight as best you can!"

But all the intimidation I'd already received now broke my hesitation, as I longed for help against Father. I rang the bell. An older girl opened the door. I said: "I'm looking for Mr. Würtz." She disappeared, and soon I heard her voice from another room: "The little Azarel kid is here."

I could hear doors opening here and there. Older students peered out — boarders. The stifling smell of carpet dust and cooked cabbage hit my nose — how different this was too! How very different from the smell of our cabbage, of our carpets!

Now Mr. Würtz appeared. The bespectacled, bathrobe-clad figure shambled toward me with a long pipe hanging from his mouth. He spoke in a freckled, phlegmatic voice.

"Hey there, sonny, what's up?"

Blushing, I said: "I only came because I want to ask you a favor, Mr. Würtz."

And he: "Well, well."

"My father," I began, "got angry during lunch, because I asked him about God."

"You see," he replied, "I told you not to be such a wise guy, Azarel."

I went on. "You were right, Mr. Würtz, now Father's angry, and tonight in synagogue he'll ask you if I said anything bad in school about God. But please, Mr. Würtz, please don't tell on me!"

He fixed his piercing mousy eyes upon me.

"All right, then," he said. "Don't you worry. We'll have us a little chat with him."

It was getting late. The door I'd left open was closed.

I was terrified. No matter who shut it, I thought, I've got to go in; I must ring the bell.

I took care that the bell should ring as softly as possible. Maybe Father wouldn't hear it after all, and somehow I could slip unnoticed back into our room.

At first I touched the bell so softly it didn't make a sound. Then I pressed a bit harder. But it still made no sound. I held my breath and tried again, pressing as softly as could be. What horror, that instant, ear-splitting noise! Now immediately I heard the study door open, then close, just as Father always opened and closed it. Then his steps. There was no way out, no way out. . . . *He* opened the door. And was he ever annoyed.

"Where were you?"

I shrunk back.

"I went down . . . just a little. . . ."

"Don't you know that when we're sleeping you're not to roam about?"

I said nothing.

"Didn't you get enough of a lesson at lunch?"

I stole away from him through the kitchen. He returned to the study. It seemed he didn't suspect a thing. I figured, yes, it probably wasn't even him who'd closed the door. Relieved, I hastily opened the Bible to resume the translation. Loudly I recited: "In the beginning, God created the heaven and the earth. . . ."

Yes, now I wanted Father to hear me studying, studying about God just the way he wanted.

Hardly had I begun, however, when Father entered the room.

"*You*," he said, "get over here."

I stood before him with a sense of foreboding. His steely blue eyes gave me a piercing look.

"Did you go see Würtz up there?"

I wanted to lie, but it was too late. I blushed, and he noticed at once.

"So, you *were* there!" And he yelled: "Tell me this minute what you were up to!"

Although she heard the goings-on from the other room, Mother was afraid of yet more upheaval, and so didn't want to come out. From inside she called out: "Papa, come on in here!"

Father didn't go in, but only stopped by the open door and called inside with irritation.

"You see? I *said* this child was lying."

Now Mother also came to the door. In a soft but angry voice she said: "Let him be. Let him stew in his own juices. There's no point bothering with him, he'll meet a bad end anyway. Come on in and shut the door."

Father just stood there for a while, but in the end he didn't give in.

"If you don't want to hear it," he told Mother, "stay in there! Just stay in there! Things can't go on like this with this boy, we've got to break him of the habit of lying!"

And he shut the door. Now he stood before me in a menacing posture.

"What did you tell him up there?"

Gruffly I replied: "Not to tell on me."

"And what did you say to him in school?"

"I only asked where God is. And why he doesn't show himself."

"So then," he said, "I was right, you *were* acting up even in school."

I defended myself doggedly. "I didn't know that was *acting up*."

"Is that so? You didn't know that a rabbi's son mustn't ask things like that in school? You think that's all right? You don't know this? You have the face to deny it?"

Now Mother came in after all. Father continued.

"Where God is? And why he doesn't show himself? What business is it of *yours?* I'll show you!"

He turned to Mother, who now wrung her hands.

"Do you want to make things completely impossible for your father? Haven't you thought what people will say if they find out? That our child, the child of the rabbi and his wife, of all people, happens to be asking questions like that? Aren't you worried that the other children will all tell their parents? Do you want to bring shame and humiliation upon us? To deprive us of our bread? To ruin our whole lives? Then I'll be the first to say, it's best if your Father just beats your brains out!"

At this, Father fell upon me and struck away.

"He'll ruin our lives," Mother cried out, "ruin us. What will become of us with him around?"

"*I'll* break him," shouted Father, "pull him out of school. He'll study at home under my direction."

At which Mother said anxiously: "But he won't want to."

"Then I'll enter him somewhere as an apprentice. That kind of work will teach him what life and God are all about."

Mother had her doubts. "I couldn't take the shame of my son being an apprentice."

"Then," Father yelled at me, "I'll lock him in and beat him till he's got just one breath left in him. But he won't bring shame upon us so long as he's in our home."

At this Mother spoke again. "Wouldn't it be better if he didn't even exist, after all, instead of being the way he is?"

I couldn't take the blows any longer — which is one reason I now cried out: "Go ahead and beat my brains out! Because I won't be any different anyway!"

At which Father fell upon me again.

"Won't be any different, will you?! No?!"

He squeezed me into the nook between the cast-iron stove and the wall.

"I'll smash in your skull," he shouted.

"Go ahead," I grumbled, "smash it if you want, I won't be any different even then."

No longer could I feel his blows —I only kept repeating: "Hit me all you want, all you want, all you want! I'm still right, I still won't be any different, I'm still right!"

Mother sobbed. "That's enough, Papa!" she finally said. "Enough. There's no point anyway. You'll only bring ruin on yourself."

Father left off the beating while I grumbled on anyway, just to irk him more.

"All you want, all you want. I'm still right, you know: there is no God. And you two know it too. You're nothing but liars."

Father raised his fist: "Will you shut up?"

Mother spoke. "Ah! Let the crazy boy talk! Let him, Papa. Obviously he's not all there. Come on in. Come on."

Taking Father by the hand — he'd turned completely pale — they went into the other room.

Yet I followed them inside and kept grumbling.

"Yes, there is no God, and you two don't believe in him either. But that's what you live on. Which is why you want me to pretend too. And because I don't want to pretend, you go and smack me. But you can do it all you want, yes, because I'm gonna tell everyone there is no God, and you two don't buy it either. Because if you believed, you wouldn't go hitting me now and other times. Because that's in the Ten Commandments too. You only preach *unselfishness,* the Ten Commandments, and God — in synagogue. But meantime you hit me, because I know the truth and say it too. Now I'll go tell everyone everything about you two. And *right now.*"

Father fell upon me again.

Mother tried restraining him. "Papa," she cried, "you'll end up killing him!"

Father refused to yield. "At least," he retorted, "then we'll be done with him."

He flung me to the ground and went on hitting me there.

I didn't dare even move anymore. Go ahead, I thought, go ahead and kill me. Here's a rabbi for you! A true rabbi!

He began strangling me. "I'll kill you with my bare hands," came his rattling howl, "I'll wring your neck. . . ."

I was unable to make a sound. Finally Mother forced herself between us. "Don't, Papa," she cried out, "it'll stick to your soul! Don't!" At this Father let go. Mother added: "God will thrash him — much more roundly than we ever could. Just leave it . . . to God. *He* knows that we always wanted what's best for him. *He* knows how much we've suffered on account of him. *He'll* thrash him, he will. Why should it be on our conscience?"

Gasping for air, I turned to Mother.

"And *you* talk about God? You didn't do anything unselfish either! You didn't love me unselfishly. And no one else, either. All you love is lovely clothes. And being proud. And Father's *job.* Nothing else. All you want is for me to obey Father. To be like you two. And if this God *did* exist, the first thing he'd do is smack the two of you like you did me. Because I'm bad, and I don't deny it, but you two are even worse, and you go denying it even though you're a rabbi and a rabbi's wife. So if this God *did* exist, he would've smacked you two long ago, and would've said, 'Don't go preaching in my name.' But that God doesn't exist. You two are rotten stinking liars."

At this Father stood, squeezed his hands to his temples, and cried out to Mother: "Get him out of here, because I don't know what I might do."

Mother stepped over to me in terror and bustled me out of the room.

I didn't resist. Once out in the hall, I collapsed on the carpet. And that is how I remained, my face brushing against the floor, grumbling: "There *is no* God, there isn't, and you two are rotten stinking liars."

In anguish and rage I bit into the carpet, and my whole face hurt.

"Let it hurt," I grumbled, "all the more. Why not. There's no God anyway, and you two are rotten stinking liars."

Again and again I bit into the carpet until my teeth started bleeding.

"There's no God anyway, there isn't, there isn't . . . rotten stinking liars."

Now I heard Father open the door behind me, but I didn't even stir. He stepped over me and locked the door, then I heard him take the iron bar, lay it across the door, and place a lock on it.

Mother came out too. Father spoke to me: "Don't you touch that lock. That's all you'll hear from me. Otherwise you won't get out of here alive. Even if your Mother wants you too, not even then."

"He won't leave," Mother commented, "and couldn't if he tried. Besides, he's had enough of being smacked. I'm sure of it."

Father returned to his study. Mother addressed me in that soft voice of hers.

"There's no point lying here anymore. Go to your room, you loathsome little thing."

I didn't stir. Presently she too left the hall.

I lay there for a while yet, but, awfully tired, no longer did I bite the floor.

Then I heard Ernuskó. He made as if he was just passing through the hall for some reason or other. And he said to me: "Why don't you get up? This won't help anyway."

Then came Oluska's voice: "See? You had it coming."

I offered no reply, but only lay there motionless.

Now Lidi came from the kitchen. "You'll be in the way out here."

She proceeded to lift the pile carpet that was all around me, rolling it up the way she did every night. It stank of dust. When she'd rolled it up to me, she spoke again.

"Move it already, I've got other things to tend to."

I didn't stir. "Leave it," I said.

"Look," she replied, "as far as I'm concerned you can lie here till tonight. Just let me pick up the carpet."

She yanked it out from under me. "So there," she said, "I always did say you were a little devil all right."

Her face now turned toward the inside rooms and she said, more softly and chuckling: "But there's no denying: You really let your father have it. You and that dad of yours! From the same barrel of rotten apples! Real godless sorts. I always knew it."

Wanting to be alone somewhere, I got up. Without a word I entered our room and cowered in the corner by the stove. There I sprawled as if I'd just fallen down the stairs, I hurt so much all over.

I waited for Mother to call, "Time to go to synagogue with Ernuskó." She didn't. Ernuskó went to synagogue alone.

Oh sure, I thought, they won't let me go to synagogue, because they're afraid I'll tell everyone, just like I said I would.

Then it began getting dark. If only it would get dark soon, I thought, darker and darker. If only light would never come again. It's all over anyway.

But then it was bright again. Mother had come in, turned on the light, then began to set the table for supper.

In a soft, tearful voice she said: "Do you realize what you've done?"

I thought: Why should I even answer her? I'm tired, and by now she knows just what I think of them. It's all over anyway.

As she went about setting the cold, empty plates, my head and entire body were hot and throbbing from the blows I'd received.

Mother spoke again. "I always said you've got a screw loose, and there's just no other way I can explain to myself what you did."

I said nothing.

Oluska now materialized, handed a tray bearing the food to Mother, who put everything in its proper place — first the toasted rolls by Father's place, then the wine and mineral water.

She continued speaking. "It seems you want your Father to die from all the distress. Or else to fall into sin because of you, to beat you to death. What is it you want? Since you were born you've made our lives one bundle of anguish after another."

Now she set the silverware.

"Seriously now," she continued, "I'm beginning to think that you're not even our son. That some bad spirit brought you among us. To our undoing."

She stopped and cried out: "To talk like this with a father and a mother! A *child!*"

And even louder: "A *Jewish* child. A *rabbi's* child!"

Only now did I notice that Mother had left my usual place empty. So they don't want me eating at their table, I thought. Fine, then.

Now she set the glasses.

"So, you think you can just pronounce judgment on your father? Even if you were a hundred times older, not even then. Don't you know that? That there's no greater sin? In the whole world. Even if your father were a hundred times worse than he is good, not even then. A father is sacred. Why, I never so much as dared think anything bad about my father. God bless his soul. Nor of my mother. Nor your own father about his. And I'm sure your brother and sister have never had such thoughts either. God will never forgive you for what you've done. You'll see. Someday you'll think back to all this. To my telling you. You'll see what your life will be like. You'll cry when you remember us, when you think back to this day, to when I told you this."

Finally she finished setting the table.

"As of today," she said, "I'm through with watching out for you. I've always defended you. You know that best. But starting now, this is over. God wouldn't forgive me for defending you anymore. Your father can do what he wants with you. There's nothing he could do that would be so bad you wouldn't deserve it."

She stepped closer. Maybe she'll hit me too, I thought, drawing back.

"Don't worry, I won't hit you. No, I don't want you ever saying your mother laid a hand on you. And I know there's no point talking. You'll just bring curses and shame upon us anyway when you grow up. Though I can't say I know why God made a child like you. And why he gave him to us. When both of us have always led upright, honorable lives."

Looking me in the eyes, she cried out: "Oh, you wretch! You think I don't know that even now you're just thinking 'Yeah, go ahead and talk'?"

Now she left me, her face all red, and circled the table.

"Your father suffers from indigestion. And all the fuss doesn't do him any good. Not to mention that you've ripped holes in my heart, which is weak to begin with. Yes, I've already gotten heart trouble on account of you. Ever since that time you climbed up to the window, every time I wake up it's to the beating of my heart. You know this full well. Because you hear often enough, and you see, that the doctor pays me visits. He asks: What's the matter? What am I supposed to say? Can I tell him what a child God cursed us with? So he'll go spread the news everywhere he goes? No. What's more, we can't say a word to a soul. We've got to keep this shame of ours — meaning *you* — a secret, so as to keep envious, mean-spirited folk from besmirching your father's honor when he's got enough enemies in the community — our community, Jewish folk like us — to begin with. And why? Because your father is upright and beyond reproach. And he doesn't bother about anything aside from his duties. All the envious, mean-spirited, self-seeking folk out there simply can't stand this, they'd snatch the bread right out of our mouths if they could. And all we need now is for someone to stand up at a congregation meeting and say: This is how the rabbi raises his son. To say such things in school about God. And about his father and mother. What sort of rabbi *is* this, to have raised his son this way? Why, if the Orthodox folk find out, that other congregation, they're not beyond attacking your father in the papers: These are the Neologs for you, they'd say. Their rabbi can't even raise his own son to be a good Jew. And they'll be delighted to do him ill. Why? Because even with them, your father's always wanted to do good. The first thing he wanted on coming to this city was that all Jews should stick together, love one another. And then he of all folks has a child like this. Even thinking what you might have said in school makes me shudder. But now your father is down there in the synagogue, and he'll find out. Thank goodness your father's the school principal, too, so no doubt Mr. Würtz will show him due esteem. He knows and respects your father, he does. And he knows that we raise you as best we can to be a good boy. He's seen how different Ernuskó and Oluska are. But the other folks out there, the envious, mean-spirited ones and everyone in general, believe that a child can only be as good or bad as his father has raised him."

Now Oluska officiously brought in my plate and silverware. She stopped with them in front of Mother, and asked: "So, where am I supposed to put his?"

"Just take it out to the kitchen. From now on he'll eat out there. That's his punishment." Mother turned to me. "And afterward you're to go straight to the parlor — that's where you'll sleep, because your Father doesn't even want to be bothered with the sight of you again. And I'm not sorry, either, because I'm not defending you anymore."

Now Lidi came in, squatted down, and stoked the fire in the stove.

"Lidi," said Mother, "from now on Gyuri will eat in the kitchen."

Lidi replied: "Sure thing, ma'am. There's enough room out there."

And Mother: "All I want to say is, leave him be. And it's best if you don't even say a word to him."

At which Lidi: "For all I care he can sit there for months. Long as he leaves me alone."

Lidi poked at the fire once more, then rose.

"Ma'am, if you'll excuse me, I'd like to say something. If I may."

Mother waited.

"I," continued Lidi, "as you know, ma'am, always did say that the devil himself is in the young master ever since you brought him back from the village. You always said, ma'am, that he'd improve. Someday he'd surely improve. But I said: I don't think so. And that's how it is, too. Because of . . . well, ma'am . . . you understand what I'm getting at, ma'am? Seeing as how I nursed him and all? I often get to thinking: See, Lidi, it didn't help him much that you were the one who nursed him. Other times I'm plain ashamed of myself because of this. And I thought just before, too: What can be done with the boy so he gets better? I'm saying this because I thought I'd ask you, ma'am, if maybe your people also do what we do in the village I'm from, because then you can pray for him. The master is a priest, kind of. I know this helped kids in our village, more than once the devil cleared out of them."

"That's all right, Lidi," replied Mother. "We don't do anything of this sort. But somehow things will work out."

"Too bad," said Lidi, "too bad you folks aren't Catholic. Then you could."

Mother turned red. "Don't talk such nonsense. Don't you know that you mustn't say such things in our home? You've been serving us for a pretty long time."

"Ah . . ." said Lidi, "forget I said a thing, ma'am."

And she left the room.

Watching her exit, Mother spoke, loud enough for her to hear. "The last thing I needed today was that ninny."

Now Oluska hurried out, returning in a flash. "Father's home!"

Mother looked at me. "Go on out to the kitchen, then. You don't have a place here anymore."

Without a word I went out and took a seat at the kitchen table.

I was exhausted and getting really hot. Much of what Mother had said remained on my mind. The more pronounced it was, though, the more resolved I was not to bother with it.

And when I saw Lidi carrying in the tray, I thought: Now that's more like it. At least things are just like I always figured. I'm not their real kid anymore.

Like I never was. Fine, then. And let's never have it any other way. They'd better not want to see me ever again. All right. So finally they'll chase me away. I never did have the guts to leave on my own. Now it'll happen anyway. And till then I'll eat here in the kitchen every time. With Lidi. Until they chase me off. I can forget about fourth grade either way, for if they don't send me off somewhere as an apprentice, I'll leave all the same.

Let there be darkness, so I can think things through.

Lidi brought me the meal, but I hardly touched it. I didn't need it. Then I went right to the parlor so the darkness would come all the sooner. So I could think things through.

Oluska brought in the bed linen.

"Well," she said, "you had it coming."

I turned to her angrily.

"I'll tell you a thing or two also, don't you worry. Not just them."

She too was angry.

"Don't you worry, either. They'll fix your problem. You won't be going to school anymore. You can go be a 'prentice!"

"I'll tell the truth anyway. That you're just a girl, you don't count for nothing. A green-eyed monkey, that's what you are! Jumping up and down in front of the mirror all the time. That's it. Now you can go tell on me again."

She turned red.

"Yecch, you *'prentice!"* And with that she left the room.

All she'd brought in was the duvet to go on top and a sheet to lie on; the pillow was missing. What did I care. Nor did I want the duvet. And I sure didn't want to lie on the divan. I'd be an apprentice anyway. They sleep on the floor.

Just as I was, I lay on the carpet. Hardly had I turned off the light, however, when Ernuskó came in with the pillow. He stopped and studied me intently.

"You won't get anywhere doing that. Why are you always doing this sort of thing?"

I sat up, intent on finally telling him the "truth" too.

"Sure," I said, "all you care about is being a good student. But you don't care about whether I'm right, nope. That's all the same to you. *Why are you always doing this sort of thing?*'" I said, mimicking him. "Just tell me: Was I right? Or not? Tell me that much. Because I don't care about the rest. Was I right or not?"

"Of course you're not right! You've got to keep in mind that Father's a rabbi. You can't go saying that sort of thing. Especially not the way you did. I really don't get it. Mother's right saying you've got a screw loose. That's what I told her too."

"I talked that way only because Father was hitting me. And why? Because I'm not supposed to ask questions and speak the truth? Just because they're who they are, and our parents? And because they give us food and a place to sleep? On account of that, I shouldn't speak the truth?"

"You can talk all you want, but you're not right about a thing."

"Not even about Father just acting like there's a God and just talking, Mother too, when they both know there's not? Aren't I right about this? And about them never really being unselfish, and them always just thinking about their money? Is that all right for a rabbi, I mean? A *rabbi*, who's always mentioning God? Aren't I right?"

"Of course you're not right," he replied. "They know how things have to be. And not you. Whatever you say, you can't argue with them. You can't hurt them."

"Just like that? Only they can hurt me?"

"Yes indeed. Only they. If you behave the way you did today and always do. Because they're our parents. If you don't understand that, you don't have any brains."

"That's not true," I replied, "because I have got brains, I do. And everything is just like I said. Sure, maybe I'm wicked, I don't deny it and didn't deny it to them. But they're even more wicked than me. Only that they don't admit it! But I do, yes: I'm *wicked*. So there. And? At least I don't deny it. But if they were more good, I would be too."

"You just keep quiet," said Ernuskó. "You were always bad; you badgered Oluska often enough, you did." Now he turned red: "And all the times you said to me, 'Oh, you good student!' But I didn't bother with it. As far as I'm concerned, you can do handstands if that's your thing," he said, swelling with pride, "but don't upset Mother and Father. I'm talking to you only because things will just get worse for you. Even worse than now. If you've got brains, like you say, you know this anyway. Do you want to be an apprentice?"

I too was caught in the grips of pride.

"I don't give a hoot about your brains and good marks. I'd rather be an apprentice. And if I want, I'll be even more wicked. Once I'm grown up, I'll give back every whack I get."

Mother opened the door. But she didn't come in.

"Leave that wretched creature be," she said to Ernuskó. "Come on."

Ernuskó left the room. Mother called inside: "You're staying in here, and from now on no one's going to give you the time of day."

"Well then, they won't," I replied, and she shut the door.

I lay back on the floor and turned off the light. But on feeling the rug underneath me, I got up once more, moved it to the side and lay down on the cold wooden floor.

They want me to die anyway, I thought. *I can't say I know why God made a child like you* — so Mother had said. Fine, then, he won't stick around.

In the dark I took off all my clothes, even my shirt, and lay naked on the cold floor. The smell of wax hit my nose. I thought: I'll catch a cold, then maybe I'll die. I won't have to go be an apprentice either. And they can be glad to bury me.

I thought back to the day I wanted to fall out the window. Back then I figured they'd cry at my funeral. But if it happened now, I know they'd be glad. But not even then would they have the guts to show it. No, they'd put on a show of being sad, for they'd be ashamed, seeing as how they're "those good parents," the "rabbi and his wife." Father would give a speech by my grave, a speech full of lies about God; Mother would cry and so would my brother and sister, though deep down they'd each be thinking: We're free of him at last. Oh, how good it would be, I thought, to cry out at my own funeral: "Liars! Liars, all of you! And you're glad!"

Now I let the darkness fall upon me. Yet even with the quiet and the darkness and the exhaustion I couldn't get to sleep.

You're completely alone, I thought; no one will bother with you anymore. Everyone you really have anything to do with is angry at you. There's no one among either your teachers or classmates who'd bother about you or whom you'd bother about. You're completely alone, just the same as when you didn't have the guts to fall out the window; and when afterward you got a hiding but didn't have the guts to run away. Because you were scared. You won't have the guts to run away even now, nor to go off as an apprentice. Of course it would be good to catch a cold and die. But you won't have the guts for that, either. In no time you'll get your shirt back on, lay down again on the divan, and even pull the duvet over you. So you don't get cold. Then you'll only cry again in secret. You chicken. Weren't you one all along?

"I was, but not anymore."

"But you will."

"Nope, just for that I won't."

I dug my fingernails into the floor.

"Anyone who's faced so many whacks can't be a chicken. I'll face more too."

And I began hitting my head against the floor while saying aloud, syllable by syllable: *"I am not a chick-en. I am not a chick-en."*

"Oh, come on, scaredy-cat — harder!"

"Hard-er, hard-er."

And with every syllable I hit harder.

"Bet you don't have the guts to hit with all your might, to 'smash in your skull' like Father said he would."

My head stopped.

"True, I don't."

"You see? And that's why you don't have the guts to run away, either. And to think that you're already past nine years old and in your tenth year. Old enough to be an apprentice. There are eight-year-old apprentices too. You've seen them often enough on the street, carrying all sorts of things, whistling as they go along. Now, *they* could really care less about school. *They* really leave their parents behind. They're Christians, you say? Of course they are, which is why they hoot amid their whistling: *'Feiger Jud!'* — cowardly Jew, that is, for that is what you are. Not just now, no, you've always been one.

"And every time you heard them — those *poncikter** kids — call out, you went to the other side of the street and thought: 'If only I had the guts to beat them up!'

"You didn't have the guts. And how much smaller they were than you. They wore big boots and little brown frocks, like the grown-ups among them wear; not to mention a whip and a pitchfork on each of their shoulders, and any one of them might already be driving a whole oxcart, meanwhile crying out at the beasts, *'Ha du, na ha!'*

"And the oxen obey them. *You* wouldn't even have the guts to stand next to one of those oxen, not to mention drive one of those carts. They go out to their fathers in the fields and

---

*A regional name for German-speaking people, mostly vintners and farmers, who formerly comprised a sizeable minority in the region around Sopron, western Hungary. — Trans.

vineyard-covered hills and work there; they dig, hoe, and lug manure. They could really care less about school, and if their fathers beat them, they just get up and leave, or throw mud or stones at them and then run off, never to go home again.

"And they don't think, like you, 'Oh my, where will I sleep?' . . . and: 'I'm scared of the dark!'

"And: 'Who will feed me?'

"And: 'What about sweets and toys and storybooks?'

"And: 'Oh my, what grade will the teacher give me?'

"But look, you, it's like this: you're a *feiger Jud*. And your father knows that's what you are. Which is why he figures he can get away with whacking you. He knows you don't have the guts either to run away or for that matter to die! Yes, he knows full well you couldn't take that sort of work anyway, in bad clothes, in mud — 'No thanks,' you'd say, 'that sort of work just isn't for me.'

"All you want are storybooks and sweets. And if you do run away, you'll be scared that some screaming-yelling *poncikter* kid will see you. Or any kid. That he'll shout at you: *'Feiger Jud!'* For then you only blush.

"But the last thing you want is for darkness to come. Why, you're scared even going as far as the Weiszes' store after supper if by chance your mother or father sends you down to get something because Lidi has a lot to do. Because the first thing you think is this: 'Oh my, what's going to jump out at me from the dark?' And when you turn at some corner: 'Oh my, what's waiting around the corner, in the dark?' No, no way, you'll never go off on your own as an apprentice, not even after all that's happened, because you're a bigger chicken than any Christian boy.

"But even among the Jewish boys you're neither the first nor the second bravest, but among the least. Rót and Züsz — they're much braver than you. But there are others too. And you're worth less than even the bigger chickens, because at least they study and gladly go to school. But you'd do even this only because you've got to, and so that you could be a little proud.

"Except that you're too lazy to do even this much. Not like Ernuskó.

"Only stories will do for you. *If things were now like this . . . like that. . . . My funeral would be like this . . . like that. . . . And if now there came: a mysterious king . . . or a magician . . . and a wizard, a magic table: 'Table, set yourself.' And all at once the table would be set and covered with the finest dishes. . . .*

"You're too craven to be a Christian. Too lazy to be a Jew. And so your father can go on whacking you. You're all talk. But no action: you didn't have the guts to run away at once. Only to say: *I'll go tell everyone everything . . .*

"But you didn't have the guts to hit back or run away. Not today, not tomorrow. Never. You'll stay here and be pleased as punch if you can lay down again in your old bed, yes, you'll kiss their hands like a good little boy and be obedient, not to mention study, until they well please. Because they won't send you off to be an apprentice, you know that full well. They'd be too ashamed. They'll hate you, but you'll apologize, and everything will be the way it used to be. . . ."

I sat up naked on the floor.

"No, this won't be, it won't! I'd rather catch a cold here on the floor and die!"

"We'll see, we will."

"We'll see."

At this I lay back on the floor and let the silence, the darkness envelop me anew. But not for long. For the questions came again: "What's this God to you anyway?

"You know full well — you said it yourself — that you're wicked.

"How can you go on talking about God, then, about whether he *is* or he *isn't?* And whether your father knows or doesn't know, believes or is just a liar, or whatever. . . .

"You could talk about all this only if you were better than your father.

"But this is all you say: Sure I'm wicked, but so is he. Let him be first, he's bigger, after all, and then we'll . . .

"But nowhere does it say in the Ten Commandments: *first him, then me.* So then, you have no business talking about God."

"I don't want to, either," I whispered, "because there is no God."

"You have no way of knowing this. Maybe he *does* exist. But only for good people, the sort Abraham was, and, yes, Jacob."

"That's just a story," I said. "They weren't good — *no one* is good." My thoughts then went something like this: There are only folks like — on the one hand — my parents and I, like Ernuskó and Oluska. The Jews — who are mostly just shame-faced cowards and good students, and are loath to fight — because "you can do more with the mind than the body," as Father likes to say. Then there are others, like the Christians, who are braver; who, if they are hit, hit back. And, sure, some of them are good students, but most aren't. Then there are "girls" and "women." They are either "mothers" and obey their "husbands" — Mother's like this — or just "girls." Girls are meek too. Both girls and women like clothes and looking at themselves in the mirror; and they're happy if someone compliments them or their clothes, calls them pretty. But other people? *Good?* As "unselfish" as Würtz put it? No, there are none.

"Just because there are no good people, there might still be a good God."

"All right, maybe so — but then God doesn't like everything down here one bit."

"He'll send a flood, like in the Bible."

"But why? When he 'created' the whole thing, after all? Didn't he know that what he created was bad? If he's God, he knew. And he has it in him to make a flood anyway. Is this a *good* God? Can't be. He's of a sort like Father. Father's known for quite a while now that I'm bad. But instead of setting a good example, he smacks me.

"Nor did God create a good world. No, he created something

bad. And then he strikes. He makes a flood. This is not a *good* God, but only of the same stripe as Father. Or even worse.

"Because Father did not create me. I only happen to live with him. Yet *that God* created him, Father; and me too. What a fiasco! All he does is give out whacks!

"Why, then, do folks call him good? Sweet talk! Maybe, they figure, it will help them.

"And God destroys other folks; which saves those he hasn't *yet* destroyed from having to do it themselves.

"Mother talked like this too, when she asked Father not to 'beat the life out of' me: *'Don't, Papa. . . . God will thrash him. . . . Just leave it . . . to God.'*

"In synagogue, one of the prayers asks God to 'strike down upon those who trespass against us, those who harm us.'

"Maybe the Christians pray like this too. This sort of God does, perhaps, exist. But a *good* God, that's just hogwash. And if I don't want to be a cowardly Jew anymore, I'll tell everyone. First in the Jewish church and then in the Christian one.

"Then if someone hits me, I'll hit back. Even Father. If they beat the life out of me, even then. And if I'm more afraid than ever, even then."

But only a single answer kept resounding in my head to all this: "All talk."

"No," I replied.

"Oh yes."

"No."

"Get going, put on your shirt."

"No, no, no …"

And though I felt cold, and was getting even colder, I kept repeating: "No, no, no, I'm not cold, I'm not."

"But if you catch a cold and die, you can't do what you said."

At this I sat up and fell into thought.

"All right," I replied, "that's true. Then I'd rather not catch a cold."

Whereupon I put on my shirt.

"But no more!" I thought, "No blanket, no divan." And I lay back on the floor in my shirt. Again I let the darkness come, now resolved to really hide within it.

It worked like a charm: I fell asleep. But before I knew it, I awoke again. It was terribly dark, even darker than when I'd fallen asleep. I was shivering.

"You'll catch a cold and die all the same. The shirt's not enough. Lie on the divan, tuck yourself in good with that blanket, or else you won't be able to do what you want to do."

"Oh, all right. But just because, that's all. So I can do what I want."

Sleepily I climbed up onto the divan, and hardly had I tucked myself in when I fell back asleep.

The light that streamed into my eyes as they opened prompted me to think at once: "Ah, so here I am on the divan, under my duvet."

"It would have been better, after all, if I'd managed to stay naked down on the floor."

Now there came the resounding peal of church bells tolling: *Don't for-get what you prom-ised. Don't for-get. Come tell us too that it's all a great big lie. Not just your people, but us too: the Christians.*

I sat up and said aloud, as if to the bells: "You bet I'll tell you too, because you people lie just the same as we do."

But the bells answered forthwith.

Whenever you happened upon some Christian holiday procession, you never even had the guts to go take a closer look.

"That's true," I replied to the bells, "because I didn't want to kneel and remove my cap — we don't do that."

At which the bell: *You were afraid someone would say: "Look! What do we have here? A Jew! How dare he come here when we are kneeling! Hit him, stone him . . . beat him!"*

Another voice: "Not just any Jew boy, but the rabbi's son."

And a third: "He thinks we're idolaters. He's secretly laughing at us, all the time. And now he has the gall to come over here? How dare he, when there are a lot more of us, and we're so angry with his kind! On your knees, Jew boy! On your knees, your knees, your knees. . . ."

"True," I replied, "I won't deny it — I was always scared. But not anymore. I'll do what's right."

Now now, said the bell, *if we so much as begin to smack you around, you'll be cowering in no time.*

"That's true too."

So now you want to tell us the truth too?

Tell us? tolled the bell, *Tell us?*

And then there came another bell, and a third, a fourth, a fifth.

Tell us? Tell us? When there are so many of us? Careful now, our blows are a lot harder than your father's.

Bimm! Bamm! Bumm! We won't send you to the parlor, but underground, in a cage, yes, in a dungeon, with iron chains, behind bars as thick as the ones you used to see at the city tower when visiting the market with your mother; when you — you were holding the bag — asked one time:

"What's that?"

"That's the jail, where they lock up thieves, robbers, murderers, and arsonists. That's where they're kept under guard, and they don't get a thing to eat, there's no light, and they can hardly move."

Yes, but you'll end up there too if you tell the Christians the truth too. Be warned! For the Jews won't stick you in there if you tell them the truth, no, they'd react just like your father: They'd be ashamed of you and say you've got a screw loose. They'd only shut your mouth, and hand you over to your father, then they'd say: "So, most honorable Rabbi Azarel, you've got a son like this? Go ahead, give him a good hiding." But the Christians will lock you up in jail right away, and you'll have neither light nor food; you won't even be able to move, and every day they'll come by and say:

"Aha, so this is that stinking Jew boy who said: 'You're liars just the same as us, because *God this God that . . . idols this idols that . . .'"*

They'll beat you till you're black and blue.

Well now, still up to it?

"You bet I am," I replied, "and I'll say to the Christians even in jail: 'Go ahead and beat the life out of me if you want, but it won't do any good.' Just like I did to Father. I swear I will."

I rose from the divan and got dressed. Every single piece of clothing had to get a word in.

But you're hungry!

"What do I care!"

You want a nice warm cup of chicory coffee with sugar and lots of milk, and a roll.

"What do I care!"

Well, you just be careful.

"I still don't care."

"Because you know full well what will happen if you touch their coffee and their roll. The coffee will say: 'Ah! How good I am to you, do stay here, forget all this "nonsense" and "unruliness," as your father likes to say.' This is what the coffee will say, and it won't be the first time it has done so when you've thought of running away. So do be careful!"

All at once the door opened and there stood Father, in a greatcoat and with a phylactery on his arm, as always in the morning when getting ready for synagogue. He looked me over with utter gravity.

"Now you'll go out and wash up, then come straight back here. You'll stay here all day. Is that understood?"

I said nothing. Careful, I thought, don't be a cowardly Jew!

Father asked again: "Is that understood? I'll break that wicked soul of yours, you can be sure of that. You are to stay in here and you may leave only when you must use the toilet. And then you are to knock. Otherwise you'll stay in here, and get nothing to eat."

With this he shut — and locked — the door.

Well then, I thought, I don't have to be scared of the coffee anyway.

Now I heard Father call Lidi. He said to her: "The child is to stay in there until I return from synagogue. Here's the key. I'm putting you in charge. If he's *got to go,* accompany him. But the child is to go nowhere else. You'll be held responsible. If he gets unruly and doesn't want to return to the room, hit him, beat him, wherever you can. You're a strong enough woman."

Lidi replied: "Well, if anything happens and I've got to, I can handle him. Until you return, sir. But if he's such a devil, and you all don't want prayers to be said for him, because that's not allowed among your people, then give him over to someone else, let him go out in the world."

"This is not for you to understand," said Father. "Just do as I say."

Lidi didn't reply. I heard Father leave. Soon there came Mother's voice, asking Lidi for the key. Mother stepped into the room.

Her eyes were red from weeping. Go ahead and feel sorry for yourself and for Father, I thought. It's all the same to me now.

"Gyuri," she said, "you're still not in your right mind?"

I said nothing.

Now Oluska carried in a tray with the coffee and the roll. As she did so, she cast me an ugly glance.

"Put it down," Mother said to her, "and go."

Next Ernuskó appeared in the door, schoolbooks under his arm. But he only stood there looking serious, uttering not a word to me, as if he was thinking, "As far as I'm concerned, you can do handstands if that's your thing, but why are you making our parents all upset?" Now he turned to Mother.

"Ma'am," he said by way of a good-bye, and left.

Oluska headed off as well. Now I should be going to school too, I thought, but don't you think of this anymore, nor of that chicory coffee with sugar and lots of milk, or else things won't be as you'd promised yourself.

Mother closed the door and spoke in a voice soft and laden with worry.

"Your father even forbade me to come in here. But I feel sorry for you, though you don't deserve it. I still believe that you're not — that you can't be — as evil as you were yesterday, and that maybe last night you came to regret what you did. Go ahead and eat your breakfast now, then go to school like a good boy, like usual. I'll take care of the rest with your father. He's a good man, if you don't get him all riled up. And if I ask him to, he'll forgive you. He'll forget what you did."

I listened in silence.

"Go ahead and eat, now, then go on to school. And let's not have another word about the things you talked about yesterday, then everything can still be okay."

I looked at her and at the coffee.

This is my mother and this is my chicory coffee with sugar and lots of milk, as so many times before, and that's my school down there, which I'm late to as it is.

Yet I thought: If you listen to her now, you can't do what you want. And you'll go back to your old routine of doing whatever Father says. And if he wants, he'll go ahead and smack you again.

"Well," said Mother, "don't you want to eat?"

"No," I snapped back. "I don't want to eat with you people anymore."

"Then what is it you want?"

"I want nothing from you people. Just that you let me go away."

I cast a sharp, sidelong glance at Mother, who replied: "Let you go? But you're still little. It's better if you study, for a few more years at least. You don't understand this yet. But later you'll be grateful. You'll see. Listen to me."

"I don't want to listen. And I don't want to study here either."

"Where do you *want* to study, then?"

"I don't want to study anywhere."

"You'll be really sorry if you talk like this. I know, I'm your mother. Don't gentle words mean a thing to you anymore? Nor love? Gyuri, Gyuri!"

"Why don't you people just stop bothering with me. Let me go."

"You don't understand. We can't just let you go *like that*. So long as you're so little, we're responsible for you."

"Responsible?" I shot back. "Now what's that supposed to mean?"

"We're responsible for upholding the law. If we just let you go where you want, why, you'll end up in the gutter in no time, you'll become a street kid, you'll steal and do God knows what, then the police will catch you, take you to jail, and they'll call us down to the station."

"And then," I interrupted, "you two will be ashamed of yourselves. Because that's what's important to you people anyway."

"Every respectable person," Mother replied, "is ashamed if their son becomes a juvenile delinquent and winds up at a police station when he's nine years old."

"Just don't you people bother with me."

"But we've *got* to bother with you. And if you wind up there — I'm saying this only so you know well in advance, as long as gentle words, love, and forgiveness don't help — if you wind up there, we'll have to put you in reform school."

I vaguely recalled having heard of this before — reform school. Yet I didn't really know what it was like there. All the same, I didn't say a thing. Mother continued.

"Then once you're in reform school we can't do a thing for you no matter what. Because that's the job of the police and the courts. And there you won't have a free moment, and you've got to study and to work, just as they want you to, and if you so much as say a word against them, they'll hit you, and hard, not like your father does — who did it out of love and fear, after all, to keep you from going to the gutter, even if you don't admit this, and afterward I bring breakfast in here to you, and you can go to school, yes, it's all up to you — but then in reform school the folks are like cops and gendarmes, there's no breakfast and forgiveness afterward, not there, only hunger and then jail. Is that what you want? Because if we just let you go, like you want us to, that's what would happen."

You can sweet-talk all you want, I thought, but there's no way I'm getting scared. Now I spoke again.

"Just don't you people bother with me. You yourself said you don't know why a child like me even exists. Because you two don't like me. Then this child shouldn't be here with you. But when I say, all right, let me go, then you, Mother, go making threats about the 'police' and 'reform school.' But I'm not getting scared anymore, no, I've already been scared enough as it is by Father and the Christians too, by the dark and the quiet, I won't deny it anymore, but I've had it with being scared. Yesterday I put up with all those whacks, and I'll put up with hunger too, just like I'll put up with it if you two go asking the cops to take me to reform school. The same goes for jail. Because I thought it all over last night, even though you sound so sure when you say, 'You don't understand.' But I *do* understand. And more, too. I also understand what that God is like, *if* there is a God. And what people are like, all of them; and I mean Jews just as well as Christians. And that's not all. Because I thought everything over last night. But I'll never say all this again, never. You people just let me go. You can try scaring me all you want with reform school or whatever, it won't do any good."

Mother's mouth fell open, like when she was upset.

Yes, I thought, that's all that concerns her. That she's scared about what I'll do.

Indeed, she said: "You want to be an apprentice, do you?"

Scrutinizing her expression, I thought, Aha! So now she'd let me go! But as an apprentice! To get at what she was thinking, I asked: "And won't you be ashamed of that?"

"Very much so. But if a child doesn't want to study when so young, what's to be done? We'll hand you over to some decent, respectable Jewish tradesman or shopkeeper." Again her eyes glistened with tears.

"Is this what we raised you for until now?" she called out quite suddenly, but then turned to me with a tender look: "Gyuri! Why, wouldn't you be ashamed of yourself?"

Again I gave her a sidelong glance, and just to see what she'd say, I declared: "No!"

"Well then, we'll hand you over to someone. It's still better than having you go completely to the gutter. Wouldn't you rather go to a shop? To Koppel's place, the shoe store?"

"No," I replied, "I don't want to go anywhere where folks count the way Father does."

"But there you could learn shoemaking, if you want to. You'd be there all day and come home only at night. They know your father well, and respect him."

"No," I shot back, "I don't want to set foot anywhere where they know Father and respect him. And if all the Jews around here respect him, I don't want to go to a single one."

"But where, then? There's no Jewish place around here where they don't know us. Maybe among the Orthodox. But they're our enemies. Don't tell me you want to go among them?"

"No," I said, "I'm sure not going among people with earlocks."

"Where then?"

Another sidelong glance. And I thought: What I'm about to say will hurt you. I spoke: "Then I'd rather go be an apprentice among . . ."

Mother fixed her eyes on me. "Where?"

I said it: "Among the Christians."

She turned completely red, and fixed her eyes angrily upon me. "So you bring disgrace on your father and end up converting?

No! No!" she yelled. "Better you go to reform school. I say so myself."

With this she left the room, and I heard her say before the door: "And what are *you* doing eavesdropping here?"

Lidi replied: "I'm not eavesdropping. The master told me to stand watch with this key I have here. And to close the door."

"There's no need," said Mother, "I'll hold onto the key. You just tend to your business in the kitchen."

"It's all the same to me."

Lidi left, as did Mother.

Only my chicory coffee with sugar and lots of milk remained with me.

It shot me a knowing glance. "I'm cold already, but I'm still tasty, you know, plus you're hungry."

"No," I replied, "I don't want to eat a thing, not here."

"You ninny," said the chicory coffee. "Drink me and eat up the roll. We'll make you strong, so you can face whatever comes next. Then you'll be better at bearing the blows still coming your way."

"That's not true," I said, "If I drink you I'll just be more of a chicken."

"All right," said the coffee with sudden docility, "but so long as I'm here you'll surely drink me."

"Then get out of my sight," I said, opening the window, pouring out the coffee, and then tossing out the roll. I followed them with my eyes: the roll's golden brown face seemed to sneer back up at me from midway down as if to say, "You'll be sorry!"

There it lay on the cobblestone street in the autumn mud.

Looking left and right, up and down the street, I thought: Of course — I should run away. Because now they're even worried I'll go off to the Christians. No doubt they'll send me to reform school. And I don't even want anything to do with the Christians. With no one. I only want to be wicked, that's all, wicked and more wicked, and never to be afraid.

I stood before the mirror and bared my teeth.

There, I thought, that's it, I'll be like a "mad dog," as Father once said.

Indeed, as if Mother had sensed that never would I fear again, she soon came in. Yes, she was worried about my going off to the Christians.

She spoke: "Gyuri, listen here, this is the last time I'm coming in. If you don't come to your senses right now, you can go be any sort of apprentice you want. If you want, you don't have to go to a place here in town, you can go to some other city, where we have relatives. Relatives are important just so you wouldn't be completely on your own and you wouldn't end up among bad boys. I'll take care of all this with your father too, just stick to your senses and don't tell him any nonsense about wanting to go instead to some Christian place locally, wanting to convert."

Giving her a searching look, I thought: I'll talk about them — about the Christians — just for that. And I'll praise them, just for that. So it'll hurt you two. Now I spoke.

"Why shouldn't I tell him? There might be some folks there who are much better than Father, you know. Not every one of them throws stones, yells at me, and knocks my hat off, no, it's mostly the *poncikter* kids that do that, but not even all of them. Yes, maybe the others are better. Up till now I only heard about them from you two, about them not liking us, them thinking this and that, all sorts of bad things about us. But why should I always believe what you two tell me? When you go and hit me. Maybe the whole thing isn't even true, and you two tell me that stuff so I don't talk with any one of them, so I keep being scared of them and then you two can be right, like always. Why? And even if it's true, if they're all out to fight all the time, they have the right idea; at least they're not cowards like you people and like I used to be, but won't be anymore. And if they're drunks, so what? Let them be drunks, if they like fruit brandy! I'll be one too if I like it! And about them not loving their families, well, I bet their families, well, I bet their families are just the same as them, and why should they love them, after all, why, when I don't even want to love you two the way you are. And if they don't write everything down, like Father, if they don't count everything the way he does, all the better. I'll find out everything there is to know about them, from them."

"I'm not saying," said Mother, "that you shouldn't speak to them. Why, you can see for yourself that even Ernuskó goes to school with them already. All I'm saying is, if you want to go be an apprentice, there are plenty of good Jewish places, and if you don't want to go somewhere local, you can go to some other city. That's all I'm asking. And that you not say such nonsense to your father, nothing about you wanting to go convert to Christianity."

Just for that, I thought, and said: "Why not? If I grow up and want to convert? Why not?"

Again Mother turned completely red.

"Why not? Oh, you wretched little thing, you ask such a thing, like this? *Why not?* You ask me, your mother, a rabbi's wife, such a thing: *Why not?* A rabbi's son." She sat down and wept.

I felt kind of sorry for her, but I was glad too. Now at least she knew that, yes, I understood everything full well. And that I had the guts to say everything on my mind. The only thing that bothered me now was that she swallowed whole my words about converting.

"You see," I said, "you believe everything about me! But let me tell you something, ma'am: I spoke about the Christians to hurt you two. Just like what you two say hurts me. But don't think the reason I don't need the Christians is that you two don't like them, and because you're crying, ma'am, but because I'm too proud for that. That's why I don't need them. But I don't need the Jews either. And let me tell you something: I don't want to be an apprentice either. Nowhere. All I want is to be wicked, completely wicked. Like a mad dog! The mad dog that Father thinks I am. But even worse."

At this Mother fell back to tears. I watched.

Careful, I thought, don't you be sorry about the whole thing. Go ahead and let her cry.

And I spoke: "You can cry all you want. I cried a lot more often because of you two."

She tried wiping away her tears and stared at me. Her face was now so tender that it hurt me all the same. I went on.

"You're crying and scared, that's all. But really you're still on Father's side, even now. Take my side! Completely!"

"But haven't I defended you enough?" she said through more tears.

"That's nothing," I replied. "If you were a real mother, you'd say to Father when he comes back up here — and you'd say it right in front of me — 'Papa, you were really nasty. Now promise him that you'll improve. And never hurt him again.' And if Father doesn't want this, you'd have to say, 'If you don't do that, Papa, I'll side with him, and I'll go off with him too.' Yes, that's what a real mother would do. And then Father would either promise that he'd be better, or else the two of us would take off right away, leave everything behind, and then I'd gladly be an apprentice or whatever, and you'd be whatever too, but we'd never return."

Though she didn't say a word, it seemed to me from looking at her tender face and eyes that she too wanted, if but a little, what I'd proposed.

And I thought: Oh, if only it could be!

My cheeks turned all the more fiery red as I went on. "And if you do it, ma'am . . . Mother, don't think I'll stay just an apprentice. Then I'll study, too, however I must, you'll see, and you won't have to be ashamed of me all the time. Do you understand, Mother? Promise you'll do what I asked."

I stepped closer.

"Hm? Hm? Exactly like I asked?"

I looked into her eyes. She seemed lost in thought. After a while she spoke.

"All right, just to show you how much you don't know I love you, though your brother and sister are much better than you, I'll make an exception of you and ask your Father to promise not to hurt you ever again."

"That's not a whole lot," I replied. "Tell me, if Father doesn't agree, will you come with me then? Forever and ever?"

"There won't be any need for this silly nonsense," said Mother. "Things are like that only in storybooks. Ah . . ." she sighed, "life's completely different. You'll see once you grow up."

"All right," said I, "if all this is just silly nonsense and is only in storybooks, then I won't say another word."

I turned away. Mother, still sitting in the chair, stared at the empty mug and said: "Come on over here and listen to how my heart is beating because of you." Again she sighed, "Ah . . ." and I noticed that once more she was all worried about that heart of hers. "You know what misery is, you do."

I said not a word. Now Father's steps could be heard as he approached the study.

I whispered to Mother: "Be a real mother! One last time!"

Hardly had I said this when Father entered. His face was ashen. Sternly he said to Mother: "I told you to leave this child to himself!"

"Wait," said Mother in a soft, frightened voice. "My heart."

Father shook his head angrily. "What do you expect," he said, "if you come in here and upset yourself with this wretched little brat! Leave the room now, and lie down till it passes."

Mother didn't move. "Wait," she said, "it'll be over in a minute."

Father paced back and forth by Mother without so much as glancing at me. I only watched them.

A minute or two passed this way, and I thought, like so often before: What's that "heartbeat" of hers like, after all? I'd like to feel it too. Maybe it's really some illness, some "misery," and so I should feel sorry for Mother; but now it's too late for that, besides, Father's here, so I couldn't do it anyway.

Father went on pacing. And I thought: Maybe she just doesn't dare be a real mother, after all, and that's why she's worried about that heart of hers. Yes, maybe she's just a coward plain and simple, and that's why she doesn't have the guts to be a real mother, or she doesn't want to be one.

Now she spoke again. "A-all right, it's over. Come on, Papa."

He retorted: "Just go in there alone. I've got to take care of this child. Things can't go on like this. I can't put up with this commotion and upheaval anymore." I sensed in his voice that he was angry again.

If he smacks me now just one more time, I thought, I'll bite him. No matter how hard he hits, I'll just go on biting. And if he beats the life out of me, why then, I'll stick to his soul.

But now Mother spoke to him. "Just don't go yelling again," she said, standing up and calling after him. "Come on, I want to talk to you a little."

They left the room, but Father left the door open. I could see that he wanted to return right away to "take care of" everything. And I reminded myself: if he smacks me, I'll just *bite and bite*.

Suddenly there came the sound of Mother's laughter. Yes, I thought, she's already sweet-talking Father. And so I was really angry at her. I only listened. And I heard Father say: "Oh come on, don't tell me you think *I* should be promising *him* something?"

Mother chuckled like that once again: "But Papa, Papa . . ."

No doubt she then whispered something to him, and from Father's response I realized what. He shot back angrily, aloud: "Not even in jest! You've got to be kidding me! Perhaps I'm to go apologizing to him?"

Yes, I thought: the way she asked Father, it was like she was joking and just laying on the sweet talk, not the way I asked her to. But he won't do it even in jest.

All right, I kept saying to myself, *bite, bite,* if he smacks you, *bite. . .*

At this they both entered. Father said sternly: "I've had quite enough of this business. Do you want to behave normally and obey us, or not?"

This was the eleventh hour, I felt. My heart was beating wildly. And I thought: So this is the heartbeat she feels too, this is that cowardliness.

Fixing my eyes on the floor, I thought: You just be careful, don't be a coward! And I turned not toward Father, but Mother, with the words: "You see, I may be little, but I know why your heart is always beating the way it does, like it is now. It's because you're always so scared. Which is why mine is beating now the way it is. . . . But I'm not going to be scared of Father, and don't you be, either — no, be a real mother, like I asked."

But I said this in vain. She replied only: "I've already had a word with your Father. Now it's up to you. Promise him like a good boy."

Bitterly I turned toward her. "Me?" I said, "I knew that's all you want!"

Now Father began again. "I'm asking you for the last time, do you want to behave normally?"

"I don't want anything," I replied, "just let me go away."

His face ashen and his voice stern, Father shot back: "Go ahead! But completely! And you will not cross this threshold ever again. Not even if you starve to death. I've ceased to exist for you."

Now Mother spoke. "Let him go. He'll think things over down there."

"He can't come here anymore," Father responded. "It's all over."

"All right," I said, "let it be over."

And I headed off. But I was scared, because I sensed that he'd want to give me one last hiding, one for the road.

Indeed, hardly had I stepped to the door than he reached out and grabbed me by the arm.

Mother cried out: "Papa!"

Then I said, trembling: "If you smack me, I'll bite you, even if you beat the life out of me, plus then I'll stick to your soul!"

"Let him go," said Mother. Father obliged.

"No," he said hoarsely, "I'm not going to sully my hands anymore with you. Get out of here!"

With this he hastened into the bedroom. Mother shot me a glance as if to say, "Get going and stay out there."

But I called back. "You didn't have the guts to be a real mother. You didn't, I'm telling you! It's all over, you know!"

Out I went, bareheaded, through the hall, down the stairs into the courtyard, out onto the street. It was terribly muddy out there, muddy and cold. I paused in front of the building.

There, now you finally had the guts to do what you've wanted to do so many times. At last! At last!

But don't you get scared of catching a cold like you did at night, and don't give a second thought to being hungry, don't you be afraid of anything, just go straight ahead, ahead, all night, and then it'll be Friday night anyway, so you'll come on back here, to the synagogue, and you'll wait outside listening until your father speaks, and right when he clasps his hands together and looks up at the sky, and says, "Dear God, almighty and good, watch over the poor, orphans, children, and all those who suffer. . . ." — then all of a sudden you'll go inside, stand up in front of everyone, and shout: "All lies, every word of his! And the Good Lord is just like him, too, yes, he hits his kid because of God."

And then everyone will turn toward you and mutter, "What's that? What's that?"

And your father will run down from that pulpit, angry and ashamed, wanting to get hold of you, yes, he'll run after you just like he is, in that high velvet hat of his, but you'll run away between the benches, shouting: "Ha! See, everyone? That's what he's like! Ha!" — and you'll be running all the while — "before it was 'watch over the children'" — you're running, you are — "and now he wants to beat the life out of me here and now. Ha!

But don't you folks let him, because then all of you are just like him, no, don't let him. . . ." — and you're running here and there; his gown is really long that he doesn't have a chance of catching you, so you just go on shouting: "Listen to me, everyone. I'll tell you everything, all about what he's really like."

And when you notice that not even they protect you from him — no, they're outright scared and ashamed, not listening to a word you say but just out to catch you and give you back to your father so he can go on smacking you — why then, you'll take to biting and kicking and shouting, and you'll run out of the synagogue straight into the convent's church next door, which is open all night long and where there's always someone on hand, and, no, you won't be frightened there either. And if they ask you, "Whadaya want here, Jew boy?" you'll say: "I'm here because I *said* this and that, *like* this and that, *on account of* this and that, to my father and the Jews in the synagogue. Now I'm here to see what you people are really like. Do you all hate me and all think bad things about me, like those *poncikter* kids, do you figure I stink, that I'm a coward, and that I'm some junk dealer's kid, just because I'm a Jew? Or will you protect me from my father and the other Jews, who are all ashamed of me and want to give me back to my father just so he can go on smacking me?"

And if those Christians say: "Sure we'll protect you, kid, all you got to do is convert and pray to these paintings and statues and this cross here. Off with the hat, and on your knees!"

At which you: "That I will not do. Protect me just for the sake of protecting me!"

At which they, now more sternly: "And why *won't* you do that?"

At which you: "Because I'm too proud, I am, to convert just because there are more of you, and because I'm afraid, and because they beat me at home."

At which they: "Oh yeah? Well if you're that proud, then scat, you hear? Get a move on back to the other Jews."

At which you: "So that's how it is. You folks are no different from Father! What you are saying is 'Obey me or get out of my sight. . . .' Yes, you people do nothing either but lie left and right about the 'Good Lord.' I knew it, I always knew it!"

At which they: "Hear that? To the dungeon with him, with the Jew boy!"

And they seize you.

At which you: "I knew it, I knew that too, but I'll just go on biting you folks until you beat the life out of me and I stick to your souls."

Such were my thoughts, although in fact I was still standing there in front of our building. And what did I notice all of a sudden in the mud before me, but a roll — my roll, which I'd thrown down there from up above.

Its golden brown face peered at me from the mud, and again it sneered. "You'll be sorry. You're hungry. Come on, wipe me off and eat me. They won't know anyway."

Whereupon I stepped over and stomped it farther into the mud.

"I'm not about to get scared of you, you lousy roll. You belong to them too!"

But it only said: "There's a long way to go till night. You plan to go hungry? 'Sustenance spells strength,' remember."

"I don't need it," I replied, and stomped it even deeper.

At which it said through a laugh: "Ha! Are you ever hungry!"

That's just how it was. But now, before I could have started off, Lidi stepped before me. Mother had sent her down with my cap and overcoat.

"Here you are," she said, "put them on."

The cap and the coat both gave me a sharp, sidelong glance, as I was in the habit of doing to Father.

"Get a load of how cold this kid is," said the coat. "He's not anemic, is he?"

And the cap: "Think you can keep from catching a cold if you go around bareheaded like that?"

"Come on now," said Lidi. "I've got other things to tend to."

"I don't need them," I replied. "I'm not afraid of anything. Tell that to my mother. I'm sure not taking a coat from anyone who's not a real mother."

Yet I took the cap all the same.

"Not because I'm scared, you know, but just so there'll be something on me. So folks won't stare as much."

"Whatever," said Lidi, already on her way.

Good, I thought, so this is over too.

Looking about the street, I thought: If you move about, you'll keep from getting cold.

These words, just like those that the roll and the overcoat and the cap had already spoken, had etched their way into my mind straight from my parents; and now I was no more keen on hearing my parents than such words. What's that? I thought. You're talking to me even now? Well, I'm not going to "move," and I won't get cold either!

At this I headed off, but ever so slowly. Passing by the synagogue, I took a long look at the building, on which, well above me, these words loomed large:

AND I LIGHT THE WAY BEFORE YOU,

DAY AND NIGHT, SO YOU DO NOT FEAR

Ha! I thought. *He's* talking too? *You* light the way? But for whom?

For my father, the wicked rabbi, and for my mother, the cowardly woman who is anything but my real mother. And for Ernuskó too, because he says, "Don't you bother about anything but your homework." Not to mention Oluska, seeing as how she says, "You had it coming, you know." Then she goes on looking at herself in the mirror.

But you light the way for Lidi too, because she says, "I've got other things to tend to." And for Mr. Würtz, because he says, "Don't get smart, Azarel." Not to mention the schoolmistress, who for her part knows full well: "A child who doesn't love his mother belongs in the corner."

But what do you light for me? I took up a stone and threw it hard against the words on the building's facade. There, I thought, this is what I'll do from now on. But even as the stone was hurling toward its target, I trembled with fear. What are you trembling for? Isn't this how you want to be wicked, like a mad dog? Go ahead, throw another stone, just to show you can!

I didn't throw the other stone there, however, but at another inscription, by the entrance to the meeting room, which read:

I HAVE GOOD ADVICE AND SOUND WISDOM

"There," I said as the stone left my hand, "so what kind of advice do you have for me, huh, God?

"You'd tell me to go on back and kiss my wicked father's hand, huh? Yes, because you're no different from him. You say in the Ten Commandments, 'Honor thy father and thy mother.' Of course it doesn't matter to you if a father is wicked and a mother a coward who laughs at her kid all the time. Honor them, that's all. But there's nothing in those commandments about honoring and loving little boys."

And another stone whizzed through the air.

"But I've already told them, and now I'll tell you too, God. So there. I've had enough of fearing you, every Saturday, of not daring to tinker with fire or touch pencils, kreuzers, leaves, of thinking *Oh my, should I? Or shouldn't I? Maybe I should anyway, maybe just maybe!*

"No more of this! Go ahead, hit me if you want. Come on, show yourself and smack me. But you *don't* show yourself, no, you say it's quite enough that my father's there, yes, you say, those folks of yours have smacked you enough as it is, so why should I bother appearing before you?

"*Of course* you don't show yourself, because you don't even bother giving me the chance at least to say to you: 'You're no different from my father!'"

And the stones flew.

Yet it seemed as if every stone had this to say in response: "It's easy enough for you to act like a big boy now. But just try dishing it out to me — that's right, me, *God* — at night, yes, try throwing stones at me *then*, at night. When you don't have anywhere to sleep."

At this I stopped throwing stones, and only shouted to the sky: "Come on, *you*, Night, come on Darkness, I'll go on telling you off and pelting you with stones."

Now it occurred to me that all of my third-grade peers — not to mention Oluska, in fourth grade — were sitting here in the school, next door to the synagogue. Ernuskó was not far away on the other side of the street, in his first year of secondary school.

This is what I thought: I'll go knock on every door, I'll go inside and tell everything I now know about God, about my father, God's rabbi; not to mention about the Jews and the Christians — but then I didn't do it anyway. And thought: Why should I get bogged down somewhere now that night, darkness, is coming, and I want to dish it out to God, pelt him with stones. Then I'll go into our synagogue and do what I want to do.

By now I was really cold, and again father's words sounded inside of me: "If you move about, you'll keep from getting cold."

"All right," I said, "I'll move about until darkness comes — but not the way you want. The way *I* want."

And so I ran about whistling all the while, because, as I'd been told not once before, "Decent lads don't whistle on the street."

But even this was not enough. I thought: I've had it with being afraid of getting muddy. So I tried doing cartwheels on the muddy street.

And I ran my way down the Bástyakör, that boulevard with the most shops, which is to say, the most Jews. Let them get a load of this, I thought, let them stare and wonder what's happened to me.

Yes, until I began going to school, and during breaks once I was already in school, it was down this very boulevard that I went with Mother and Lidi to the market, carrying one of the bags, always like a "good little boy" who obeyed his mother's orders, "Don't step in the mud, Gyuri," and "Let's go on the sidewalk" — those of a mother to whom the shopkeepers, when they saw us pass, gave a greeting and said: "How fine you look, ma'am." Or . . . "We're really proud of Rabbi Azarel, what a fine sermon he gave." Or, looking at me: "What a fine little lad."

That's right, because my mother shopped there and they were proud of my father. Sure, because Father didn't tell a single one of them, from the pulpit: "You folks sweet-talk only those who shop in your stores."

And while turning cartwheels, I shouted: "How fine you look, ma'am! . . . What a fine little lad! . . . We're really proud of Rabbi Azarel!"

But it was cloudy and cool, so not a single shopkeeper was standing in his doorway, and then it began to rain again.

Yes, I thought, God is wicked all right; he wants me to catch a cold and die, so I can't say all I want to say tonight in the synagogue.

No, no, go ahead and rain! I'm not taking shelter in some doorway. Again I whistled away. Rain all you want, but I'm not even going to run anymore, not now.

Looking at the display window of the storybook shop, two fairy tales came to mind — one about a journeying prince disguised as a pauper, and another, about an orphan prince. And I thought: In a minute I'll find out if the shopkeepers are as wicked as their rabbi, my father, if that God of theirs created them as wicked as himself. Anyway, I was good and muddy, even my hair and face, and so no one would recognize this prince in disguise, I made as if my legs were lame and one of my arms were crippled. To top it all off I squinted resolutely.

Standing there by the bookshop entrance, I thought: Now I'll see if you still say, "Ah, what a fine little lad." . . . "Does he want a little sweet?"

But before I opened the door, Father's voice rang shrilly in my head: "The nerve!" And Mother's: "How shameful!"

"Well, well," I replied, "now you can talk!"

Once I'd assured myself that no police were about, I opened the door and stepped inside.

There sat Reich — fat, ratty-voiced Reich, as I thought of him — reading a paper while his two older sons were working, or so it seemed, in the storeroom.

"Hmph, whadaya want?" he asked, but fortunately didn't recognize me.

Whining and squinting as best I could, I said: "I'm an orphan, and the Good Lord sent me here, the Good Lord, who watches over orphans and wipes away tears."

"Hmph," he muttered, nudging his glasses back up his nose and reaching into his pocket. He put a kreuzer on the table.

"Hmph, take it. Kids like this are begging too!"

He went on reading.

Having pocketed the kreuzer, I suddenly felt hungry, so I said: "But that Good Lord also said I should go to Mr. Reich, for he would give me a good lunch."

"What?" he said. "Lunch? That I don't have."

He kept his eyes on me. Now I added: "But that's what the Good Lord said."

His eyes still on me, he remarked, "Well, he said it in vain. You on such good terms with him?"

"Even Rabbi Azarel said so."

I cast him a sharp, sidelong glance: let's have it!

"That where you're coming from?"

"Yes," I said, "he's the one that said it, and he gave me a good breakfast too."

"I don't have any lunch for you," he replied, "does this look like a restaurant? Go to Blau's place."

And he put another kreuzer in front of me. "That's all now, so beat it."

Not knowing what else to say, I opened the door to leave.

"The Good Lord bless you."

Outside it was raining harder. I thought: Two kreuzers, so that's what his sort gives. One because I lied that God is good, and one because I lied that the rabbi, my father, is good.

And I began to laugh with delight over what I'd done. I was exhilarated. Over just two kreuzers. Holding the coins up toward the sky, I thought, See, you wicked sky? Rain all you want, but I've already got two kreuzers.

On I went, from one shop to the other, and the more kreuzers I got, the harder it rained. The more I laughed, too, and the more glad I was about the kreuzers and my courage and the whole game, it was so much fun that I couldn't help but skip about and run in circles.

"Go ahead and rain!" I shouted to the sky. "Make some thunder and lightning, too, if you want. But I'll just keep getting more kreuzers anyway."

By the time I'd finished skipping, laughing, and begging my way down the Bástyakör, I had more than forty kreuzers. With wild delight I jingled the coins in my pocket, thinking: With all this lying about God I'll just collect more and more! I'll have kreuzers galore. And then? Then my father can be as wicked as he wants, I'll still be able to buy myself all sorts of things. And why should I go only to Jewish shopkeepers? What did I have to fear anymore? I'd go to the Christians too! If I'd squint like up to now and wrinkle my nose real good, why should they notice that I'm a Jew? Maybe I'd even whimper those words I heard Christian beggarwomen say so often in front of their churches, "Glory be to Jesus Christ."

But I thought twice about this.

No, I wouldn't say that after all. Not even for begging and fun and kreuzers. The "Good Lord" would do.

In vain did Father and Mother call after me again, their voices resounding in my head, "Oh God, he's going to the Christians too." In I went.

While turning the doorknob I thought: If they notice all the same that I'm a Jew, and they say, "Outta here, you stinking Jew!" — why then I'd spit a big one and run away, just like I saw a Christian beggar kid do one time when he was chased out of a Jewish shop.

Once again luck was on my side. I neither had to spit nor go away without a kreuzer. See? I said to myself, laughing, you didn't even need Jesus. From now on, if you don't want them knowing that you're a Jew, you'll just wrinkle your nose and squint. But never will you say a thing about Jesus. And you won't have to go convert either.

Maybe by evening all my kreuzers would add up to a forint even. Then I'd go somewhere and ask for lodging, as did the prince in disguise: "Give me lodging, because I've come a long way and I am going to my father."

Yes, I'll have a place to sleep. Tomorrow I'll go farther, every which way and beyond. And I'll buy storybooks all the time, not to mention cream puffs or frankfurters. Never again will I have to bother about my parents and brother and sister or anyone. I'll neither have to go to school nor give myself out as an apprentice. That will be the life. And I'll let everyone know I don't give a hoot what they think.

And so I went on begging at Jewish and at Christian shops alike. Deep down I was roaring with laughter.

And where I didn't get even a kreuzer, I shouted my very own curse: "The Good Lord will whack you good!"

And before evening, before the shops would have closed, I bought cream puffs — *five,* that is, of the sort that we got on Saturdays, but never more than one. Immediately I wolfed down several. Then I bought a brand-new storybook, nice and thick at that. Not to mention three — three! — pairs of frankfurters, wrapped in a cornet. Then, since I was sopping wet, I entered a Jewish bakery's courtyard, where a fire was raging in the oven. Like the orphan prince, I said: "In the Good Lord's name, I'm coming from a long journey on my way to see my father. Please let me dry my clothes by the fire, and let me sleep here a bit, anywhere will do. . . ."

The journeymen bakers — young fellows, they were — readily agreed. And so I undressed, leaving on only my shirt; and they let me hang my clothes on a long shovel by the oven.

There I crouched in my shirt, watching them in the covered courtyard kneading dough into loaves of bread and into rolls. One of them was hardly older than I.

Why not join them? I thought. This was immediately followed by a second thought: But why? So *they* go bossing me around, too? And *smack* me sooner or later? I can go around getting a kreuzer here, a kreuzer there, till it all adds up, not to mention a place to dry my clothes and get some rest, and no one can tell me what to do; but if I start working someplace, before I know it the shopkeeper will be bossing me around, smacking me, and no doubt he'll want me to think the way he does, just like my father did.

So it's best like this. I've got everything I need, there's no one bossing me around, no one is smacking me, and I don't have to bother with anyone. All I've got to say is: "The Good Lord bless you, I'm on a journey to see my father. . . ." Or else: "May the Good Lord whack you good!" . . . Yes, I thought with a chuckle, I've got it all, and I can tell him just what I think of him, pelt him with stones, if I want. And I can go where I want. Ha-ha, ha-ha! I was so overcome with good cheer at such thoughts that it was all I could do not to jump about and laugh aloud; instead I only crouched there and watched the fire, tightly squeezing the frankfurters under my arm. Even at home I'd always liked frankfurters, but never had I been given more than a pair. Get a load of this, I thought, Now you've got no less than three pairs, why, you don't even have room for them, those cream puffs were so filling. And then there's your storybook, brand-new and so thick!

But I didn't say a word to anyone. You guys go ahead and work, I thought, I'll just go on laughing to myself.

Yet I made sure to squint hard so as to look half-blind, and saw to it that my legs and arms should look suitably lame. In one hand I tightly held the five kreuzers that remained.

Finally my clothes dried, and I got dressed. No sooner had I done so than the head baker called over to me: "Well, if you want, you can lay down in the straw in the storeroom in the back. But just for tonight."

I thanked him. At which one of the younger bakers spoke up. "I'll show him where it is."

Now the head baker called to his wife, in the back. "I'm off to synagogue!"

Then he turned to one of the guys. "You can come along, too, Ignác."

They went into his flat, which was just off the courtyard, to get properly dressed.

This took me aback.

Gee, I thought, I should be off to synagogue right about now too, where I must *tell the truth* — to Father and the Jews and to God — and then go on to the Christian church, to tell the Christians the truth too. But first to give God a piece of my mind in the dark. Yes, all those kreuzers, the storybook, the cream puffs, the frankfurters, the warmth of the fire, not to mention this good place to lodge and all my secret laughter, had taken my mind off the whole thing.

Sure, sure, I thought, but why go now, after all? When I've got everything I need? And I already know what I'm going to do from now on. I'll be a beggar, and then, every day when I've got enough kreuzers, I'll read my storybook and bum about wherever

I please. So why should I go to the synagogue to tell the truth about Father and about God?

Only so Father can catch me, or if he doesn't, so the Christians can, so they can give me a beating and lock me away in some dungeon? I'd do better just to be glad I'm through with it all. And I stretched out contentedly by the oven, watching the fire.

But the fire now had its say: "Gee, *this* sure took a lot of courage. Begging! And then wolfing down all those cream puffs; buying that storybook; clutching those frankfurters, those kreuzers; drying your clothes, and getting ready for a good night's sleep in the straw."

And of course, in no time Father's voice intermingled with what the fire was saying. "This took a lot of courage?! All *this* took," he'd say, was "*some* nerve," or else being as "cheeky as a cock sparrow," not to mention as "dumb as a real freeloader."

And I felt as if Mother and Father could see me, that they knew everything I'd done and thought since leaving home; that they were talking among themselves like this: "You see? Told you I knew him inside out. *God?* Now, he himself could sure use a dose of God, but *he'll* 'tell' the truth to the Jews and the Christians! Him? All talk, that's him. No, he didn't want a thing, just to be a shamefaced beggar, to stuff his face and live like a freeloader, to loaf away his time with a storybook, while others, decent folk, knead dough and study, sweat away beside an oven, have their noses on the grindstone! While he does nothing but laugh to himself."

I was getting hot.

And I snarled back at the fire: "You won't be right, you bad father. You won't. Just for that you won't!"

"Now, now," said the fire, "I know you inside out!"

And in the fire I saw, exactly, Father donning his gown. While Mother said: "Come on, Papa, let me brush off the lint. What's going to become of that boy?"

At which Father: "Don't you worry. I know him inside out.

For now he's still begging, but then he'll steal, break in, rob, and explain it all away by saying he 'just wanted to know if there's a God.' Of course, his real aim was to be 'wicked,' as he himself put it. That's *all!* The rest was just an excuse. I know him, I do!"

In the fire I saw him putting on his high velvet hat, then going into our room with Mother. There Mother prepared the holiday candles. She spoke.

"Papa, you hit him too much all the same, I just had to tell you before you go to synagogue."

"Oh come on!" Father proudly replied, "Just let him beg if that's what he wants, and let him be the shame of the earth."

And Mother: "Oh . . ."

And in the fire I saw Father giving Mother a kiss, then heading off to synagogue while saying to himself, as I so often did: Just let him be the shame of the earth.

I got up from beside the fire.

"No, you wicked father," I snarled too, "he's not going to be the 'shame of the earth' — *you* will." And I saw him going down the stairs, holding his gown up in front lest it should get dirty.

At this I got up from beside the fire, so as to head off. But first, like the orphan prince from the story, I said to the others: "Thanks for everything. You'll hear word of me yet."

They laughed. One of them spoke.

"Hey, aren't you gonna stay here in the straw?"

"No," I replied, "I've got one more 'big job' to take care of."

"Go on ahead," said the fellow, "then if you want to come back after ten, rap hard on the outside door and I'll open it up."

"Thank you," I said, then practically recited the words: "*I shall avail myself of your kind offer.*"

Whereupon he: "Wait a minute, pip-squeak, where you off to? What's that 'big job'?"

And he stood before me with his huge, half-naked body, batting his eyes.

"Hey, didn't you run away from home?"

They all now gathered around me.

I thought: Well then, I'll just have to introduce myself; then it's off to the synagogue to take care of things.

And I spoke, as befits an orphan prince: "Well then, you should know that I am neither a beggar nor on any journey, but that I am the son of the wicked rabbi."

Opening my squinted eyes nice and wide, and straightening myself out, I said: "But I can't say anything more, not now. The rest is a secret. But if you come to the synagogue, there you'll find out everything."

They laughed.

"Well, I'll be damned!" cried one.

And the other: "We sure can't go there, not now, we gotta work."

"In that case," said I, "farewell." And I hurried off.

But out there on the darkening street as I hastened toward the synagogue, the darkness spoke — of course, once again in Father's voice.

"*You* — with your shameless begging, frankfurters, and a storybook under your arm, your last five kreuzers in your hand — *you* want to tell the Jews about God and about me? To tell them this and that? You'll think this through yet. I suggest you do."

And I said to myself as I walked quickly along: "Talk all you want from the dark, go ahead."

The more Father snarled those very same words in his oh-so-familiar voice, the more I hurried, until at last I'd broken into a run; and before I knew it, I was dashing up the stairs right into the synagogue's lobby. Here, however, I stopped dead in my tracks. Gasping and trembling, I watched the huge swinging doors. Inside, Flussz, the cantor, was already well into singing:

> Draw near, O Queen, and here abide;
> Draw near, draw near, O Sabbath bride.

"See there?" came Father's voice from the swinging doors. "All talk, aren't you? And already you're so scared."

I was shaking and gasping terribly. *Oh dear, oh dear.* Was I still such a coward? But I'd already gone and begged! Even from the Christians. What's worse, I nearly entered with my bag full of goodies in hand.

I looked upon this bag. Now Father's voice, his mocking voice, came from right inside of it. "That's right! First we hide what we shamelessly scrounged, yes, we deny it, lie about it, then we go inside to rail against those who 'earn their bread through honest work, and aren't some sort of freeloaders.'"

"No," I replied to the bag, "I'm *not* hiding you, and even if I'd scrounged for you a hundred times over, I'm still going in there with you in my hand, and I'll tell it all. Just *let* them find out that I've gone and begged, that I've gone to the dogs — yes, I'll tell them it was because of you, you wicked father."

So intensely and suddenly did I grab the doorknob, my whole body shaking, that my hand all but stuck there like glue. I couldn't even have gone in, had Father's voice not now come from the door itself.

"We'll see, we will."

At this I frantically flung open the swinging doors and nearly plunged straight into the synagogue.

The fright and all the effort hardly allowed me to move, and I only stood inside there gasping for air. I didn't dare look about, but only stared, headstrong but still trembling, at the floor and at my bag: So I *had* in fact brought inside the fruits of my begging. Even now I could not move. It seemed my bag had grown, and I felt as if everyone suspected by now: *What? So, that beggar is the rabbi's son?* Especially my father, who was no doubt casting me a stern look.

In no time I imagined his scolding voice: "Someone so shiftless wants to criticize others?"

At this I looked up anyway, though trembling still. Take that!

My entire body was burning, pins and needles, with my knees and the bag trembling in particular; but I kept standing there anyway, staring into the light with my head held up high, thinking, let everyone see and know who this beggar is.

Glancing to the side, my eyes now fell upon the bench farthest to the back and closest to me, where sat those who "live on the congregation's charity." Gathering up my will, I went straight over to join them, for I already belonged there anyway. And there I only stood and stood once more, taut and trembling, still not daring to take a good look about. With the bag still in my hands, I thought: Maybe Reich or Blau will come over here all of a sudden and put me to shame before I have a chance to say even a word about my father. But no one came. All that happened was this: The poor have-not beside me put his prayer book before me and pointed to where the cantor was. The other, bowing gruffly, wasted no time throwing a prayer shawl over my neck. I looked upon them. One was squinting above eyeglasses that clearly didn't quite serve their purpose anymore, the other had broken into a toothless smile.

Sure, I figured, they're still thinking, "What a fine little lad," and "He's the rabbi's son."

Now I finally dared to move my eyes all around, at first only in sidelong glances but then more directly; only that I didn't look up *there* — where, I knew, Mother was sitting with Ernuskó.

No one returned my glances. It seemed they hadn't noticed me and perhaps didn't recognize the "beggar"; or perhaps the sole reason they didn't want to humiliate me here went like this: "We're really proud of Rabbi Azarel, what a fine sermon he gave." Now I put the bag down behind me, well into the corner. Of course this didn't allow me to feel any more proud, and against my will, my leg just kept trembling away. Once again I heard Father's voice, now from the yellow, tattered prayer book I was staring at.

"A beggar whose leg is still trembling like this has no business talking about his father. . . ." At this I leaned over and held my legs by turns — first one and then the other, that is — to keep them from trembling.

"No," I snarled under my breath. "Are you going to obey *me*, leg, or my father?" But hardly had I let go when my legs started trembling again, and calling to me in Father's voice. "You're not even master of your own legs, yet . . ."

Let them tremble all they want, I now decided, I won't bother with them anymore. But my ears were ringing, too, and from inside them I heard, again in Father's voice: "He who isn't even master of his own ear . . ."

Fine, I thought, you all just go on listening to my father if you want, I'll talk about him anyway. And now I began paying careful attention, waiting for Father's prayer; there were four prayers to go, I reckoned.

Finally I looked up at Father. Yes, it seemed he'd been watching me from the start. He nodded, indicating that I should go up there to him. And I could hear his voice inside my head. "Enough of this street-kid stuff. Get up here, and now. And then it'll be all right with me, seeing as how you've atoned on your own."

At this my legs nearly started off toward him on their own, so I had to grab the edge of the bench. I held myself down as best I could in spite of the trembling of my legs, the pitter-patter of my feet.

"I'm staying put," I snarled under my breath, and no longer looked at Father but only at the prayer book. Having regained some composure, I began to count again. "Two more prayers, then it's his turn. . . ."

So that I couldn't possibly hear Father's voice inside my head, I began murmuring the prayer from the point we were at.

But of course all I thought about was what, after all, I would say. Laying it all on the table, begging included, seemed really hard.

Or maybe they haven't even recognized you as the beggar? I thought. Then maybe you can get away with not talking about *that*. Only about your wicked father. Yes, that would be easier.

No sooner had I thought this, however, than I noticed Reich cast me a sidelong glance. He'd recognized me, he had. And Blau? Him too.

Then it doesn't matter, I thought. I'll have to talk about my begging after all. How I went to the dogs. At this I turned around, and in a sudden fury I reached out my trembling hand, wanting to take everything out of the bag, so they might see for themselves. I didn't care, for I'd talk about it all the same. About everything.

But now Mother's snickering voice called out from inside the bag. "Gyuri, Gyuri, you nincompoop! Why, you'll make a laughingstock of yourself with those frankfurters and cream puffs! Do you want that?"

I didn't reach for the bag. Desperately I looked straight ahead instead, as Mother's voice came again. "You are *so* ridiculous! Don't you even realize? If you so much as open your mouth, they'll burst out laughing. You silly little thing!"

At this I wanted to cry, for, yes, this was the worst of it all — that they would laugh, because I was a little kid, *little, little, little,* and my begging was little together with my bag, the frankfurters and the cream puffs and the book, all little and ridiculous, as was the talk, too, that I wanted to give about myself and my wicked father.

Again came Mother's voice. "Oh, Papa, how can anyone be angry at him when he's such a silly little thing? The whole thing is so ridiculous, believe me, Papa!"

At this my tears began to flow against my will. Then, so no one would see or hear my stifled tears, I squatted down under the bench and began blowing my nose.

But now Flussz's singing suddenly rang out loudly once again. It came as a warning: one more prayer, then he's up. At this my tears stopped at once in fright. I only stood there frantically clutching my handkerchief.

And I thought: No more crying, because I'll make a fool of myself. There's no point, none at all. I'm little, and what I'd tell them, that would be little too.

No one, nothing, not even my wicked father, could say anything as disturbing as my ridiculing mother. Again I only stared at the prayer book.

And there, in the final prayer, I saw written in great big Hebrew characters:

THE LORD OUR GOD

Dumbly I stared at the words.

And now *He* spoke. "Now why did you go railing at me? At your father, sure. But why at me? Why did you pelt me with stones and taunt me with those coins? And you see, now you've got no one. Not a soul."

Dumb, awfully tired coward that I was, I muttered to myself: "But I only pelted the synagogue, the letters, the wall; and I held the coins only in the air."

"Come now," pronounced God, "this is nothing but cowardly quibbling. You might have asked me for some help against your father. But not even now, here in the synagogue, do you ask, but you only stare dumbly ahead, and the final prayer's already here. Afterward your father will come down and take you straight home; he'll notice the bag and, well, you know the rest anyway."

He continued, "Now, let's see here, why did you say that God created people, Jews included, all as wicked as he himself and his rabbi?"

God added after a pause, "And you see, I didn't even make them so terribly wicked, all of them gave you a kreuzer, even the Christians, which is why you have this bag here with you, your shame. And you see, had you not railed at me the way you did, right now you wouldn't feel so little."

"But what can I do anymore?" I muttered.

"What? Ask me not to let them laugh at you when you show them the fruits of your begging and tell them the truth about your father and yourself."

"But I already asked you, so many times, and you always helped my father, my wicked father."

"Just give it a try. One last time."

"But you don't care about me anyway."

"One last try, come on."

"And if it doesn't work? If they laugh all the same, and my father comes out the winner, and humiliates me again, takes me off and locks me away in reform school like some 'panhandling loafer'?"

"Then you'll say, 'Now I've really given everything a try, so from now on I'm not going to bother with anything, yes, from now on I'll really be a wicked beggar forever if I get out of reform school.'"

"All right," I replied, "so be it. One last try."

I looked up at the ceiling. "Look, God, I really didn't mean to get you angry, it was only because of my folks that I said everything I did. But I didn't want to offend you! Maybe you really do exist, and you're good!"

But God snapped back: "*Maybe?* Now that's not saying a lot."

"No, no," I said, "I believe that you really do exist! Absolutely sure you *can* exist. That you *do*. And I'll do anything you want! Just help me this one last time so they don't all laugh at me, so I won't be so little, and my father won't be right."

"All right," said this God, "but you know what this requires: to unselfishly keep the Ten Commandments, just the way Mr. Würtz said and like it says in the Bible."

"All right," I consented, "though I don't know all of them by heart, I swear I'll keep them all the time."

"That's better!" said God. "But *unselfishly!*"

"Unselfishly, then," said I.

"But then," God replied, "you can't go asking me to make sure that you're in the right here and that your father isn't, because you know full well that you're wicked just like him. Which is why I won't say either one of you is right. That's the plain truth."

"So," I said, "you're not good, but just."

"That's right, and that's exactly why all you should be concerned with is railing against yourself. That's number one!"

"All right," I responded, "I want to do that anyway. But then who will rail against him? Against Father? He sure won't do it to himself, not here!"

"Leave that to me," said God, "you just go on out there in front of the pulpit, and before your father starts talking, fall on your knees and cry out: 'I'm a wicked, wretched beggar! And I led my father into sin.' And then he'll come on down from there and say, 'You're better than I, for you're little, after all; and all of you, the faithful gathered here today, should know that he became a wicked, wretched beggar because of me.'"

"Ah," I said, "he won't do that. The folks here will only laugh at me, I'll only cause a 'disturbance' — that's how Father will put it — and then everything will be even worse than before."

"Then," said this God, "just don't believe."

"But it's so hard for me to believe this about him! Give me some kind of sign that it will definitely be this way."

"That's not possible," said this God.

"Even a little one, just so *I* know it's you! Have everyone fall asleep all at once, say. Just for a minute!"

"Whoa there!" said God, "Now that's asking a lot!"

"Well then," I bargained, "have those two old men beside me fall asleep, seeing as how their heads are drooping anyway. Or if that's too much, then have the candles flicker out, right now!"

But this God wasn't about to do even that much.

"Either you believe everything I say," he said, "unselfishly to a fault, or not. There's no bargaining. Now go to it before your father begins his sermon."

"But he'll think I'm doing it only because I want to cause a 'disturbance' and a 'sensation.'"

"It doesn't matter what he believes!"

"And he never did love me! You know that full well."

"It doesn't matter that he never loved you! Do it!"

"But if I'm too embarrassed? I'm afraid it'll just come off badly."

"Shut your eyes and go out there like that, then fall to your knees and cry out."

"But what will happen? *What?*"

"If it's not like I promise, why then, I already said you can rail at me all you want and be wicked forever. Understand? But enough of this. And be careful, because your father's getting ready to talk. Now shut your eyes, and do it!"

Frightened to death, I shut my eyes and felt all at once that I had no time to lose, that I had to cry out, that no longer could I *not* hurry and *not* cry out.

And so I began to shout: "In God's name I declare that I'm a wretched, wicked beggar and led my father into sin!" And from the beginning, again and again.

The cantor fell silent. My eyes being shut, I couldn't see my father; I only heard his voice along with those of many others.

But I didn't care about a thing anymore, and only kept shouting. "*God* told me to shout! *God* told me!" Then I fell, and stayed like that.

My eyes were still shut, and now I felt my father clasp my hand in his.

"Come at once!"

But I just kept shouting like until now, at which Father picked me up and carried me out of the synagogue.

Not for a moment could I rest, I felt, no, I had to keep crying out; for if I didn't, afterward things would just be worse.

Suddenly there came Mother's voice.

"What is it?" she shrieked. "Has he been hit by a carriage?"

But I just kept shouting. "*God* told me to shout, it was God, God!"

And when Father lay me down in our room, straightaway I ran over to him, jumped about, and kissed him where I could. And I kept yelling, "I'm shouting in God's name, in God's name!"

Then I ran over to Mother, to kiss her too in God's name. But she stepped back in fright, and cried out: "He's gone mad! My God, the boy's gone mad!"

She darted away into her bedroom, so my attention fell on my brother and sister, whom I likewise ran over to and covered with kisses where I could, except that they too stepped back in fright, and joined Mother in the other room. At this I ran back to Father and went on kissing him, at which he held me tight.

"Now, now," he said, "it's all right. There there. I love you too, we all do, just calm down like a good boy."

Now Mother appeared on the threshold, but without saying a word Father gave a firm wave of the hand to signal that she should just go on back into her room.

There, locked in Father's arms, I anxiously waited to see if he would say what God had promised me that he would; that is, for him to dish it out to himself. As long as he didn't do so in the synagogue, I figured, maybe here and now he would.

But he just kept giving me this odd look. Neither stern nor gentle, no regret either; no, instead he only seemed to be watching me. Yet he said nothing of the sort that God had promised, only this: "It's all right, everything's all right. Come on now, sit down. Then we'll talk. Aren't you tired?"

"Yes," I said, "I'm tired, but I did speak in God's name, you know."

And again I said what I'd already said so much, only softer, for I was completely hoarse and exhausted. Yet Father still didn't say what God had promised.

"It's all right," he said, putting the sheet and a duvet on my bed, "now you just lie down, and if you lie there nice and calm, you'll get whatever you please."

I thought: Lay down, and . . . you'll get . . .

So he thinks I'm sick, and that's why he's promising to give me "whatever you please," and says, "Hey, it's all right." And Mother's cry just before she darted away now came back to me: "He's gone mad!"

And I said: "Thank you, but I'm not sick and mad. It's God that spoke to me, he's the one who told me to say all this."

"All right," said Father. "But do lie down. Once you're snug in bed you can tell us all about what God said to you."

Watching Father, I wondered whether to tell him what God had promised. I kept watching him until an inner voice whispered: "Careful, don't tell him what God promised you about him — that he'd confess his wickedness, too. If you tell him that, he'll stop thinking of you as sick and instead just like he did before, as a wicked little boy who does nothing but cause 'trouble,' and he'll be even more wicked to you. Careful! Now that you've seen that God hasn't kept his promise, better you just be sick, or rather, 'mad.' That's much better!"

It seemed as though the voice that told me all this was entirely different from all those that had previously spoken to me and from inside of me. I felt that all would be well if I paid heed to this voice, and was secretly pleased with the fair warning.

Yet Father, it seemed, must have noticed something about me straightaway.

"Hey, what are you smiling about?"

Worried that he might figure out the warning I'd received, I hastened to say: "Oh, nothing. . . ."

I was still unable to move and get changed for bed, because, I noticed, Father was watching me intently. Even more than until now.

"So then," he said, "don't you want to go to bed?"

"Yes," I promptly replied, "now even I know that I'm sick, or mad, so I'll go to bed."

I began to change for bed. But not like before, no, not quickly, because the voice whispered, "Don't you hurry now, because you're supposed to be 'mad,' or 'sick,' not to mention tired."

And so I paused now and again while changing, but as I saw that Father was watching me even more intently than before, and would figure out sooner or later that I wasn't sick, or mad, suddenly I picked up my pace. And I slipped into bed even faster, and wanted to pull the duvet completely over me, so he couldn't watch me anymore, but I didn't dare. Maybe that would tip him off to the rest. And how frightened I was when he sat in a chair awfully close to the bed, and watched me ever more closely. And he said: "Well, then, now you can tell me what God said to you."

Again that voice: "Careful! His face and voice are that gentle just so you won't know how much he's watching you, but be careful, because all of a sudden he'll lunge at you for not being 'sick' or 'mad' after all, and . . ."

This thought frightened me so much that I couldn't even speak; I just watched and watched my father. Until finally he asked: "What are you watching like that? What are you frightened of? What do you see?"

Whereupon the voice: "Careful! Don't go telling him it's *him* you're afraid of, because then he'll figure out everything right off, and you're in for it!"

And I shrunk back in bed in ever more terror.

"Hey there, stay put now," he said, reaching after me.

Yet again the voice rang in my ears, ever more slowly, Careful, he'll lay his hands on you!"

And then I shrank back even farther, but there was the wall, and the voice now came from the wall: "Don't look at him anymore, because he'll figure everything out in no time; hide your head, because otherwise you'll die at his hands, he'll strangle you, he will."

At this I buried my head in the pillow and stayed like that, panting, while Father kept talking to me louder and louder, and so I figured he was threatening me with that voice of his, because *He already knows everything*. And I buried my head ever deeper into the pillow, until his voice suddenly faded away.

Now I knew it was all over, that he would strangle me in no time. But I couldn't even bring myself to move, no, I only felt as if my father's hand was twisting, slowly, around my neck from inside the pillow. I gasped for air, then suddenly all was completely silent; and once again I heard that third voice, but more softly than ever: "Well, that's it: you're dead, finished, you can't get up anymore, and never again will you open your eyes."

"And then?" I asked, without opening my eyes. An entirely different voice replied.

"Gyuri, Gyuri."

And I thought: Isn't that my mother?

"Yes," whispered the voice, "it's she, and she's glad you're finally finished, so you just let her be glad, because it'll be better for you too like this, if you're dead."

At this Mother's voice came again. "Come on, Gyuri, open your eyes! Look, it's us."

The voice: "Go ahead and open them, but make sure to stay dead, it's for the best."

Open them I did, but with great difficulty, and I hardly saw a thing, I was so tired. Mother was sitting there by my bed and asking through her tears: "How are you? Do you feel well?"

And the voice: "Just say you're dead."

Softly and awfully tired, I spoke: "Me, Mother? Don't you see I'm dead?"

At this Father came in too.

And the voice said at once: "Don't be scared, there's nothing he can do to you anymore. Because you're dead, finished, you can't get up anymore; your eyes are open, that's all. He can't hurt you anymore."

He stepped over to my bed, and asked: "So, feeling better?"

I replied: "I'm dead, finished, my eyes are open, that's all."

Suddenly I noticed that Father wanted to hold my hand. At first I wanted to pull away, afraid as I was, but the voice encouraged me again.

"Let him, he can't hurt you anymore. Like I said, you're dead."

And so I let him, and I said: "I'm dead, and no one can hurt me anymore."

Whereupon he said: "Hurt you? certainly not. And you're not dead, you were only a bit faint."

Looking at him, I thought: He doesn't want to admit he did *that* to me, that that's why I'm dead!

And I watched Mother too, who was just watching as well. And I thought: Does she know what Father did to me? Or doesn't she want to face the facts either, because she doesn't want any more "excitement"? Should I ask her?

But the voice then said: "Tell her whatever you want, just not what your father did to you, because then your mother will again think you're 'mad' — sick, that is. And your father will again lock his eyes on you. That will be really bad. Just as bad as before. Better to just be dead, since that won't raise any eyebrows." So I didn't say a thing.

Father spoke again. "Indeed, you fainted, and from naughtiness at that." He smiled, and patted my hand. "But now, thank God, you'll get back in form." And again he held my hand; perhaps I had a fever?

At this Mother said anxiously to Father: "But why is he always saying he's dead?" Again she wept.

Try as I did to watch them, I was so hot and tired that I could barely open my eyes.

Father replied: "Oh, for heaven's sake, he just feels *tired*, that's all. This is natural after such a fainting spell. That's what he means by being dead."

Mother cast me an inquisitive look. "Do you feel really weak?"

I only returned the stare. Again I thought: Fainting? Do you really have no idea what Father did to me? Or are you just deny-ing it, too, like him?

She now tried getting me to talk. "Do you want to say some-thing? Go ahead, you can tell us anything, no one will hurt you, no one will be angry. No one! Right, Papa?"

"Of course — no one!" replied Father. "So go ahead and talk, what is it you wanted to say?"

Again the voice: "Tell it all, just not that one thing, that your father strangled you, that that's why you're dead."

"Well?" asked Mother. "Go ahead, Gyuri, talk."

And I said: "I can tell you everything, just not that one thing."

Mother leaned closer. "What?"

And Father: "Well?"

"That one thing," I replied, looking at them and thinking, Whew, what a show they're putting on, pretending to be curi-ous. When they know anyway. Father, he knows for sure.

Now Father spoke again: "Come on, say it. Don't worry one bit. You can tell us even that one thing. Anything."

I looked upon him until my lips started moving on their own. "You know anyway. . . ."

Yet the voice cautioned me straightaway: "Careful! Don't you say it! Because then things'll be really bad. Again."

"What?" asked Father. "What do I know anyway?"

But still I didn't dare. "Only that . . . nothing."

Smiling, Father whispered something in Mother's ear. Whereupon she too smiled, and began to nod.

Yes, I thought, they're glad I'm dead.

Father now stood, however, walked vigorously into the other room, and returned with a bag. *The* bag. Full of what I'd begged — well, the storybook alone.

Ah yes, so they figured that *this* was the one thing I didn't want to say; that I feared this. But I had nothing to fear anymore about having panhandled, for I was now dead anyway.

Father placed the book on my bed and spoke. "It's all taken

care of," he said, "we saw to that. There's no problem. And this is now rightfully yours."

And Mother: "Is this what you wanted to ask about?"

The voice whispered: Say it is! You don't want them asking more questions, and you then blurting out the one thing you shouldn't."

"Yes."

Whereupon Mother said: "Everyone got back what they gave. Even the Christians. Every single kreuzer."

The voice whispered: "Say a nice thank you. You're dead anyway."

And so I spoke. "Thank you, seeing as how I'm dead anyway."

At this the tears came again to Mother's eyes. She turned to Father. "See? He said *that* again."

Father replied: "But you've got to understand, Ida, that he doesn't even know what being dead is. All this means to him just now is that he's tired. Just like I already said. Right, Gyuri?"

At which Mother turned to me. "Right?"

And the voice from within: "They know that's just what you are. Dead. But they don't even want to upset themselves with that. So best you just leave it to them to decide that you're tired, or else they'll keep firing away with questions. And it's best for you if they don't."

Thus when Mother asked again: "Yes? Are you very tired?"

I replied: "I am. And it's best for me if you don't keep asking questions."

Mother nodded. "All right. Then just get a good sleep."

At this the voice: "Shut your eyes. Let them think you're tired, that you've fallen asleep. It's all the same to you, right? You're dead anyway."

And I shut my eyes.

Now the voice was encouraging: "It's best in the dark, alone, completely alone."

I heard them slowly rise and leave my bedside.

And the voice kept whispering, ever more softly: "It's best in the dark, *a-lone, com-plete-ly a-lone.*"

The darkness was thicker and thicker, heavier and heavier, pressing against me so hard that before long I felt that I was lying motionless in the ground, in a box. Yet my eyes were open, and I could hear my parents calling my name. I thought: Let them call me all they want, I don't want to get up. No, no, no. But things got worse and worse in that box, so I wriggled about as best I could. Suddenly it turned light all around me, and I saw myself lying in bed in the room I shared with my brother and sister; my parents were sitting beside me. It was daytime. Not morning, it seemed, but afternoon already. I looked upon them in bewilderment. So I'd only dreamed being underground.

Father began. "Well, you better already?" But I only looked at them again in bewilderment.

How I'd ended up in my bed, I had no idea. And why I'd been asleep when it was daytime and maybe even afternoon — again, no idea. It seemed I'd been sick.

And so I said: "I don't get it. Was I sick?"

At this Father turned to Mother and they exchanged a glance. "Why, he doesn't even know what happened to him!" He broke into a smile.

And I thought: He's glad I'm no longer sick. Because that's a big pain.

Now Mother, to Father: "Think he doesn't know anything about what happened to him?"

Father turned to me. "So tell us, do you know what happened to you?"

Curiously they looked upon me. And I at them, in bewilderment. Then I just stared ahead and racked my brain. But this only tired me out, and nothing else came to mind but my dream. That I'd been underground, in a box. And that before that I'd gone panhandling and into the synagogue to "tell it all." As to just what had happened there, however, I couldn't remember.

Nor could I remember anything that had happened since Father had brought me home. I'd completely forgotten the delirious state that fear and exhaustion had muddled me into, not to mention the specter of my strangulation and of being dead. The dream that had occurred after my "death" had submerged it all into my subconscious, and only years later did it reemerge from there ever so slowly in my dreams. But on opening my eyes that day I remembered not a thing. I only racked my brain over why I'd gotten sick. Not even *that* did I understand, however.

Mother now said in amazement, in that soft voice of hers: "He really doesn't know!"

And to me: "But you feel refreshed by now, right?"

Refreshed? I thought, looking about. "I don't feel a thing." Again I looked about: everything was just the same as on other mornings, only that it seemed to be afternoon.

"If he doesn't feel a thing," said Father, "then everything must be in order." He reached for my hand, which drew back slightly by itself, but I was immediately ashamed of this, and Father didn't notice a thing. He held my hand and turned to Mother.

"I think his fever's gone, too."

He brought the thermometer, which I put in my underarm. Then they had a look at my tongue and took my pulse. "Everything is in order," they pronounced. The thermometer didn't even show a fever. When Mother asked if I had an appetite, I accepted the soup and the soft-boiled egg she offered, and ate it with relish. Father was satisfied with this too. Only now did I hear that it wasn't even afternoon, not yet, but well short of noon.

Father showed me the time on his own watch. Indeed, it was just eleven.

"Of course," he said, "you can't possibly have a feel for the time when you were sick in bed and asleep for so long."

Good, I thought, no doubt this is how things are supposed to be — how would I even know, when this was the first time I'd been "sick in bed and asleep for so long"?

So then, it was morning still. Now Father began asking questions.

"So, let's see . . . what's the last thing you remember?"

At this, Mother sat down by my bed, too, although lunch was well underway out in the kitchen. I could see that she was curious, and as always, anxious.

"What do I remember? The last thing?" I said. And I thought: Why shouldn't I tell them my dream? Yet I hesitated a bit all the same, not even I know quite why, except maybe because they'd never before shown any interest in my dreams.

Nonetheless, finally I told them what I'd dreamed: that I had died.

At this Mother got up and gave a vigorous wave of the hand, as if she didn't want to hear another word, not one, for she'd definitely had enough excitement for one day.

"It's all right, everything's all right," she said. "So don't you say another word." She stepped over and suddenly kissed me. "It's all over, thank God it's over. No need to talk about it." She patted my face and left my bedside just as suddenly. "What's important is that everything's in order, and that you've recovered."

My questioning look must have been too much for Father to resist giving a bit of an explanation.

"You caught a cold down there," he said, "and were delirious for two whole days, raving away. You kept saying *we want to do God knows what with you.*"

Mother cut in: "Papa! Like I said, we don't have to talk about it!"

"About what?" I asked. But Mother answered.

"Nothing, okay? It's over. Now you just get some rest. Look." And she showed me that finest fruit of my begging, the storybook.

"Read a bit instead, if you feel like it. Then, in a day or two, you can get up. Till then you can read all you want, and you must eat well. Right, Papa?"

At which Father said: "Just don't overexert yourself reading."

I took the book in hand, then Father retired to his study and Mother went out to the kitchen to see to lunch.

I remained alone with my book. Turning it about in my hands, I thought: What else is there to do? As long as I'm sick and I've got to stay in bed for a few more days anyway. I kept moving my eyes over the room, trying to get a sense of how in fact I was. But once more all I saw was that nothing, absolutely nothing, had changed around me.

I was *delirious,* I thought. For two whole days.

But that was just a word.

I simply couldn't understand how two whole days could have passed with me doing nothing but being delirious, raving away about nothing less than: *"We want to do God knows what with you."* And what, exactly? As for this: *"Like I said, we don't have to talk about it!. . . It's over."* I really would have liked to have known what it was I'd gone "raving away" about. Meanwhile I happened to glance at my hands, which held the storybook. Seeing that they were thinner than before, Mother's words came back to me: "You must eat well. . . . Then you can read all you want." Oh yes, I thought, I'll really have it good until I'm well. So as to get a better look at myself — maybe I'd find something — I threw off the blanket. Examining my entire body precisely, even my feet, I found nothing out of the ordinary, except that not only had my hands gotten thin, but so had the rest of me: the outline of my ribs showed clearly on my skin. Wanting to give walking a try, I got out of bed, but hardly had I done so than I felt unusually lightheaded — weaker, that is. I thought: This must be the "dizziness" Mother's always complaining about. Frightened, I slipped back into bed.

My ruminations continued: See how brave you were? You left home, threw stones at the synagogue, went begging even at Christian shops, asked for "lodging," and went to the synagogue to tell it all. And now you're a coward again, and little as well. You don't even have the guts to get out of bed. I was terribly sad.

That's right, I thought. But why? Because *that God* hadn't kept his promise. He'd pulled one over on me. But now there came another voice.

"Sure about that? Did you do in the synagogue what you promised God? Did you confess all your sins?"

For all I tried, I could remember only one thing: although I had indeed wanted to confess all my sins, I'd no longer been able to do so. Instead I'd done nothing but shout — just what, I couldn't even remember that anymore. It seems, I now thought, that I'd been "sick" even then, because I'd "caught a cold," so that must be when I'd turned "delirious" and begun "raving away." So then, maybe that God hadn't duped me after all, for neither had I done as I'd promised. But — I thought — maybe I had.

I'd find out, all right, what had happened down there in the synagogue.

And since Father just happened to be passing through on his way to the kitchen, to Mother, I asked: Father. . . sir, what did I shout in the synagogue?"

He smiled upon me. "All sorts of silly nonsense."

"But what?"

"I sure don't know," he said, stepping over to me and putting my pillows in order, exactly, then the duvet, especially by my feet; he even produced another duvet and placed it atop the first.

"There," he said, "now you take care not to catch another cold. Turn the book toward the light when you're reading."

His voice was so tender.

Suddenly I thought: Now I'll tell him what I wanted, what God had promised me he'd do; yes, I'd tell him the whole thing just the way it happened, as far as I can remember. Exactly. He might as well know everything, and I'll see what he says.

"Father . . . sir, I want to tell you everything exactly and really seriously, everything that happened to me, and especially" — I paused — "about God, but the rest too. So you and Mother know the whole thing."

Father raised his eyebrows, just so, but I saw it. Especially at the point where I'd said "especially about God."

He said: "Why, son? We already know everything. About what happened to you. Exactly. It's best if you don't rack your brain about what happened; about what *was,* because you'll just get sick again."

Once more he went about putting my bed in order. "We've forgiven and forgotten it all. Your mother, and me too. The whole thing was an illness, as far as we're concerned. Over and done with." He continued emphatically. "You just look at it that way too, and now forget the whole thing, the way we've done, yes, that'll be for the best. Because, believe me, if you were to get sick again, you wouldn't get better so easily anymore. That would have a really damaging effect on your growth and on your whole life. So it's best that you just forget everything, *understand, my little lad?*" And he repeated, even more emphatically: "*Everything, my little lad.* No need to ask about this anymore."

With this he stroked my head, in a grown-up sort of way, like usual, then went out into the kitchen, where he'd been off to anyway.

Watching him go, I thought: No matter why he said it, *what he said does seem true.* For him and for me too.

And I thought it all over one more time ". . . *an illness, as far as we're concerned.*" Everything. All the way from the point where I'd begun badgering them about God. An illness. Not naughtiness, like usual. And they want to cover up the whole thing. They've "forgiven" me, they say.

And it seemed the reason they didn't want to get angry at me over the whole affair is that they figured I'd already been "punished" enough — by being sick. Not such a bad sort of punishment. . . .

Again I mulled over what Father had said. You just look at it that way too . . . and forget the whole thing. . . . Everything. . . . Everything, *my little lad.* He'd never called me that before. I thought: So it seems I must have been awfully sick after all. And they really do want to forget it. All right, I won't talk anymore about it all. Fine, so let them think of that God as an "illness," not to mention the naughtiness and the begging, and everything that happened. Let's forget it all. I'll read a lot and eat like a king.

And so I did, until my brother and sister got home from school.

I could tell immediately from how they behaved that Father had told them, too, to regard the whole thing as an illness, to "forget" it all. Ernuskó offered to help me study so I wouldn't fall too behind in school. For her part, Oluska tried to a fault to hide her envy over my having it "so good," getting to eat well and read all the time. Instead she brought me pictures she'd begun collecting for herself. Although I knew they meant this not for me, but for my illness, I thanked them all the same. At least I'd have it good for now.

Lunch passed as did every other lunch. Hardly had the soup bowls been taken to the kitchen, but Father pulled out his slips of paper to do the counting on.

Of course I was ashamed even now, but thought straight-away: An illness . . . *You* just look at it that way, too . . . and *forget the whole thing, my little lad. Everything. Everything.*

Yes, I thought, I'll think of Father's constant counting — and Mother's accompanying fear — as an "illness," too; not to mention Mother's habit of always serving Ernuskó before she did either me or Oluska, and serving him more.

And when, after lunch, the usual profound silence had to reign in the flat, I thought of this as an "illness," too; and I reminded myself, *illness,* when Ernuskó, still chewing his last mouthful of food, already buried himself in his books, while Oluska was where else but in front of the mirror, combing her hair. And there was Lidi's favorite expression, "I've got other things to tend to." In no time I'd added Mr. Würtz and the schoolmistress to the list. And this is how it was that day and the next and on those that followed: anything that got me angry or ashamed, anything I didn't like, that goaded me to blurt out brash words right away; of anything like this I now thought, Ah yes, illness . . . forget the whole thing. Just eat well . . . and read.

The only thing I tried not to forget was what happened to me. While reading from my storybook and after meals I strained to remember everything ever more precisely.

But memory invariably got me no further than the point where I'd begun bargaining with God in the synagogue. And if I strained to remember beyond this, suddenly my head would begin to hurt.

You see, I told myself, this is what Mother suffers from so often. Now you know this, too.

So then, this God is really an illness, or at least a headache.

And afterward I thought: Forget the whole thing.

But then I still couldn't forget it, it's just that I stopped racking my brain once I reached the point where I'd begun to talk to God in the synagogue.

What remained of all this would make a good story, I thought. Something like the one about the prince in disguise and that other one, about the orphan prince. But it would be called: "The Rabbi's Son: Pauper and Orphan."

No sooner had I thought this than I began to compose the story in my head:

"Once upon a time there was a Jewish priest — a rabbi — and his wife, and their three children. And they loved both their older children more than they did the youngest. They gave the youngest at first to Grandpa, who was covered from head to toe in black hair, and who never let go the fringes of the little boy's prayer shawl, not even when he was asleep. But things got no better later on, either, back at home; for this youngest child wanted so very much that his parents didn't, and that not even his brother and sister did.

"His brother wanted nothing but to study, and so he was

called the Good Student. His sister was just a girl, and wanted nothing but to comb her hair and be green with envy all the time, and so she was called the Long-Haired Girl.

"Yet the third, the youngest, wanted neither this nor that, but only wondered why his mother, father, the furniture, and the paintings didn't dance, and why they didn't make music. And why they didn't speak to him, not *really*. Yet he wanted other things, too, and so he was simply called the Selfish Child, or Unruly Child.

"And he wasn't supposed to do anything at all. Not even to fall out the window, so he'd be 'finished.' Not even to ask about God, to ask: Why doesn't God show himself? When he asked this anyway, he got such a good hiding that he got really angry at his wicked father, his ridiculing mother, and even at God, and was resolved to wander off into the world, forever, so that he could be truly, completely wicked, like his father said he was. But first he wanted to go to the synagogue and there tell the truth about everything; for first he'd thought things through, about the Jews, the Christians, and God, too, not just about his wicked father and ridiculing mother.

"And this would be the ruin of the Selfish Child, his wanting to tell the truth in synagogue. For at first he'd had the courage to pelt God with stones and to go begging even in Christian shops, and to buy a storybook and cream puffs, and frankfurters too, and to ask for lodging, and everything would have worked out just fine; but then his father started after him, yes, his father's voice began speaking to him from the fire in the baker's oven. And from the dark and from the synagogue doors, too, this voice spoke and spoke and spoke, until it convinced the Selfish Child to enter the synagogue after all, to tell it all. And there, not only did his father chase after him, but so too did his mother, with her ridiculing voice; and in vain did the Selfish Child implore this God, who promised that everything would be fine; the end was to be only illness, delirious raving, and headaches."

I can't remember the rest. Only that in this story I was then just as much of a cowardly Jew as before. The whole thing ended like this: "Forget the whole thing, my little lad. I'll forget it too."

Ernuskó gave me some paper so I could write down the story, because I didn't want to ask Father for money to buy some with; and Oluska loaned me a pencil, because I'd already sharpened mine down to a stub while in bed. And I said to them: "Thanks. Forget the whole thing, just think of me as sick."

Whereupon Ernuskó said: "That's why I gave you the paper, even though I've got to ask Papa for it, too."

As for Oluska: "And that's why I lent you the pencil." She added, "But when you're out of bed again, just don't start it all over again."

But on looking over the story I'd written, I no longer cared for it one bit. For I wondered: Who got taught a "lesson," after all? Like in stories? And where's the ending? Only illness? A story can't end like this.

And then I thought: In stories there are witches, dwarves, fairies, and wizards, but this God is in not one. He is only in the Bible — or rather, in the stories of Moses. So then, this whole thing is more like the stories of Moses. But not that much, for God *keeps* the promises he makes in them.

As I mulled over this, again there came a voice from inside of me: "*God?* What is it you still want?! You know full well that God is just an illness, or a headache. And when you 'spoke' with him, you were already down with a 'cold,' yes indeed, you were 'delirious' and 'raving away.'"

And so I gave the story a different ending, as follows:

". . . The Selfish Child thought he'd spoken with God, who'd promised him all sorts of things, although by then he — the Selfish Child — was sick. He wound up in bed. Even so, his father, mother, brother, and sister still lived on God for the rest of their days. As did the Selfish Child."

Only when no one was in the room did I work on this story.

I didn't want them to know about it as long as everyone had forgotten the whole thing already. Still, I was scared that one time Mother or Father would notice me writing, or remove the pages from my bed while I slept.

Which is why I figured that maybe the best thing would be to just throw the sheets of paper in the fire; for it wasn't such a good story anyway. And so I did. But, I thought, someday I'll write a real one, too.

I watched the flames. From within them came Father's voice again, as at the bakery.

"You're just lying around being 'sick,' you know, while others work all day and study hard."

His voice was more gentle than at the bakery, but it was reproachful enough as it was. But now this reproach came not only from the fire, but in actuality, from Father just the same as from Mother and from my brother and sister.

They called the doctor, Büchner, to take, as they put it, "one last good look at me." He came, too. His beard was long, even longer than Father's; his hands were redder and colder. He had less hair; so little, in fact, that Mother remarked, "At night he packs away every single strand," and "He's like some maniac, he rubs so much ointment into his beard. . . . He's so vain . . . ." He smelled strongly of pomade and medicine, but I liked this. It was just his cold red hands that I didn't care for, especially since they really were terribly red, and hairy too.

"So what's up, lad, what's up," he muttered. "Back in one piece, are you?"

Since it was already winter, he lit the lantern. Then: "Head doesn't hurt a bit anymore?"

I replied: "Not anymore."

And he: "Don't get even a bit dizzy anymore?"

Whereupon I said: "No, it's just that I'm still kind of light-headed when I get out of bed."

He gave a wave of the hand. "That's nothing."

Then he brought the lantern over to the bed, and began peering intently into my eyes. Just why, I couldn't have said, but I didn't like this one bit. I began getting scared, although we weren't alone in the room. Mother and Father also stood by the bed.

The doctor noticed. "Got scared?"

I blushed. "Of course not. But there's nothing in my eyes anyway."

He replied: "That's for me to say! You just tell me if you're jittery. Hmm?"

"Not me," I said, my face all red. Now I opened my eyes wide, so he could look as deeply as he pleased.

And so he did, saying: "Don't strain your eyes like that. Just look at me the way you usually do."

I looked at him, and he smiled.

"There we are," he said, stroking my head and smiling. But he kept scrutinizing me, then stroked my head again and smiled. "All right, nothing wrong at all."

Father nodded, and I thought: What's all this stroking all of a sudden? And that smile? Because they *pay* you?

At which the doctor asked: "So now, tell me what happened to you when you left home."

I looked at Father and said: "I've already forgotten everything."

Father nodded again, and the doctor said: "Well, all the better." And then: "I'd like some water, then. For my hands. Hot water!"

He washed his hands and went into the other room with my parents. I thought: Now he's getting his precious, hard-earned money.

That very day I got out of bed, and two days later I would return to school. I was worried about the embarrassing reception I'd get.

But Father told me not to worry, that he'd "taken care of things" there as well. Indeed, on seeing me, Mr. Würtz came right over.

"Hey," he said, "nothing happened, nothing at all. Now be a good boy and go take your seat."

And I sat down even prouder than before, lest anyone should say a thing: What business was it of theirs what had happened to me?

No one said a thing, either. There was just one kid. He came over and mimicked me, wrinkled his nose and squinted, like I'd done when begging.

"You dummy," I said, "I was sick."

He laughed, and went away. Yes, I thought, they all know that I wanted to run away, to go out into the world. That I'd tried but failed. And they figure I got sick because I was a coward.

But still I didn't say a thing to any one of them. Half of them would fail anyway by the time we'd get to fourth grade; and half of those by the time we'd wind up in secondary school, with the Christians. And a lot of them would just drop out. That's just what happened with Ernuskó's class. So why should I have said a thing to them?

Learning now seemed to go better. It seemed even the subjects had forgotten everything. Even math and Hebrew translation, which had always been the hardest. Of course, it was easier now because I didn't spend as much time as I used to thinking of "bumming about."

And why?

Because I didn't want to go outside on the street on my own as much as before — I went only if absolutely necessary. And even then, I now avoided the whole length of the Bástyakör with all those shops if I could, figuring this was for the best, even if Father had "taken care of" everything.

Perhaps the Jewish shopkeepers wouldn't have said a thing. But maybe the Christians would have. And why should I have been ashamed?

Only when winter had passed into spring did I try my hand again at the Bástyakör.

And then it did happen, after all, that one among the many shopkeepers — what's more, not even a Christian — remarked: "Well, well — so when are we begging again?"

But he said it with a smile. Of course, I thought, he's thinking to himself, What a fine little lad. And: He's the rabbi's son. . . . We're really proud of Rabbi Azarel!

I proudly replied: "I was sick, and don't remember a thing."

On I went. He just stood there, smiling away. I thought: You didn't smile like that when I was just a beggar, did you now?

And I hurried home.

ABOUT KÁROLY PAP

KÁROLY PAP WAS born in Sopron, western Hungary, on September 24, 1897. His father was chief rabbi of Sopron's largest Jewish community and a literary historian. Pap is believed to have died in the Bergen-Belsen concentration camp in early 1945; his parents and older sister also perished in the Holocaust, while his older brother survived the war and emigrated to South America.

After high school graduation Pap volunteered for military service in World War One, both out of idealism and to counter a popular perception of the time that Jews were disinclined to put their lives on the line for their country. In 1919 he took part in the revolution that saw the brief ascendance of a communist regime in Hungary, and for a short time was military commander in Murakeresztúr, a small city in southwest Hungary. After the toppling of Béla Kun's government and the ascendancy of the right-wing regime under Admiral Miklós Horthy, Pap was imprisoned for two years on a charge of having looted a wealthy landowner's property while with the communist forces. Following this, he emigrated to Vienna, from where he returned to Hungary after a couple of years and worked as manual laborer and an itinerant actor.

Pap's literary debut came in 1925, when his poems and stories began appearing in the era's most famous journal, *Nyugat* (West), established by a leftist Hungarian circle that, like Pap, had spent time in exile in Vienna. His first novel, entitled *Megszabadítottál a haláltól* (You Redeemed Me from Death), appeared in 1932.

In 1930 Pap was nominated for Hungary's most prestigious literary award of the time, the Baumgarten Prize, but lost out

at the last minute when an acquaintance on the prize commit-
tee told his fellow judges of Pap's criminal record — which
was, in effect, synonymous with his leftist, revolutionary past.

Despite the missed opportunity for such recognition — the
financial support would have come in handy too, but reportedly
Pap had considered giving the entire sum to a friend whose
daughter was seriously ill — Pap continued writing away in
Budapest cafés while supported by his wife, a short-story writer
who held an office job. In the cafés he frequented, Pap befriend-
ed and earned the respect of many fellow writers and poets,
including some who were to become Hungary's most famous literary artists in the decades after the war.

Pap's second novel, *A nyolcadik stáció* (The Eighth Station),
was published in 1933.

The year 1937 saw the publication of the novel many consider
his best, *Azarel*. Critics have lauded it as a universal — and
largely autobiographical — tale of rebellion, yet one that also
sheds light on the experience of a young boy in a religious,
decidedly bourgeois, Hungarian Jewish household at the turn of
the twentieth century. Published in the same year was *Irgalom*
(Mercy), a volume of short fiction. Although Pap published
nearly 120 stories in his lifetime, this collection, comprising sev-
enteen stories, was the only volume to appear before his death.
Most notably it included semi-autobiographical works that were
part of the "Azarel" cycle, focusing on the childhood of a fictional character named György (or Gyuri, the diminutive form)
Azarel, who is also the narrator-hero of the novel of the same
title. With its publication, Károly Pap secured his reputation as
one of Hungary's finest short-fiction writers.

Amid growing anti-Semitism, Pap made no effort to conceal
his Jewish heritage, especially not in his writings — in contrast
to some other prominent Hungarian artists of the time. In 1935
he published an essay, "*Zsidó sebek és bűnök*" (Jewish Wounds and
Sins), which stirred considerable debate.

Beginning with the rise of Hitler, partly on seeing how little real impact art had against the increasing terrors of the time, Pap wrote less and became increasingly depressed. Several of his literary mentors had died; two had committed suicide. Gradually he turned to playwriting, seeing in it a vehicle to express his beliefs that was safer than what he was really inclined to do — publish anti-war pamphlets. With the cooperation of actors banned from participation in Hungary's theatrical life, a few of Pap's plays were performed at the Goldmark Theatre, in Budapest's Jewish ghetto.

On May 23, 1944, Pap was taken to a labor camp within Hungary. In November of that year he was deported to the Buchenwald concentration camp, after a letter from the Swiss embassy that might have saved him failed to reach him; this came only days after he wrote a final letter to his wife, expressing optimism about the future.

Decades later his wife quoted the writer Dezső Keresztury as having said, "On November 2, 1944, [Pap] was taken to Buchenwald, where the number 72,713 was tattooed on his arm. His fellow internees recognized him and wanted to help him escape, so that through his writing he could let the outside world know of their plight. He refused the offer, opting to stay among them. On January 30, 1945, he was still counted among the living. It is presumed he was then taken to Bergen-Belsen, where he vanished without a trace."

A LITERARY TRIBUNAL CONSIDERS KÁROLY PAP'S NOVEL *Azarel*[*]

TRANSLATOR'S NOTE: As readers of this novel cannot help but notice, Károly Pap's relationship with Judaism was anything but smooth. Yet Judaism — or, better put, the staggering burden of one's heritage, of the *past*, upon the psyche — was Pap's lifelong obsession. In this he stood apart from most Hungarian writers of Jewish descent, who in their works did not distinguish their particular heritage from that of their intended readers. Nowhere — not even in Pap's many stories, some of which were the precursors of *Azarel* — was this more evident than in *Zsidó sebek és bűnök* (literally, Jewish Wounds and Sins), a frank and impassioned sociohistorical essay analyzing how Hungary's Jews had arrived at their situation and what they could do to better their lot. Its rejection not only of fascism but of Zionism must have rankled. And in 1937, Pap topped it all off with *Azarel* — a novel whose protagonist-narrator flatly accuses his rabbi-father of being not only a hypocrite but an also atheist, and tries his utmost — albeit with limited success — to climb out from under the whole of his burdensome Jewish past. To make matters worse, it was clear to most everyone who knew a thing or two about Pap that the fictional father was inspired by the author's own father — one of Hungary's most distinguished rabbis.

---

[*]From a report by this title in a 1938 issue of the Jewish cultural journal *Múlt és Jövő*, which was published in Budapest before World War Two and, after an extended haitus, later resumed publication.

All this set the stage for the "literary tribunal" recounted below. This was a trial without legal consequences, without literary consequences, as many of Pap's readers, and most vocal fans from the ranks of famous writers, were not Jewish, and without even the possible consequence that Pap would henceforth be an outcast in the Jewish community. Although the influential Hungarian Zionist Association called the proceeding, Pap had supporters even among its prominent members. In any case, Pap, who in his own way yearned to be a voice for the Jewish community, must have felt he had no choice but to respond to the summons and take part. Reportedly, neither of his parents was present.

Pap's statement in his own defense is remarkable for making a startlingly convincing case that he, the artist, by delving into (ultimate) "truth" and all its troubling contradictions-revelations, actually serves the interest of those who look no further than absolute truth; and what's more, that in doing so he bears the burden of heritage more profoundly than do his "pious" critics. All writers — indeed, all who have ever questioned the purpose of art — would do well to remember his words.

Azarel was vindicated, if ambivalently: the case was put on hold.

DRAWING ON international precedents, the Hungarian Zionist Association established a "literary tribunal" to consider the matter of Károly Pap's book *Azarel*. Presiding over the court, Mr. Miklós Gyula summarized the case and then, in a concise and engaging manner, the content of the book itself. Then he called on attorney Mr. Dénes Friedmann to present the prosecution argument.

Having emphasized the eminent author's illustrious literary achievements, Mr. Friedmann declared that he had taken on this thankless role not for the sake of bringing an accusation against a congenial and learned man, but so as to debate the serious problems of the book under consideration.

Mr. Friedmann opened by taking exception to several aspects of the novel. All writers, he observed, generally magnify their parents' characters. Károly Pap belittles them to an uncommon degree — this, notwithstanding that no one may transgress the Fifth Commandment. Nor does the book speak of the rabbinical profession with great esteem. Mr. Friedmann ascribed the concealed accusations raised in the book as an error of form, in that the adult narrator hides behind a child's personality and voices his exhorting, admonitory, critical — and, as the author himself has put it, ruthless — words from there. The book's anti-rabbinical slant is all the more disagreeable, he said, given that the merits of the elder, most esteemed rabbi who in the book is Rabbi Azarel are widely known and recognized across the nation. Not even the author denies that in a land where Judaism is a state religion, this book would have come before not only a literary tribunal.

Afterward, Mr. Béla Dénes, counsel for the defense, set forth his arguments, citing the sovereignty of the literary perspective and quoting from a presentation by Dr. Beneschofszky, a rabbi from the Buda side of the capital, on the book.

"'[The novel's] portrayal of man and of Jew is that of art. The truth of this portrayal is not the mechanical fidelity of photography, but that of a vision. Whenever I open any of Károly Pap's books I am struck by the rapturous wind of vision. This is what I feel: *numen ades*. Thus the commotion beginning to stir about his new book is born of a half-baked perspective and of misunderstanding. Scandalmongers are nosing about. They establish a tribunal to judge the book, but they do not ask if the book is good, beautiful, and true according to the laws of inner plausibility — in other words, if it is true in terms of art. Instead they ask, is it true word for word, are things like this in real life? As if the real "princess" from a fairy tale we know and love were being examined based on Weber and Fechner's laws of stimulus-threshold — is it possible, after all, for sensory nerves to be so condensed as to allow someone to perceive a single pea through sixty-six mattress covers? Yet even *that* story is true, for it is beautiful; and it is beautiful because its truth is rooted in our souls. Károly Pap's vision of Jewishness is immense, staggering, and beautiful, and so it is true. Yet the nature of this truth is different from that of a scholarly study or a newspaper article.

"I believe that the conscientious reader need not think that all Orthodox Jews are like Papa Jeremiah. Or that all Neolog Jewish rabbis are like Rabbi Azarel. Or that all Jewish households are like this, or perchance all Jews. I believe that we need not draw lessons directly from the content of the book. All artistic portrayals describe individuals, for the conflicts that works of art present are convincing only if girded by experience — or rather, by an air of singular experience. As for the peculiar fact that the more individual and unique a person and his conflict, the more generally and deeply human he is, this is the secret of artistic creation.

"In writing his book, Károly Pap did not consider what the Christians would say, what the Jews would say. He knew neither compromise toward his duty as a writer nor indulgence toward himself. This is why the Christians respect him too."

At this point Károly Pap, being the author of the accused work, read aloud a poetic statement containing, among others, the following words:

"What I've been criticized for and will yet be criticized for is completely true — this book is ruthless. Yet it was precisely and only through this ruthlessness that I could achieve what I wanted, which was for my book to make itself felt all the way down to that depth of the Jewish soul beyond all economic angst and beyond all societal angst: to the place inhabited by collective and eternal humanity, wholly independent of birth and of the currents of the age. The fact that this level of consciousness is buried so deeply in the Jew, that the ruins of ghettos and so many instances of assimilation have buried it so deeply that it is impossible to reach this eternal, human aspect of the Jewish soul with a gentle hand — this pains me most of all, I have suffered the most from this ruthless fact. Who could be pained more than I by the fact that the best of my people's soul is accessible only through ruthless words and writing? Who could this hurt more than me, who am of this people's innermost soul? I, who am this people's writer? And could I be so if I didn't rouse myself with a knife every bit as ruthless from under the ruins of the mendacity, duality, and self-deception, as that with which this book rouses all its Jewish readers?

"Oh yes, I know all too well what it is for the Jewish soul to be awakened from comfortable, mendacious dreams, I do: the helpless agonizing dread, the terrified flight into even more mendacious dreams, the rage that bares its teeth even during the flight; the unctuous cries of sanctimonious self-love bundled up in the love of one's own kind; the ever doubting, obstinate self-consolation; the resigned or cynical wave of the hand. Yes, I know it all: the singular sounds of the Jewish soul as it recovers its senses. Yet I know also that aspect of the Jewish soul that doesn't shrink from recognizing itself, which neither flees nor lies nor shuts itself off from the world in spite of all its hurt, but rather says the following in horror on facing that which is itself: Dear me, I am completely naked and a stranger far and wide, I am a stranger in myself and a stranger everywhere else. Oh, dear God, dear Father, show the way to my native land, the world of my tranquillity!

"To this I reply: Happy is he who shudders yet does not hide; happy, he who feels great pain on encountering himself but does not cry and never grits his teeth; happy, he who has recognized that he is a stranger in himself and in others, everywhere; happy, I say, for he is the only one among us who is truly at home in himself and at home everywhere, in the lands of all people and under all skies, at all times, even in death, for he is the only one who, wherever he may be — is there in the name of God, speaks in His name, whatever he may say, and whose words are welcomed by all peoples."

Following the author's presentation, a witness, József Patai, pointed to the book's literary value, which he said was the deciding factor in this case. He testified that inner struggle guides Károly Pap to consider the problem of Judaism. Speaking as an expert witness, Endre Sós criticized the work for serving as material for the enemies of Judaism. Dr. Ernő Szinetár, in his capacity as a medical expert, drew light upon the work's psychological background from the perspective of psychoanalysis. A Zionist witness, Ákos Epstein, then analyzed the work. In the name of young people Farkas Weisz declared that a Jewish writer of such great talent can rightly be expected to demonstrate a more profound immersion in, and factual knowledge of, questions pertaining to Judaism. The nearly overflowing crowd in Herzl Hall* listened with taut interest until the trial closed with Miklós Gyula's announcement that the tribunal would postpone its decision until the appearance of subsequent volumes on the *Azarel* theme.

---

*Named after Theodor Herzl (1860–1904), the Hungarian-born Austrian founder of Zionism.

3665 31